Sins of Thy Mother 4:

Maybe I'm Just Like My Mama

By Niki Jilvontae

Dedication

This book is dedicated to the great mother who raised me and the great mother I've grown to be. Being a mother is not easy. This job comes with no instructions, no off days, and often no help, but we do it all because we love our kids. I just pray and wish every day that every child in the world could have that type of mother. So I dedicate this book to other great mothers as well. Keep being great because there are too many "so-called" mothers like Denise in the world!

Acknowledgements

I just want to thank the Most High for this incredible gift. I'd also like to thank my Pen Hustlas family, True Glory family including mentor Shameek Speight, RDP, BDP, MLP, HSP, and all of our other sister companies. I'd like to thank my family: mom, brother, daughter, son, and aunt Debra for their endless support on my literary journey, and my beta reader bestie Latoya Ms. Climaxxx Brown. Thank you all. Also thank all of my readers and supporters. It's so many of you all, but I love and appreciate each of you!!

Prologue

I spent my eighteenth birthday the year my sister and I killed our mother, wrapped up in Jerrod's arms, staring into my daughter's eyes. Despite all we had been through and all that I had done, I was lucky to have the happiness I had always dreamed of. With my mama and Lee gone, the house completely burned down destroying all evidence, and Lieutenant Black helping me out, Terricka and I were able to fade into the background as victims and begin normal lives.

A full year went by with me living happy with my family, building a life for myself and working my ass off, trying hard to forget the past. I married Jerrod in a big beautiful wedding on Christmas day and I was right beside my sister to help when she had her first child. They ruled my mother and Lee's deaths as a murder /suicide that next year and set my weary mind at ease. By then, I was happy and back home with the Robinson's close by and with Jerrod and A'Miracle with me where they belonged. I didn't want anything to change that.

Finding out we would each gain a half of million dollars following our mother's death was the icing on the cake, which came in the form of certified letters as we prepared to go out to celebrate my 21st birthday that next year. I can still remember the look on Terricka's face when she got that envelope in her hands and began planning what she would do with it. Buddy was right there with her as he helped her to spend money in their minds that she didn't even have yet.

I wanted to step forward and say something, but I figured who was I to tell her anything with all of the fucked up decisions I had made. Hell I had wanted to say something when Terricka got pregnant with her second child before she had even had her six weeks' checkup, but I couldn't. However, as I sat there besides Jerrod later at our house, and watched my now pregnant with her third child sister ignore one, chastise one, while drinking beer after beer, poisoning the other, I thought about how the apple never fell far from the tree. I couldn't help but look at my sister with some of the same disgust I once looked at my mother with when I heard her tell my nephew to sit his stupid ass down. A tear fell from my eye as I rushed over to pick up my barely walking, crying nephew Ryan and tell him how much I loved him. I held him tightly to my chest while I watched A'Miracle play with Rodney Jr., Terricka's first son, and Jerrod came up to rub my back.

"What's up with Terricka?" Jerrod asked me as my sister's drunk, belligerent voice suddenly got louder and everyone in the room turned to look at her.

For the first time in my life, I felt embarrassed to call her my sister, as I faced a fact I knew all along.

"Maybe she's just like our mother," I said to my husband as I shook my head while I hugged my nephew tight, and hoped that I wouldn't have to slay a dragon of my own.

Four years after that day, Terricka and I began to drift apart and I moved off to California with Jerrod to start our new life. Life in Apple Valley, California was beautiful. It so much different from the chaos I lived in Memphis, so much so that I often wondered was all of the horror that haunted me in my dreams simply in my head. The scars all over my body and those mental stains that would probably never go away were the only things left to remind me that life wasn't always so good. Those scars reminded me that there was still pain in the world, and in my own family for that matter.

Although I had Sha in the same state as me after he had moved to Sacramento with his father, there was still Terricka hundreds of miles away projecting her own sins on her children. With four kids, our mama's insurance money gone, and a baby daddy who didn't work or provide, my sister had slipped into the sticky web of drugs, violence, and despair furnished by the underbelly of Memphis. I rarely talked to my sister at this point, but when I did it was never pleasant. That's why I knew all of the things I had heard about her were true. I knew they were true because even when I did talk to Terricka I never felt that unbreakable bond we had always shared. Usually our talks were short, but never sweet because Terricka always seemed to have this chip on her shoulder. I can remember our last conversation perfectly, all of the malice and ignorance still rings in my ears.

"Shut the fuck up stupid muthafuckas. Don't y'all see I'm on the phone?" Terricka yelled as she cursed at her loud, playful kids in the background.

Their giggles and laughter quickly stopped and they left the room as soon as Terricka opened her mouth and I felt rage ignite inside of me as I held the phone to my ear. That was an anger I hadn't felt in five years because it reminded me of the horrible life I had before. I guess that's why I had subconsciously pushed as far away from my sister as I could.

I couldn't help but to run away from the person she had become because it reminded me of the horrible person our mother once was. The 25-year old successful woman I had become just didn't want to go back to that life so I avoided anything related to it. Everything except Sha. Over the years I had stayed in constant contact with him as I monitored his progress while I ignored the sister I once admired who was nearby.

Terricka was the last person I wanted to talk to because she was always negative, which is why I wanted to just hang up the phone at that moment and end all the ugliness that she represented. I didn't want all of her misery to shatter the happy world I had created. I wanted to see her and deep down I missed her deeply, but I just couldn't bring pain into my world.

Suddenly, all I could do as I sat there in my office at my publishing company, was think about the three kids who begged for help as their mother gave them the worse that the world had to offer. In my heart I knew that the rumors were true and that

Terricka's kids were living some of the same horrors we had lived. That was enough motivation for me to swallow that twinge of fear of what could happen that dwelled inside of me and face the devil my sister was about to become head on.

"Yea, who the fuck is this?" My sister yelled into the phone finally as I tried to think of the right words to say.

Nothing I thought of at that moment seemed right though because I knew Terricka would be offended by anything I had to say. After a few seconds I gave up on the plan of finding a tactic to avoid Terricka's rage and flipped back into the smart mouthed, don't take no shit girl I had become shortly after my mother's murder.

"You know who the hell this is, it's your sister. You would have known that had you not answered the phone with all that bullshit. So wassup T? What's going on with you maine? Why are you hollering at those kids like that?" I asked my sister as adrenaline and anger surged through my body and I thought about the angry, scrunched up face I was sure she was making.

I couldn't believe that Terricka was repeating the same fucked up mistakes our mother had made and continuing the cycle of abuse that had almost killed us. That made me wonder if my sister suffered from the same mental illnesses our mother had. I didn't wonder about that long though because as soon as my sister spoke all hope was lost. "Awll shit, it's the bougie bitch. Y'all its Ms. Rich!" Terricka said to herself as she laughed into the phone like a fucking lunatic.

"What the fuck you want Tisha? You calling to tell me what a fucked up mother I am again? Or are you calling to brag about all of the new shit you got living out there in Cali like you rich and famous. Bitch, you ain't rich. You ain't shit Tisha just like me so don't call me on yo queen shit preaching bullshit to me when you have no idea what the fuck I'm going through. Bitch where you at? I'll tell you BITCH. You're hundreds of miles away doing you so let me do me. If you ain't trying to send me shit witcho rich ass I ain't got shit to say. So wassup with yo ass now SISTER?" Terricka yelled into the phone spewing her hate, hurt, and misery at me like daggers.

Her words felt like daggers too as they ripped through my heart and tore me apart. That little girl who loved her big sister and still lived inside of me cried a river as she sat in her big office inside of her very successful business. Even with all I had at that point and all I had gone through all I wanted the most was to have that close bond with my sister again and be the family we had always wished for. I still dreamed about escaping to a happy place with my siblings so that we could run through a field amongst beautiful flowers. I wanted them to have that same peace I had. That just didn't seem possible for Terricka though, not at that time anyway so I met her force with one equally hurtful and hateful.

"What the fuck? You gotta be kidding me. I can't believe you sitting yo big head ass over there trying to read me like that. What the fuck Terricka? We used to be so close we shared the same thoughts and breaths. Now you on some straight fuck me shit, talking to me like I'm some random hoe on the streets. Really Terricka?" I asked my sister as I stopped for a second to catch my breath and she sighed on the other end.

Her disrespect at a time when I was trying to figure out what was going on and when she had started feeling that way, really set me off as I laid into Terricka like she had done me. "Bougie bitch? Bougie? Me? See now I know you down there popping pills, getting drunk, snorting powder, and wilding just like everybody said. Bitch ain't shit about me bougie. Am I successful? Yes, but that's because I worked my ass off to get to where I am Terricka. Believe that. Bitch we had the same opportunity, the same stepping stool to change the direction of our lives and live better than we knew possible. I took that money from Denise and invested a small portion into my writing while I let the rest sit in an interest baring account. Meanwhile, I wrote and put out my own books, doing everything I could to change my life with that blood money. I remember coming to you right after we got it and asking yo funky ass to go in with me on the business. You remember what you said to me Terricka?" I yelled out of breath as I got up to pace the floor of my office.

As I walked my size 7 Louboutin heels clicked loudly on the Italian marble floor. I waited for a second and gave Terricka a chance to respond, however I quickly realized she wasn't going to so I went in again.

"Bitch I'll tell yo drugged out ass what you said. You told me to get my nosey ass the fuck out yo face. You said you had it and you knew what you were going to do with YO money. You told me to worry about my money and that when mine was gone not to ask you for shit. Remember that? DO you remember that SISTER? Bougie? Bitch I ain't never been bougie because I know just like you do that being hungry, broke, and disgusted ain't no joke."

"We came from the same hell Terricka so how can you sit here and try to flip shit on me cause you fucked up? You was the bitch in the hood buying dope like it was going out of style for your stupid ass new baby daddy, Vito to flip. Dope this nigga never fucking flipped. Y'all muthafuckas was taking trips, buying cars, and doing all other kinds of ghetto fabulous bullshit, barley buying R.J. and Ryan anything. I took care of them and you took care of Y'all Terricka. Now you got four kids, no money, and a broke ass baby daddy and you blame me? You act like you losing yo fucking mind ShaTerricka, but I'm ready to help you get it back. Bitch that's why Buddy left you or should I call him Rodney. That maine won't even go by the name Buddy no more because he said it reminds him of you."

"He knew that you were going crazy too that's why he got out when he did. Hell, yo behavior proves something wrong witcho ass. I just wish he would have taken Rodney Jr. and Ryan with him. Maybe then you wouldn't have met baby daddy Vito and started down this fucked up path. Maybe you wouldn't even have had Tania and Talaya. Maybe your life would be easier then, without yo kids. It probably would've been better, huh? I say that because I know deep down that you just like mama ain't it Terricka? You just wonna be free huh? YOU'RE JUST LIKE DENISE AIN'T YA TERRICKA?" I screamed like a maniac as I watched my secretary walk towards my door, but I waved her off instead while tears poured out of my eyes.

The moment I said that I regretted it because that was an answer I really didn't want to hear. I wanted to hold on to the tiny bit of hope that I could talk some sense into my sister. I wanted her to be okay, but I suddenly felt like I had gone about it wrong. I quickly tried to lessen the blow of my statement and possibly save our damned relationship, but my heart told me from the start that it was already gone.

"Terricka before you say anything let me tell you I'm sorry. I'm sorry for bringing up Buddy like that and I'm sorry if you think I'm bougie and trying to be something I'm not. What I'm most sorry about though is what really has you so in your feelings. I'm sorry sister. I'm sorry I left you there to wade the waters alone. I really do apologize Terricka. I tried to get you to come just like I tried to get you to invest and save your money, but sister you just wouldn't listen. I had to leave in order to live Terricka because I was dying slowly in that chaos. I will always love and help you sister so please just tell me we can be alright again. I can help you with the kids, they can come live with me, and you can go off to get help and get yourself together. I just want you to be alright Terricka. I need you to be alright. We all we got, remember? I AM MY SISTER'S KEEPER. Right?" I asked as Terricka sat silent and she held the phone.

For a second I thought she had hung up but suddenly her loud, angry to the point of deranged laughter filled my eardrums as she laughed and I held the phone away from my ear. When her laughter stopped so did my heart as my sister did damage to our relationship I feared could never be repaired. "You little shaky, bougie, ghetto bitch. Who the fuck do you think you are Tisha? Just because you saved some money and got a little company, you think you're better than me? Bitch you wouldn't have none of that shit if it wasn't for me. I was the one who took all the beatings for you, and extra dicks in my mouth to shield yo green ass from what was going on around us. Bitch I gave you and Sha my life from the time y'all was born. Hell I gave up my soul by killing our mother just so that you could live without the fear of Denise finding you and taking yo baby. I have always given up everything Tisha and what have I ever got in return? Huh, Ms. Know-It-All sister? You know what I got?" Terricka yelled as I heard her cry between her words.

"I got an insatiable hunger for drugs, fast money, and niggas that mean me no good. Bitch I am a product of my environment and so are you. The only difference is you had somebody that could make you forget the pain and you wanted to live better, but bitch I ain't you. Everybody don't make it out and have that fairy tale happy ending we always thought was around the corner. I'm fucking broken Tisha and nobody can fix me, not even you. You don't give a fuck anyway though. DO you?" Terricka yelled as she bawled and I cried just as hard while I fell back into my chair.

The pain in my sister's voice melted all of my anger and made me feel for the broken little girl she still was. All I wanted to do at that moment was comfort my sister like she had always done me and ensure her everything would alright. "Terricka of course I care. I love you sister, and I." I said as tears fell from my eyes and rolled down my peach, silk blouse and left a puddle of my pain as a reminder of the guilt I felt.

Terricka cut me off as she yelled my name and I stopped but continued to sob. Everything was silent for moments as I got lost in my thoughts and wallowed in my pain. I knew from the start what was eating Terricka even though she never wanted to admit it. However, hearing her explode like she did made me wish I could have swallowed my own fears and sacrificed my happiness for my sister like she had always done for me. I wished I had never left Terricka in Memphis alone to raise her kids by herself. She was there in the place where we endured the most pain and my selfish ass hadn't even tried my hardest to get her away. If I could have turned back the hands of time in that moment I would have, and just started back at that day our mother was killed. However, I didn't have a fucking time machine so I had to just sit there and await the inevitable.

"You don't care about shit Tisha but yourself, your baby, your husband, and y'all happiness. That's it. Since that day, that fucking dark day I slayed the dragon you decided you would erase it all. Me included. You gave up on us that night Tisha and now I'm giving up on you. Maybe I don't need kids and I could do better but bitch you ain't gonna tell me what to do and you can't have them. Fuck you Tisha. What makes you a better parent cause you don't smoke, curse, or beat they ass when they do some stupid shit? Bitch, you ain't shit. Yo baby died cause you a miserable bitch too just like me. You internalized all of your pain and in return you poisoned yo own son."

"Jerrod, Jr. died because you just as rotten as me bitch! So don't you sit yo raggedy ass over there on yo high horse and look down yo nose on me. If you really loved me hoe you would have been here. You would help me while I'm sitting here with four kids, no food, and lights in my apartment. You heard everything else, why the muthafuckas didn't tell you that? They didn't tell you the rest of my money I invested on my own is gone because I let our cousin stay with me and him and his bitch robbed me blind and skipped town. Muthafuckas didn't tell you that did they? No, but they can tell you everything Terricka doing wrong, and yet and still with all that information yo maggot ass still didn't come back. Bitch you haven't even been back to visit so just shut the fuck up SHARTISHA." My sister yelled as I sat in my desk and cried while I held a picture of me, her, and Sha at the Robinson's house on one of our happy days.

I couldn't help but wonder would we ever have that happy, loving feeling we had in the picture with our arms wrapped around one another as we looked like we never wanted to let go. I quickly found out that day probably would never come when my sister said the words I hoped would never come out of her mouth again. That was the words that would bring us full circle right back to where all the pain began.

"Maybe you're right Ms. Author, Publisher, and self-appointed psychologist Tisha. Maybe I am just like my mama and I don't give a fuck. That's the difference between me and you. You so worried about how other people see you when in reality, no matter how much money you make you will always be this little broken, girl from the projects. You're so quick to believe everything bad about me so now I'm gonna give you muthafuckas exactly what you was looking for. Now I see what Denise was always saying about the robots telling her shit because I got a little birdie in my ear too. That birdie told me to tell you go fuck yourself. You don't ever have to worry about me or these ugly ass kids again Tisha. You know what, better yet I'm gonna say this and be done. What we once were will never be again because you are no sister of mine. You are my SISTER NO MORE...and I mean it this time bitch!" Terricka said calmly before she attempted to hang up the phone and I stopped her.

"You know what Terricka? You're right. Maybe you are!" I said to my sister as she yelled out, "Fuck You, and hung up the phone.

Once the call had ended I sat there for a while and cried until I couldn't cry anymore, then I got up and went into my adjoining bathroom and cleaned myself up. After I washed my face, reapplied my makeup, and dried up the tears on my blouse, I stopped to look at myself in the mirror as I saw a flash of the horrible life my sister would have. I stood there and looked at myself as I imagined her face and finally accepted the truth that was right in front of my face. "Maybe she is just like our mama and she can't be saved." I whispered to myself as I walked back out the bathroom to my happy world, not believing what I had said or giving up hope of someday saving my sister.

That was the last conversation I had with my sister before fate, and my little brother pushed us all back into each other's lives.

PART 1

REFLECTIONS: FROM MY POINT OF VIEW!

Chapter 1

Tisha: Pain Always Finds Its Way Home

"Tishaaaaaaaaaaa, bring you stanky ass down here and entertain my guests." My mother yelled as I quickly climbed from under the bed where I usually hid to read and avoid her abuse. My mama's voice was so loud in my mind at that time that the dream I was trapped in as I sat asleep on my hammock swing in my backyard, felt real. Years later everything was still so vivid and felt so real I could actually smell the stale, musty, crack smoke filled air of the hallway in my childhood home as I made my way downstairs in my dream.

"Tisha I know you hear me calling you." Denise yelled as I slowly entered the living room with my copy of My Sister's Keeper by Jodi Picoult that Terricka had just gotten me for my twelfth birthday tucked tightly under my arm.

My legs shook as I walked into the dirty, musty living room and stared into the drunk, and stoned face of my mother. I slowly crept closer to her as I glanced at the people in the room from the corner of my eye. I noticed at least three women and four men I had never seen with either a beer bottle, blunt, or a crack pipe in their hands as they eyed me like fresh meat. The only face I did recognize in the room other than my mother's was that of her friend Lisa as she suddenly got up and walked to the door. I wanted to run after her and beg her to take me with her after seeing the sneaky, evil look on my mother's face. I wanted to run, but I didn't because I knew that it would do me no good. Instead I just stood there while I still held my book under my arm and stared down at my feet. I could feel the eyes of all of the junkies in the room on me as I stood there and my mother walked over to the door behind Lisa. "Where you going bitch. We just finna have some fun. You know kids liven up a party." My mother said laughing as I heard Lisa do a sarcastic laugh of her own.

Even though Lisa had never done anything up to that point to help me or my siblings escape the hell our mother unleashed on us, she wouldn't indulge in it either, which is why I had always felt that she was the only person in the world we had. I quickly raised my head when I heard Lisa laugh to see her as she stood in front of my mother and stared her down. "Maine Denise you a muthafucka witcho self for real. You call that baby out of bed just to dance for y'all high asses. Or at least I hope that's all. Denise that better be all for real." Lisa whispered as she stepped closer to my mama almost nose to nose.

For the first time I felt like someone was fighting for me and could possibly kill the monster that haunted my dreams as my mother stood silently and listened to all Lisa had to say before she spoke. "Ahh girl, come on now. You know we just finna have fun. Hell, if you had a child we would tell you to go get em to dance. So bitch that mean get yo ole barren ass on somewhere and worry about the kids you might never have. BYYYEEE Boo!" My mama said changing emotions so much when she talked it was like watching Dr. Jerkel and Mr. Hyde wrestle.

I watched as Lisa stood there for a minute and contemplated what she would do next. She looked back at me with a look of genuine concern until my mother met our gaze and stepped forward to whisper into her ear. Whatever my mother said to Lisa was enough to erase whatever sympathy and concern she felt for me because she quickly ran out of the door and down the steps without even looking back. I stood there for a while and stared at the spot she was standing in when our eyes met, even after my mother had closed the door. I just wished I could have kept her there for a little longer even if she wasn't gonna help me. I knew that just having her there would make my mother think twice before she went too far. However, it was clear my mother had something on her that mattered much more than me or my safety. It seemed my mother always had the upper hand and could get what she wanted no matter what it was. After seeing Lisa flee like she had done, I knew that was true and accepted the fact that there was no hope as my mother set her plan in motion.

"Can y'all believe that bougie, punk bitch. That hoe gonna try to call me out cause we wonna have fun. Fuck ha cause Tisha wonna dance. You know kids wonna dance, don't they y'all?" My mama said swaying from side-to-side as she encouraged her junky audience to chime in.

All of them agreed with my mother as they stared at me and smiled the same wicked smile she had. I felt the hair all over my arms and legs stand up as one of the men got up to go to the bathroom and let his body brush up against mine when he passed. I jumped so hard I almost knocked the only picture we had that wasn't broken off the wall and that set my mama off.

"What the fuck you jumping foe, like a muthafucka want you. Lil scary ass girl. Always got her face in a book or singing and shit. Her and her sister live in a damn fantasy world with they're lil mute brother. That other one just love the streets a lil moe. This one, she different. This one THINK she's gonna be something. Don't you Tisha?" My mama said as she walked up on me and whispered into my ear and I kept my head down.

My heart raced in my chest as I tried to decide whether or not I was supposed to answer that question. My mama was so unpredictable I never knew if a question she asked was rhetorical or not. Unlike Terricka I still didn't know how to divert my mama's evil intentions, which is why I wished my sister was there as I stood there trembling and my mother used her index finger to trace down the outside of my right arm.

"Yeah, you think you're gonna get out this ghetto and live a happy life don't ya? You think you better than everyone around here because you read for fun. This the muthafucking problem." My mother yelled as she ripped my book from under my arm and held it up in the air for her friends to see.

I stared at my mother with enough hate and malice to melt a glacier as she walked over to her friends with my book in hand to mock me. I started to run after her, jump on her back, and beat the fuck out of her until she dropped my book. However, a small slither of logic in the back of my mind calmed that rage that was burning, but I never knew I had inside. Instead of clicking the fuck out and getting my ass beat like I was sure to do, I just stood there biting my bottom lip as tears burned in my eyes and my mother finished her performance.

"See this is the fucking problem. They go off to school and these muthafuckas put all these hopes and dreams in their minds, gassing them up and shit by telling them they can live like people in these books. Then they bring they uppity asses home and look down their noses on the muthafuckas who feed and clothe them cause they think they better cause they learned something. Or cause we smoke dope and shit. This shit don't mean a muthafucking thang!" My mama yelled as she turned from her friends to face me while she ripped pages out of my book.

"This don't mean a muthafucking thang Tisha. Cause what them muthafuckas in that school and the people in those books don't know is we poor as a muthafucka. Our lives can never be the same as theirs cause we in the bottom and this is probably where we will stay. Ain't no moving off to live in the sunshine with the wind blowing in yo hair. Bitch yo life gonna always be in Memphis and that shit gonna be hard as fuck unless you listen to me. I'm trying to give you game. In Memphis you either sell dope, pussy, guns, cars, or dreams. Dancing can be yo way out but it starts with learning how to do basic dances and have fun with it. I ain't never seen yo lil uptight ass out there dancing with Terricka and her friends when they used to. Yo ass was always just sitting there looking stupid. That shit stops today tho. Today you gonna learn so show us what the fuck you got." My mama said as tears streamed down my face and her words rang in my ears.

In less than sixty seconds she had predicted and damned my whole life and as horrible as it all sounded a part of me thought that she was right. A part of me, that broken, beaten, and starved part of me knew that the world was cold and no one really loved and would help you. With that in mind I couldn't help but think that my mother was right and that my life was already destined to fail. I hated to admit it to myself but I often felt hopeless and that being good was overrated. I still didn't want to do the things my mother wanted me to do and sell my soul like her but I had no other choice.

I wiped away the tears rolling down my face with the back of my hand as 'Whoomp, There It Is' by Tag Team came on and banged loudly through the speakers by the door. I swallowed down the food that was threatening to come back up as I began to dance around the room with my eyes closed. I tried my best to imitate what I had saw Terricka and her friends do countless times before; however, the look on my mama's face quickly told me that I was doing a shitty job. When the man who went to the bathroom suddenly reappeared looking higher than he was before, my mother had had enough of me embarrassing her and quickly jumped up to stop me.

"Okay I see now why yo ass don't be out there with Terricka nem, but you'll stay upstairs under the bed all day with yo mute brother. You a fucking girl with all the right tools and no fucking sensuality about yourself at all. What the fuck wrong with you Tisha?" My mama asked as she walked up to me and we stood face-to-face as tears rolled down my cheeks.

"I know what's wrong Denise. She just lacks confidence. Hell, my son can give her that. You know how lil Main is." The big, fat, sloppy lady in blue who my mother was sitting next to and sharing her pipe with said as she grinned and slid forward on the couch.

I watched for a few seconds as her big ass struggled to get up off of the couch and no one even tried to help her. All of the other fiends sitting right on the couch next to her were so wrapped up in their drug of choice they didn't even notice that she was having a difficult time. Her light-skinned, 400 pound, umpa lumpa looking ass had to fall down on to her knees before she could pull herself up into a standing position. I almost laughed seeing her big ass stagger to her feet and waddle towards us, but I quickly lost that feeling of amusement when her and my mother agreed that adding Lil Main to the mix was exactly what I needed. "Hell yeah Pat, go get Lil Main's lil sexy light skinned ass I bet he get her stiff ass to act right." My mama said as I watched her rub Pat on the ass before she wobbled quickly out of the apartment.

I felt sick to my stomach as I stood there shaking and my mama followed Pat to the door. I tried not to look at the drugged out faces as my mama's junky audience stared at me, however, I quickly memorized every face. Each of them had that same hopeless look in their eyes that my mama had which let me know that the plea I was making with my eyes to help me would go unanswered. I quickly made it up in my mind at that point that I would just be strong and endure whatever I had to just so that Sha could stay safe. I hoped that he was still locked in his room with his earphones on oblivious to what was about to happen. Hell, I wished I was locked away somewhere far away from Denise so that I wouldn't have to be a part of her sick game. I wished and wished like I had done countless times before, and just like before my wishes went unanswered. All I could do was close my eyes and imagine myself running through that field of flowers without a care in the world. "Open yo fucking eyes and sit down." My mama yelled into my ear as she broke my daydream and made my heart race again.

I quickly shook off my shock and made my way over to the dirty, oversized chair by the window and sat down as my mother sat on the arm of the chair next to me and lit a blunt. "I know you hate me Tisha and you think I'm a horrible mother." My mother began as I shook my head no and she rolled her eyes.

"Don't sit here and lie wanch cause I've heard you and yo sister talking. It's okay though because I hate myself too, but what you don't realize is that I'm trying to help yo green ass not hurt you. These streets gonna eat yo lil weak ass up Tisha so you better pay attention to the shit I say. Now, this gonna be your way out or I'm going to have to think of something even better. I suggest you sit here and get yo fucking mind together before Lil Main gets here because if you embarrass me Tisha, I'm fucking ALL of y'all up. Believe that! Now hit this, it'll get you right." My mama said as she handed me the blunt in her hand and I refused to grab it.

I didn't want to get high and become a zombie, unfit mother who intentionally hurts her kids for her own amusement. I didn't want to put any drug in my body if it meant I would be like her. I didn't care what she would do to me, but no matter what I wasn't going to smoke with her. "No mama. I don't wonna smoke." I said as my voice trembled and the junkies on the couch laughed and mimicked what I said.

I glared out of the corner of my eye at the man they called Snake as he licked out his tongue at me like a little vindictive kid and then started flicking it in a sexual way. I quickly looked away as he winked his eye and I turned right around to a smack from my mother. Denise hit me so hard my ears rung and my teeth chattered. In fact, the lick Denise gave me was so hard and powerful I could still feel it in my sleep as I shifted in my hammock and let my dream take me deeper into my memories.

"Oh so now you too good to unwind. That's the shit I'm talking about. Y'all see what I'm saying, this lil bitch bougie." My mama said to her friends as she laughed before she leaned over to whisper in my ear. "Didn't I tell you not to embarrass me bitch? I should fuck you up right now, shouldn't I? Shouldn't I Tisha?" My mama growled in my ear as my tears began to fall again.

I gazed around the room and caught the attention of the skinny lady sitting on the far end of the couch as she looked at me with a little sympathy. I pleaded with her using my eyes as my mother stood up in front of me with her fists balled up and demanded an answer. "I should fuck you up shouldn't I Tisha?" She yelled as I slowly looked up at her and shook my head yes.

I quickly closed my eyes as soon as I answered her question and braced myself for the blows she was sure to throw. However, after two minutes of waiting and I still hadn't felt my mother's hands on me I opened my eyes to see the woman up off the couch and standing beside my mother as she whispered something softly in her ear.

"Okay you right Woo Woo, you're right. Tisha you better be glad she here cause I was about to fuck you up. I'm still gonna fuck you up if you tell me no again. So what the fuck ever I give you this time you had better take it." My mama said as she walked over to the coffee table and Woo Woo came over to me.

I stared at her as she strolled her 120 pound, 5'8" frame with big gray eyes and matted, messy hair over to me to whisper in my ear like she had done my mother. I held my breath so that I would not throw up when I smelled her alcohol, booty smelling ass breath. I had never smelled anything so foul in my life so I was afraid I wouldn't be able to hold my vomit as she stared at me face-to-face. I could feel my eyebrows and all of the hair on the left side of my face melt as she leaned in to tell me why she had saved me.

"Know this lil mama, I didn't stop Denise cause I care about you. I stopped her because I don't want to miss the show. So, I suggest when she comes over her with that glass and pill yo lil ass take it and shut the fuck up. Know that our show will go on regardless so either you gonna be beat the fuck up when you do it or just high as fuck. It's yo decision." Woo Woo said before she kissed me on the cheek and stood back smiling like she had just told me the secret to life.

I felt panic rush over me as I realized whatever my mother had planned wasn't new to them, it just involved different players. I swallowed down the lump in my throat and song our salvation song in my mind as I watched my mother walk back over to me. Just like Woo Woo said when my mother came back over she had a glass of vodka mixed with orange juice and a blue pill in her hand. She stopped right in front of me with her rotten snatch in my face and the smell almost blew me away. I had to force the pill down my throat after I took it and the glass out of my mother's hand and quickly put it in my mouth. I drunk down the entire glass of vodka just to get the pill to go down, yet it still felt like it was hung in my throat.

"Now that's all yo funky ass had to do in the first fucking place instead of making me slap the shit out of you. Now get yo dumb ass upstairs and fix yo face then get right the fuck back down here." My mama said as I quickly got up out of the chair and ran out of the living room.

I was happy to get out of there and away from the staring faces, however I knew that I had to come back or else she would take her wrath out on Sha. That realization was enough to take the pep out of my step as I slowly walked up the stairs while I thought of a way out. "Ain't no way around this shit either Tisha so don't be thinking of some stupid ass plan as you walk up those steps." My mother yelled from behind me, which made me stop in my tracks.

It was like she was reading my mind again and I couldn't figure out how she did it. "Yeah bitch. I know everything. I told you the robots tell me so yo ass better hurry up before I think you plotting. Besides, what I got planned is gonna feel good so you might as well stop fighting it. We gonna see if little Tisha can pop that coochie and get mama paid. Them niggas got some money and dope down there so it's time to Hoe up until I blow up. You hear me? Now get yo shaky ass upstairs." My mother said as she laughed which caused me to jump and then bolt up the steps.

Once I was upstairs I ran straight to Sha's door and knocked three times, then twice more to let him know that it was me. In seconds he was at the door and I could hear his little muffled breaths through the thick wood as he waited to hear my voice. Even at six-years-old my brother knew our mother was dangerous and couldn't be trusted so he hid as much as he could.

"It's me Sha and I'm okay. Just stay in there and Terricka will be here soon. Whatever you do and no matter what you hear, don't come out. Okay?" I asked Sha as I kneeled down next to the door and put my forehead on the smooth wood surface.

I waited for my brother to respond as he cried and I cried my own tears. Seconds later I heard him as he got up off the floor and sucked up whatever tears he had left. "Okay Tisha, I'll hide. I love you." Sha said with strength that helped me to get up of the floor and face whatever was about to come.

I stood there for a second as I heard Sha's little feet scurry across the floor then I turned to go into the bathroom. Inside I put on the red booty shorts and wife beater my mother had left on the counter before I washed away my tears and applied lip gloss. When I was done I stared at my bruised face in the mirror and I barely recognized the girl who stared back at me. The sorrow that I saw in my eyes sent shudders through my body as I tucked my pain deep inside and prepared to face the chaos my mother always created. By then the blue pill my mother had given me had kicked in and I felt light and wobbly all over. I tried to fight the haze in my brain the pill created as I stood with my head on the door and my hand on the knob. I tried to slow my breathing and ignore the anxiety that was beginning to build up inside of me but it was no use as thoughts of what was going to happen flashed in my mind. As soon as I opened the bathroom door my mother's voice and the laughter from the junky spectators downstairs filled my ears and I drug my lifeless legs to the top of the stairs.

"Bring yo ass on down here Tisha, Lil Main waiting on ya and he ready!" My mother yelled with her back turned to the steps before she turned to smirk at me. "Oh here she go Lil Main, looking all refreshed and cute. She about to show yo ass something so get them lil bucks ready. Yo dollars spend too up in here." My mama yelled back into the room as she laughed and I tried to make it down the steps without falling.

My legs shook violently with each step I took and my heart raced like I was on the biggest coaster in an amusement park. I tried to think of a way out but the haze in my brain was so thick everything was a blur. When I got to the bottom of the steps I stumbled a little but my mother was right there to catch me and drag me into the center of the room. I stood there in front of Lil Main as I held my breath and he stared with his red, tight gray eyes. I had to admit that he was cute with his big juicy, pink lips, smooth light skin and curly black hair; however, the way that he stared at me gave me this uneasy feeling in my heart and made butterflies flutter in the pit of my stomach.

"Damn Denise I didn't know you was talking about this one. I thought you was talking about yo dark skinned daughter. This one cute but she bougie as fuck. I always be trying to talk to her lil thick ass and she always ignore me. Don't you bougie?" Lil Main said as he reached over and flicked my hair and I stepped back out of his reach.

I quickly regretted pushing Lil Main to the side as soon as I had done it after I looked around and saw the angry look on my mother's face. I knew that was a total act of defiance that would be punishable by another smack or an ass whooping, but I didn't want Lil' Main's nasty ass hands on me. "Nah, I ain't bougie." I said to Lil Main as my mother glared at me and motioned for me to step back up in front of him.

"I just don't fuck anything." I whispered as I stepped back into my original spot and watched the annoyed look on his face turn into a smirk. I held my breath and broke my stare off with Lil Main as my mother got up out of the chair she was sitting in and went back over to the radio to turn the music back on. Suddenly, Whoomp There It Is blast through the speakers again and my heart pounded louder than the bass. "Do something Goddamit Tisha. What the fuck did I tell you?" My mother yelled as I stood there still, frozen in that spot.

A warm tingly feeling began to rise up from my toes to my head as Lil Main grabbed me in the waist and pulled me close to him. His strong, athletic arms felt good around my waist as he held me there, close enough to feel his breath on my neck. However, the nagging feeling inside of me told me that he wasn't that knight in shining armor I always dreamed would rescue me.

"You used to not fucking anything huh? Well, now you'll do what the fuck I say. This $100 in my pocket that yo mammy junky ass wants says so. Sooooo shake something lil bougie hoe." Lil Main said before he reached around to slap me on the ass and everyone in the room laughed and cheered.

Before I knew what was happening Lil Main had spent me around and bent me over as he thrust his pelvis into my butt. I had to extend my arms out in front of me to keep my balance as I stared up at my mother with tears in my eyes and silently pleaded with her to end the madness. My mother's laughter and harsh words filled my ears next as she made her way over to us and had me stand up so that she could whisper in my ear. Her breath was so hot on my neck it felt like it was searing my skin as her words melted my defiance.

"Bitch I told you not to embarrass me right? Now, I told yo funky ass he got money, $100 to tip you. SO yo ass better stand up here and dance like them bitches in the videos. Do what the fuck ever you have to do to get all of those dollars out of his hand. Do that and you can go back to yo room with yo lil mute brother and I won't fuck the both of y'all up. Can you do that Tisha or should I just beat the shit out of you now and then just let him do what he wants to you for that $100? Huh? What you wonna do Tisha, its yo choice?" My mother whispered before standing back to look at me with nothing but hate.

I could see it in her eyes that she was serious and I knew that the little money she had was about to run out. All of those factors told me that I was in a lose, lose situation so I did the only thing that I could do and that was dance. Without answering my mother, I closed my eyes and backed up until I felt Lil Main's massive manhood on my butt. My mother hurried over to restart the music as I grinded my hips to the beat in my head and Lil Main held me close. When the music came back on I felt a rush of energy that caused me to feel out of control. For a moment everything was tye-dye colored and every touch on my skin sent intense tingles all through me. I bounced and grinded my body on Lil Main with my eyes closed until I felt dollar bills as they fell down on my body. By the time the song stopped I was dripping wet with sweat and Lil Main's lips and hands were all over me. The pumped up haze the pill had put me in slowly began to wear off as Lil Main dipped his hand down in the front of my shorts and let his fingertips graze my vagina. The feeling that gave me scared the fuck out of me as I attempted to pull back but he pulled me closer. My heart raced in my throat as I pushed, struggled, and began to panic while Lil Main tried to calm me down between kisses to my neck and face.

"Shhhh girl, the fuck you hollering for. This what you wanted how you was bouncing that ass on me. Besides I paid for this pussy already. What the fuck you think I'm here for? Yo mammy didn't send my mama to get me for shit. I'm tired of burning her sloppy ass cap up anyway, so gone let me break you in Ms. Bougie." Lil Main said before he kissed me deeply and stuck his tongue down my throat.

I almost threw up all of the food I had eaten that week as his nasty, stinky, cigarette, liquor, and cigar smelling breath invaded my lungs. My natural instincts kicked in instead though as I began to claw at Lil Main's face until he let me go. I tried to break and run for the steps after I broke free from Lil Main, but before I could even move he was on my back with his arms wrapped tightly around me as he whispered in my ear.

"Ima fuck the shit out of you for that lil bitch. Right here in front of yo mammy." Lil Main said as he suddenly threw me down in the chair, face first and began to rip my shorts down.

Panic filled me as I began to scream and yell for my mother who was still standing by the radio while she took a hit from a glass pipe. A big, thick cloud of white smoke enveloped her head as her laughter filled the air and I lost all hope of her helping me. I squirmed and moved as Lil Main continued to try and pull my shorts down while I begged someone to help me.

"Mama please. Pllleaaassseeeeee Mama. Make him stop. You got the money Please make him stop. Why y'all sitting here and letting this happen. Somebody please help me. If I was your daughter, you would want someone to help. Please stop this." I cried as tears fell from my eyes and I held on to the front of my shorts while Lil Main ripped the back down.

I felt him stop for a minute and my heart stopped racing in my ears long enough for me to hear the man they called Snake as he demanded Lil Main get off of me. They argued for a few seconds as I let my head fall into the chair and tried to catch my breath while the room began to spin. By the time the room stopped spinning Lil Main was being snatched up off of me and I quickly regained my composure so that I could flee. I ran on my wobbly legs as I tried to see through my tears and people laughed all around me. Once at the door of the room I stopped for a second to turn around and stare at my mother. She stood there, high out of her mind with all of the dollars she had picked up of the floor in one hand and the glass pipe still in the other as she smirked at me with no remorse or sympathy. I felt no remorse or sympathy for what I said next either as I cried the tears of an abused little girl for the millionth time.

"I HATE YOU DENISE. YOU ARE A ROTTEN PERSON AND I HATE YOU. YOU'RE NOT MY MAMA. DO YOU HEAR ME? YOU'RE NOT MY MAMA. MAMA! MAMA!" I yelled in my dream when suddenly the word became so clear I could hear it in my own ears.

I jumped up out of the nightmare of the past I was trapped in and nearly fell out of the hammock right on top of A'Miracle as she called my name. I quickly caught myself and sat up right before I stared into the beautiful face of my daughter. At seven-years-old, A'Miracle was tall, slender and gorgeous with beautiful, flawless caramel skin like Jerrod and the deepest brown, most powerful eyes ever, just like me. I felt all of the pain and hurt that consumed me in my dream melt away as my daughter smiled at me warmly before she wiped away tears I didn't even know had rolled down my cheeks. She had that effect on me. No matter how much the past loomed over me and threatened to disrupt the happy world I had built, A'Miracle was always like that ray of sunshine that bursts through the clouds to create a rainbow. She was my new Salvation Song.

"What's wrong mommy are you sad? I bet my kisses and tickles can make you all better." My baby said as she jumped on me and kissed away all of my sorrow. Minutes later A'Miracle and I rolled around on the lawn laughing as we tickled and kissed each other into submission. We laid on the sprawling lawn with the Cali sun high above our heads as a rainbow stretched form one corner of the sky to the next, and I wished that my life could stay that beautiful forever. I laid there wrapped up in my daughter's arms for minutes as we talked about how beautiful the sky was and how fortunate we were to see it.

By the time we got up off the lawn and went into the house to go about our day, most of the sorrow my dream had drug to the surface was gone; however, I couldn't stop the vivid images as they flashed in my mind. When Jerrod got home from working overtime on a Saturday it was late afternoon and I had just finished the salad, baked beans, and spaghetti for our cookout. He snuck up behind me as he often did and slipped his arms around my waist before he kissed my neck gently. "Ummm Mrs. Hill, you're smelling mighty delicious today my love. Just waiting on daddy to come home huh? Well, I'm ready to eat." Jerrod said as he spent me around and wrapped me in his arms before he kissed me deeply and passionately on the lips.

I kissed my husband back and welcomed the warmth that only his love could bring, but my body spoke volumes by itself. I could tell the second our lips touched that Jerrod knew something was bothering me, because just like me he wore his heart on his sleeve. He quickly let me go and held me out so that he could stare into my eyes with that penetrating glance and see straight down to my soul. I tried to look away as my husband looked at me with love and concern written all over his face, but he grabbed my chin and forced me to look at him. "Tisha what's wrong baby? Don't say nothing because I know it has to be something." Jerrod said as I shook my head no and attempted to walk away from him.

I hated to hide anything from my husband, but I knew that our happiness was already fragile with everything we had gone through in the past. The last thing I wanted to do was send our world spiraling out of control once again and end up broken and alone. I wanted to keep my family just the way it was so I forced that radiant smile I usually wore back on to my face before I turned back to look at Jerrod.

"I'm okay baby just a little tired, I had a lot of work to do today on my book. I had to relive some things I wanted to leave buried, but I'm better now that you're home." I lied as I stepped back into my husband's embrace and hugged him tightly.

I could tell Jerrod was still not buying what I was saying because his embrace wasn't as tight when he hugged me that second time. However, lucky for me A'Miracle loved to make sure her daddy knew she missed him whenever he was gone, so she popped in right on time to offer a much needed distraction. "It's my daddy, it's my daddy. I missed you daddy." A'Miracle said as she popped around the corner to the kitchen and ran towards Jerrod.

He slowly let me go while he stared intently into my eyes and I tried to hide the pain that was still inside of me. A'Miracle broke our gaze as she jumped into to Jerrod's arms and his look of concern turned into nothing but happiness. Within seconds they were giggling and joking as Jerrod danced around the kitchen while he held A'Miracle tightly to him and sung I Choose You by Willie Hutch. I stood by the stove as I stirred the beans and watched the two people I loved most in the world love on each other. I couldn't help but to adore the relationship Jerrod and A'Miracle had, which was a father, daughter relationship I always dreamed of.

I wiped away the single tear that had fallen from my eye when I heard Jerod tell A'Miracle she was the best thing that ever happened to him. "And you're the best daddy ever." A'Miracle said back to Jerrod before she gave him a big kiss on the cheek and he returned the love as he kissed her on the forehead.

"Okay now that both of my ladies are okay and have felt daddy's love, I'm gonna go shower right fast and then we will crank the grill up and get the party started. Go put on your pretty dresses ladies, its dinner under the stars tonight." Jerrod said with the biggest smile I had ever seen spread across his face.

Within seconds both Jerrod and A'Miracle had disappeared up the stairs full of happiness and anxious to spend time together. I tried to feel the same enthusiasm that they felt as I climbed the steps behind them, but something deep inside kept telling me something bad was on the way. I couldn't shake that feeling even as I changed into my yellow and white sundress and went outside to sit in my hammock. I sat there and swung for a few minutes, trapped in my memories until suddenly music filled my ears. I turned around to see Jerrod as he came out of the house with the meat to start the grill while A'Miracle and her dog Binx trailed behind him. I watched Jerrod light the grill and start the meat while talking to A'Miracle and Binx like they were the audience and he was the host of his own cooking show. By the time he came to sit down beside me I was so tickled by his antics, tears rolled down my cheeks.

My fit of laughter finally stopped when Jerrod reached over to grab my face so that I could look at him. The look in his eyes told me that he knew what was going on without me even having to say a word. I told him anyway though. I sat there and revealed all of the secret nightmares and vivid daydreams I'd had in the past few months as A'Miracle ran back and forth with Binx and Jerrod listened intently. When I was done talking tears fell from my cheeks again and like every other time in my life since we were reunited, Jerrod was right there to wipe them away.

"Baby I think it's only natural that you sometimes remember the past. We have to have darkness in order to have light my love. The thing is, we can't let the darkness consume us. Don't let the darkness consume you Tisha. The past is the past. We have to just keep moving forward baby. I'm here for you no matter what and we will get through this all. I know what's really wrong. You're missing your sister and your brother. We should plan a trip back home soon. Maybe having them around for a while will let you see its okay to relive the past sometimes but you also have to look forward to the future. I love you Shartisha Hill and I'm going to tell you like I told you about seven years ago. WE GONE BE AITE!!" Jerrod said before he kissed me on the tip of my nose and I started to laugh too.

A'Miracle and Binx were at our side in seconds to join in on the fun as we all laughed and hugged for a while. After dinner, Jerrod and I sat on the deck in our glider with A'Miracle and Binx in the swing, and watched the sun set over the mountains. It was so beautiful and peaceful in that moment I wanted it to never end. Jerrod wrapped his arm around me and I laid my head on his shoulder before I sighed and released that twinge of fear inside. I felt complete and whole in that moment and that was a feeling I had never experienced before. "Do you think things can stay this perfect forever?" I asked Jerrod as I watched A'Miracle close her eyes and let the peacefulness of the moment rock her to sleep.

For a second all was quiet and I thought Jerrod wouldn't answer, but then he kissed me in the top of the head before he spoke. "I hope that it will. I will do my best to keep it this way." Jerrod promised while he looked me in the eyes and I felt that maybe it could stay that way.

That feeling didn't last long though because suddenly the phone rang and startled us out of our loving moment. I told Jerrod I would get it so he wouldn't have to get up and dashed across the lawn and into the house to answer it. As soon as I answered the phone and heard the voice on the other end I knew that the pain that I felt lurking around the corner had found its way home. I just hoped that this time I wouldn't be destroyed in the process.

"Tisha, it's me. I need to come down there for a while. Shit real ugly down her in Sacramento and I think that if I stay here I'm going to jail. Can I live with you and Jerrod for a while? At least until a nigga figure out what he finna do?" My brother Sha said frantically into the phone as my heart dropped into my stomach.

I stood there frozen in shock for a second with the phone in my hand and I tried to make sense of what Sha had just said. The nineteen-year-old man Sha had become over the years was so much different from the smart, shy boy I had raised and I didn't know what to expect. I did know that my brother's personality hadn't changed and trying to figure out what had happened with him over the phone would not be successful. SO like the dedicated sister who always acted as his mother, I swallowed the lump in my throat, smothered the cries and screams threatening to come out of my mouth and did what any good sister would do.

"Be at the bus station at 10 am Sha, you know I got you. Love you little brother." I said to Sha as I confirmed his ticket on my laptop and waited on him to respond. I could feel my heart beating a mile a minute as I stood there on wobbly legs and glanced out of the window to see Jerrod and A'Miracle still laying out peacefully. I was happy they were oblivious to what was going on and I was going to try to shield them for as long as I could.

"Thank you Tisha. You all I got because Terricka don't care about shit anymore and my daddy just as bad since he got this new bitch. I gotta go before I do some shit I don't want to T. I got to. Now I understand why you had to go when you did. Know that I don't blame you for shit big sis. I love you. Matter of fact, I love you to the moon and back Tisha. 1!" Sha said before he hung up and left me to stand there with tears in my eyes.

I stood at the sink with the phone still in my hand for a minute before my fingers dialed a number on their own. Before I knew it I was on the phone with Terricka as she yelled for me not to call again and how she didn't give a fuck what was happening to Sha. I held the phone and didn't say a word as she ranting on and on about me and Sha then went on to curse her kids out. By the time she suddenly hung up on me tears ran down my face fast and hard as my body shook from pure emotion. I felt lost as I stood there wondering what was going on with my siblings. I cursed my mother from her grave and blamed it all on her as my emotions got the best of me. Before I knew it I was throwing plates while I cried and cursed to the top of my lungs. I know I must have looked like a mad woman to Jerrod as he burst into the house and grabbed me up in his arms.

"TISHA what's wrong?" Jerrod asked as tears fell from his eyes and I blurted out everything through my tears. When I had let it all out I felt drained and lifeless in his arms as he carried me into the living room and laid me on the sofa. "Just lay here for a second baby and let me go get A'Miracle and put her to bed. Then we will get you a bath and off to bed. Everything is going to be aite, I promise you. Shamel will be here tomorrow and soon we will all be back together with Terricka. It's gonna work out baby, I promise you." Jerrod said before he kissed me again and dashed outside to get our baby.

I laid there with my eyes closed as visions of what could happen played in my mind. By the time Jerrod came back to get me and put me in the bath, I felt numb and so out of it I could barely walk. My husband carried me upstairs and to our room where he put me in a hot, bubble bath. Jerrod washed me gently as I sat there in a daze and wondered how my life could be so bleak. Once out the tub I allowed my husband to love on me after he dried off my body and tears. Jerrod and I made love to the sound of our heartbeats that night while he professed his love and devotion then I fell asleep in his arms.

My dreams were filled with happiness and hope that night, not the sadness and sorrow that had haunted me many nights before. I woke up refreshed and ready to conquer the day until I went downstairs to make breakfast and the doorbell rang. As soon as I opened the door and saw my brother as he stood in front of me 6'4", 200lb with dreads, gold teeth, a black eye, and bandages and bruises all over him, I knew that pain had found my family once again and there was no way I could turn back. I just hoped that the sins of our mother would spare Sha and I could save him from some of the pain I had felt. I hoped, but just like lottery winners in the ghetto, it seemed that hope didn't exist.

Chapter 2

Sha: Fuck Second Chances

After I hung up the phone with Tisha I just couldn't shake the monkey on my back that seemed to hold me down. Just the sound of her voice brought up memoires that I tried to bury forever. I missed my sisters and their love but the thought of them just dug up too much pain. I couldn't think about them without thinking about Denise and that was just too much for me to deal with. However, I knew I was in a fucked up situation where I was at so once again my sisters were all I had.

I sat the phone down and held my head as that intense pain my traumatic brain injury and horrible childhood brought on took over me. The throbbing was so bad that no matter how much I rubbed my temples or the massive scar that stretched from one side of my head to the other under my dreads, it wouldn't stop. Suddenly I was overcome by the most vivid memory I had, the memory of the day I almost died. In that moment I was that ten, almost eleven-year-old boy again being drug from his hiding place by a drugged out psycho mama and lead to his death.

"You little ugly muthafucka, it's you she loves the most. It's you she's always trying to protect. That bitch stabbed my man, the nigga who kept me straight so now I gotta take something from her. You what she loves huh? Well, she does but I don't. I hate you Shamel and everything you represent. If I had known you were gonna be retarded when you were born I would have killed you then, but I didn't so I will just rid the world of yo worthless ass now." My mother said with malice as she drug my small, malnutrition body out of the apartment and to the rail with her nails dug deep into my wrists while I fought, squirmed, and tried to claw my way out of her grip.

I remember how I clung to her fucking arms with tears in my eyes as I begged her to let me go. I remember the cold, evil look in the bitch's eyes too as she yanked her dirty, clammy skin out of my grip and hoisted my frail body up over her head. I could still feel the way that my heart raced in my chest and hear my own screams ring in my ears as I sat in the oversized recliner next to the window at my father's house nine, almost ten years later. That memory haunted my dreams and caused my anxiety along with the fits of rage that were almost uncontrollable. Those memories and the nightmares that accompanied them are what caused the wedge between me and my father. That along with bitch that he married and her four kids.

From the day Alice married my dad in secret at a courthouse wedding one day when I was 14 and at school, my life changed. The first two years after the accident before her, were hard with all of my surgeries and having to learn to walk and talk again. My dad missed so much work and was so worried about if I would ever recover he lost his job and we had to move in with his mother. Money was tight after that and life was a bit hard but it was nothing compared to what I had come from. My dad, Shaheim and I became closer than ever during that time and he gave me the love I needed to get as close to normal as possible again. Physically I regained my strength with my motor skills intact and started to feel like Sha again.

All that was left as a reminder of my horrible past were all of my scars and the burn that covered half of my body. That along with the mental stains that made it hard for me to trust or really get close to anyone, except my father and grandmother Rose. So for those years I had a real life while I struggled with my internal demons on my own and watched my father dwell in loneliness and guilt for never being there for me. That is why when he met Alice I welcomed the smile she brought to his fucking face and thought that I would finally get the life I deserved.

Soon after they got together though Alice moved in and everything flipped upside down. I found out she had twin sons older than me, a daughter the same age as me, and a daughter who was a year younger. All of them invaded my world and caused a rift between me and the dad I had really just started to know and love, which was a rift that could not be repaired. Once they were married after my fifteenth birthday, the bullshit began with Alice. She excluded me from shit because she said I was slow and wouldn't catch on or me and my walker was too much of a burden for her.

Sometimes when I would come into a room her and her kids were in I could overhear them talk about how things would be better if I wasn't around. I told my dad about that shit and he did nothing, just told me to suck it up and stop whining like a girl. He acted just like the bitch ass nigga I knew he was deep inside and took his hoe side. That's why I internalized my anger for a while and worked hard to get strong and in no time I did that. In fact, I was in better shape than most young boys who hadn't been inches within death.

Despite the shit everyone said I overcame my physical limitations, started to play basketball, and worked hard on the mental and social challenges I faced. I was in special education for a while as I struggled to speak and understand what I read, then one day something just clicked. Maybe it was the nightmares of my mother being alive and coming to get me or the constant verbal abuse and degradation from my father, step mother, and three of her kids. Whatever it was, that shit motivated me and I started to understand every fucking thing. I graduated high school at 17 with an honor's diploma and a scholarship to UCLA but that shit quickly went south. It was like my dad, despite what he said, didn't believe in me or want me to be shit. He was stressed at that point about paying the high ass mortgage for the house in The Fabulous Forties subdivision his wife insisted we move to so he took it out on me.

Every day for a year he would come home and find a reason to either lash out at me with his words or lay hands on me. He thought I was his own personal fucking punching bag the moment that bitch moved in, but that day was different. I was tired of him telling me I wasn't pulling my weight because I was retarded or nagging about everything I did or said. It was like he took on Denise's role to torture me and I wasn't in for another devil running my life. So I did something I thought I would never have to do and I beat his ass that day like a pussy ass nigga in the street. That shit landed my black ass in jail after his wife called the police and he pressed charges for domestic assault.

I spent six months in jail behind that shit with no one to come see me or to even fucking call. I wanted to call my sisters because I knew they would be there, especially Tisha, but I couldn't bring myself to tell her I was in jail. I knew Tisha would be disappointed so I dismissed that idea before I even let it stick in my head. Instead I linked up with a goon I had met in the hood one day I was with Alice's daughter who was my same age named Lydia, the only person who liked me, and was reintroduced to the wild side of life. This nigga Lydia introduced me to was a real fool named Toon and we clicked instantly. That nigga was like me a retard, fuck up that nobody wanted, however, just like me he wasn't actually retarded just damaged as hell with a need to belong somewhere.

On lockdown me and that nigga ran the pod, sold dope, and took out our aggression on any nigga who dared to step up. I was a different fucking person when I was around that nigga, free to inflict pain instead of receive it and I liked that shit. That's why when they finally let me out I went to North Highlands and kicked it in Cottage Meadows with Toon and his goons, free to fuck up the world. I was out there for six months just reckless. I got down with the cause and joined the lifestyle which included drugs, banging, sex, and anything else I wanted to do. I spent my nineteenth birthday in the trap with bad bitches, dope, and guns all around me. I did some shit that really fucked with my mind while I was out there non-stop, which is why I wasn't even mad when my dad finally found me one day.

Lydia brought him right to me and I came back on the promise that shit would change. It did change for a while too until Alice lost some earrings. That bitch swear I had them and that's what lead to the black eye that was still tender to the touch. That and the fact that I had a meltdown at my job at Footlocker after a bitch who looked just like Denise walked in. I couldn't control myself when I saw her, I tried to reach out and touch that hoe before everybody grabbed me and told me to calm down. After that I just flipped the fuck out from everything that had built up and I wrecked the entire fucking store.

My dad freaked the fuck out when I got home that day and yelled about how I was a retarded, fuck-up, thief because he knew I had Alice's earrings. His words as he yelled in my face that day hurt, and although almost a week had passed they still made my heart race and anger build up in my heart. I don't think it was really what he was saying that fucked with me because I didn't care what a bitch nigga like him who let a hoe run him thought. No, I think it was more so what the words represented because they reminded me of the hate I had heard all of my life. It wasn't really his voice I heard that yelled out I was nothing, it was Denise, the monster who haunted my dreams. She still had a way to ruin my life and make me pay for her sins, even from the grave.

I had to sit back in the chair and close my eyes in order to catch my breath as this realization mixed with the voice of Denise filled my mind. It was like a symphony of sorrow that swirled in my mind and ignited a rage that made me scared.

"Sha you retarded muthafucka, you are worthless. Why did I have you? You ain't never gonna be shit. I hate you." Their voices yelled in my mind as they took turns in an attempt to tear me apart.

I quickly used my hands to cover my ears to calm myself and silence the torture in my mind. I squeezed my palms deep into my ears and the side of my head as my body trembled and I gritted my teeth while huge tears ran down my cheeks. I could feel one of those uncontrollable rages inside of me as it waited on something to initiate the explosion that was evitable. I didn't have to wait long though because suddenly I could hear the voice of one of my tormentors close by.

"What the fuck wrong with you old stupid ass boy? Didn't you hear me calling you? Sha? Shamel? SHA!" My dad yelled as I slowly opened my puffy, bloodshot eyes and stared into his face.

I could tell that he was damn near drunk from the slur in his speech and the unsteady sway in his step. I knew that meant he was ready for confrontation so I quickly stood up and got ready to give him what he came for. I towered over my father at 6'4", 200lbs of pure muscle while he stood his little old, 5'7" 180lb ass there and tried to look tough. That shit didn't impress nor scare me anymore and his bitch ass could see that from the way I showed him my grill and folded my arms in front of me. I could see the bitch in his eyes too as he mimicked my actions, but he didn't back down. It was like he wanted to provoke me to beat his ass and I was ready to give him his wish. "Yeah I heard you calling me. What the fuck you want?" I said through clenched teeth before I quickly wiped away the last tear that linger on my cheek.

I was tired of the shit and ready to click so I wasn't concerned with honoring thy father. I figured fuck that because how could I honor a nigga who didn't give a fuck about me. He proved that when he left me with a devil that all but successfully killed me. Then when he did get me away from danger and with him he did the exact damn thing. Hell no, wasn't no honor. At that point Shaheim was just another nigga in the streets and I would show him that if he decided to put his hands on me.

"What nigga, so you heard me? You lil bitch ass retard. Fuck you down here crying for. Remembering the shit mommy did to you huh? Well, now I'm starting to see why she might have done it. You are a worthless piece of shit who just brings trouble everywhere you go. You can't do shit right Sha and then you stand and just stare when someone calls you on yo shit. You are that damn mute Denise said you were so I can't blame her for beating yo ass. I'mma beat yo bitch ass if you ever talk to me out of line again or act like you don't hear me. You understand that? Can you comprehend retard or should I slow it down for you?"

Shaheim yelled as he walked closer to me and I let my arms fall down to my side.

I let an evil smile much like the one my mother always wore spread across my face as tears rolled down my cheeks and I clenched my fists ready to attack. I was so fucking mad I couldn't stop my body as it began to jerk and I prepared to take off. "Oh, the lil retarded baby crying. What you want daddy to do get you a paci? What you need a hug nigga?" Shaheim said as he stepped so close to me I could feel his breath on my neck. "Don't touch me dog. For real. If you touch me I'm about to lay yo old ass out. Test me if you think I'm playing." I said as I continued to stare straight ahead and he got on his tip toes to try and look me in the eyes.

I paid him no mind as he stumbled a few times before he was almost at my eye length. "If I touch you what you gonna do ole bitch ass nigga? Have a muthafucking tantrum? Grown ass baby. Nigga you ain't gonna do shit." Shaheim said as he suddenly used his index finger to poke me square in the chest.

As soon as I felt his finger touch me I reacted and grabbed his ass by the neck before I choke slammed him to the floor. I wrapped my massive, scarred hands around his throat and began to squeeze as he squirmed like a fish out of water beneath me. He tried to apologize and beg me to get up but at that point I didn't want to hear shit he had to say. All I wanted to do was fuck him up and end my turmoil once and for all.

"Fuck you, you evil bastard. You're just like Denise. First you leave me only too pick me up and treat me worse than she did. You let that bitch and her kids talk shit about me too. Nigga you ain't no better than the junky who raised me. At least she had an excuse because she was drugged out and mentally ill. What's yo excuse though? Huh, daddy? Spit it out ole retarded ass nigga. I CAN'T HEAR YOU!" I yelled as I dug my thumbs deep into my dad's throat and pressed down as hard as I could.

For a second I saw Denise's face on his body and that shit made me go insane. Before I knew it I had let go of his throat and unleashed a combination of punches that bust his shit on contact. I lost all control as I beat my father and he squirmed before I wrapped my hands around his throat again. I squeezed as hard as I could as I stared at the blood on my hands and listened to his insults ring in my ears. I could feel the life as it slowly seeped out his body and I didn't give a fuck.

"SHA! SHA PLEASE STOP. SHAME, LET GO!" Lydia yelled as she broke my haze and began to pull me off of my dad. I didn't resist her as I slowly came back to my senses and she pulled me up. In that moment I looked down and I realized I had fucked up again. I stared down at my father's bloody, battered face as he laid there and moaned. I felt panic set in as I realized the severity of what I had done and thought about the jail time that would follow. "Sha. Sha, we have to go so you won't go to jail. Come on Sha!" Lydia yelled as she grabbed my arm and tried to pull me towards the door.

Everything seemed to slow down as I looked at her and told her to go and that I was right behind her. I watched her as she ran out of the room before I turned back to stare down at my dad. For a second I felt sorry for him as he struggled to get up, but slipped in his own blood and fell back on to his back. Part of me wanted to help him and salvage whatever relationship we could still have, but the smarter part of me knew that was long gone. That thought was solidified when my dad started to laugh and stared up at me through swollen eyes.

"You think you did something huh pussy? You caught me off guard bitch, but I'mma get my lick back. Oh yeah, ole bitch ass nigga I'mma get my lick back. I might get yo bitch ass threw back in that fucking cage, that's where an animal like you belongs anyway. Or I might just show yo lil retarded ass how a real gangsta get down and bring that shit to you. Whatever I do though lil bitch, you gonna regret the day you fell out of your junky mammy's ass. That's my word. Bitch nigga, fuck you. You ain't my son and I'm gonna show yo bitch ass that." Shahiem yelled from the floor as my rage surged again and I laughed an evil laugh of my own.

My laugh was so cold and shrill it made my father stop and stare up at me with fear and regret in his eyes. "Haaaa, you think that hurt me nigga? You right, I ain't yo son. I ain't shit to you and you ain't shit to me so I don't give a fuck if you die right now. I do care about the next child you might bring into this world and ruin him like you've done me. So for that I'm about to do the world a favor and eliminate the chance for you to reproduce. Pussy ass niggas like you don't need kids so I think I'm doing a public service." I said as my father finally caught on to what I was about to do, but it was much too late.

I used my size 12 shoe to stomp down on his groin so hard that all of the contents of his stomach instantly came up. I jumped back as he screamed and held himself while vomit continued to spew out of his mouth. I couldn't stop my laughter as I watched him waddle around in filth on the ground and cry like a little bitch. I started to walk away just as he reached out and grabbed my pants leg and begged me to stay.

"Please Sha, I'm sorry. I know I fucked up. Don't leave me like this, at least call the ambulance because you really fucked me up. Please son help me and forgive me for what I've done. I've been no better than your mother to you and for that I am so sorry. Please Shamel, please. Just give me a second chance. Everyone deserves a second chance, even you. Let's both start over son. Please Sha." He begged as I began to laugh again.

My laughter caused him to stop his pleas because he saw that shit wasn't about to work. I walked back around where he could see my face as Lydia blew the horn outside and he tried to sit up. "Nigga it's too late for sorry and what you mean second chance? I been on this earth 19 years, nigga we way past a second chance. All that shit over now though cause it's fuck you just like you said fuck me. Fuck everything about you nigga, yo bitch, her kids, this house, and most of all nigga FUCK SECOND CHANCES!" I yelled before I lifted my size twelve high in the air once again and stomped my father right in the face.

By the time I turned to run out of the room all that could be heard was his loud, labored breath as he laid unconscious in a puddle of his own blood followed by the erratic beat of my heart. I quickly ran up to my room and grabbed my bag that was packed and ready before I ran back downstairs and out of the house. I ran to Lydia's car with tears in my eyes and my laughter in the wind, and never looked back.

Lydia and I rode for a while in silence as I replayed all that had happened in my mind. I was so lost in my thoughts that I didn't even know she had tried to get my attention until I felt her hand on my shoulder. I almost jumped out of my seat for a second as my evil thoughts drifted to the back of my mind and I turned to stare into Lydia's beautiful face. Her clear, smooth apricot skin glistened in the sunlight and her grey eyes shone as she stared at me with genuine love.

"Sha I'm so sorry for everything that has happened to you and for how everyone treats you. It's not right the things they do and you don't deserve any of it. Know that I will always help and support you, and I won't let them railroad you on another charge. I'm gonna tell everything if they call the police and be a witness for you if necessary. In the meantime, I need you to just lay low over here with Toon nem. He moved to a different apartment in the complex so Shaheim won't know where you at as long as you don't hang out. Just hold on Sha, everything is about to get better. I can feel it." Lydia said as she reached over and squeezed my hand and melted my heart.

She was the only person besides my sisters who could do that to me and make me feel so loved I forgot about all of my pain. She always showed me compassion and helped me to see that I wasn't the worthless fuck everyone said I was. That's why I liked her so much. In another life and time, she would have been my girlfriend, but my father and the fucked up curse on my life ruined that too. I was okay with that though as long as I had her near, even if it was only for a short time.

"Thank you Lydia, maine you all I got besides my sisters. Real talk. One day I'm gonna pay you back for all you've done for me. I promise." I said as I squeezed her hand and she looked over at me and smiled with tears in her eyes. "Pay me back by getting on your feet and showing all of those muthafuckas that they don't know shit. Pay me back by living your life for you and leaving the sins of your parents behind. If you do that I will be more than satisfied because all I want is what's best for you and to see you happy." Lydia said as she squeezed my hand and a nigga felt flustered as fuck.

I didn't know what to say next after that because I had never been in a heartfelt situation like that with a girl I actually liked. I didn't have to feel or work hard with the thots I fucked with in the hood, but Lydia was nothing like them. She was a beautiful, smart, caring, talented, mature woman, wise far beyond her years. She was the total package, the perfect wife, which is why I knew she was too good for me. I knew that my curse would only bring her down that's why I never acted on the feelings I had for her after she kissed me at my 17 birthday party. I just blew it off so I wouldn't fuck things up, just like I did at that moment.

"That's wassup." I said nervously to Lydia before I released her grip on my hand and turned to look out of the window. For the rest of the ride we both remained quiet and just listened to the songs that played on the radio. When we pulled into Cottage Meadows Lydia took me to Toon's new apartment in the back of the complex and I quickly jumped out and grabbed my bag out of the back passenger seat. I walked around the car to Lydia's side just as she got out with a wad of cash and cellphone in her hand.

"Here Sha, and don't say no because I can't have you out her broke with no means of communication. I care about you, can't you see that and I want you to be alright. I need you to be alright." Lydia said as tears streamed down her cheeks. To see her cry like that made my heart melt just like it did whenever I saw one of my sisters cry. Before I knew it all of that fear and awkwardness I felt in the car was gone and I had stepped up to Lydia and wiped her tears with my thumb.

"Don't cry Lydia, I care about you too. As a matter of fact, I love you. I said before I could even think about it. As soon as the words left my mouth I felt like my ass was gonna pass out as all the blood rushed to my head. All I could do was let my natural instincts kick in as I grabbed her chin in my hand then leaned down to kiss her. What I felt when our lips touched was enough to make a thug change his life. All of her love and passion pulsated through my body and went straight to my heart as she wrapped her arms around my neck. I dropped my bag quick as fuck and wrapped my arms around her waist as she pressed them double d's up against a nigga. We got lost in the moment as our hearts and love intertwined and I felt maybe there could be hope for a happy future.

When our passion subsided, I let Lydia go and stood there and stared into her eyes. I wanted to tell her everything I felt bad as fuck, but I knew I was in no position to start anything with her. My life was nothing but heartache and pain and I didn't want to drag her into my hell. I felt she was too good of a person to indulge in my misery so I fought my need for her. "I love you too Sha, I really do. So what does this mean for us?" Lydia asked as I thought of the perfect way to tell her that I was too fucked up for anybody to love or be with, especially someone as good as her.

I searched for the right words but as soon as I was about to open my mouth Toon's 2015 Chrysler 300 pulled into the parking lot followed by three other cars filled to the capacity with goons. All of them jumped out with guns in hand as they yelled about who they were going to kill. I knew that meant some shit had gone down and that it probably wasn't over so I told Lydia to go.

"Look Lydia, I can't get into all that right now and further more I don't think you want to go there with a fucked up nigga like me. I'm rotten baby, to the core so maybe you should find somebody better. I love you enough to let you go Lydia. For real. Now get the fuck outta here before these niggas start shooting." I said as she grabbed my hand with tears in her eyes and I tried to snatch away.

I tried, but not really because honestly I didn't want her to go. I couldn't help but let her wrap me in her embrace again as she kissed me and tears ran down her face. "I don't care what you say, I love you. I love you and I want to be with you. I will wait for a lifetime if I have to because you deserve love and I deserve you. You're worth it Sha, you're worth love, so I'll go, but I will never leave you. EVER!" Lydia whispered in my ear before she kissed me on the neck and quickly hopped into her car.

I watched her drive off as my niggas crowded around me and filled me in on what was going on. "Maine them niggas rode down on us in broad daylight my nigga Sha. Them bitches tried to take me out. You ready to ride nigga?" Toon asked me as he handed me a kush blunt and I thought about the love that had just drove away.

I deeply inhaled the kush as an internal battle broke out between the side of me that just wanted to love and be loved, and that side that just didn't give a fuck. I thought about what would happen if I left and tried to be with Lydia, then I realized I had nowhere to go and that the police were probably looking for me. I knew I had that ticket from Tisha that would be at the bus station the next morning, but that didn't do shit for the situation I was in at that moment. With all of that in mind I made a decision to just live for the moment and say fuck how it would turn out.

"Toon you my nigga, the only nigga who ever fucked with me like I mean something. So if you need me to ride nigga, you know I got you... God help any nigga who gets in our way." I said as I handed him back the blunt and grabbed the AR15 he had in his hand. "That's what I'm talking about, my muthafucking dog. Let's go smash on these niggas Sha." Toon said as he showed me love then threw my bag in the backseat as we all loaded up.

We rode around the west side of Sacramento for hours as we looked for the niggas we were prepared to murder. As the sun began to dip lower in the sky we all realized we weren't going to find them so we headed back to the hood. Part of me was relieved the niggas hadn't crossed our paths because I knew what I would have done if they did. With all of the hurt and pain inside of me I knew that I wouldn't have been able to control my rage and I probably would have killed every nigga in sight. I sighed in relief when we pulled up back in front of the house because I had saved my soul from hell for another day. I felt numb and high as fuck as we walked into Toon's apartment and the party that never ended raged once again.

In minutes the house was filled with thug niggas and bad, project bitches half naked and smelling good as fuck. I quickly found me a corner and posted up with a bottle of E&J in one hand and a blunt in the other as I surveyed the room. I knew that I wasn't supposed to mix the meds I took for my migraines with alcohol but at that moment I was at the point of no return. I had to do something to dull that pain in my heart and silence the voices in my head so I drunk and smoked until everything moved in slow motion. About an hour after we got back and the party was in full swing, one of the homegirls I fucked with tough named Peaches came over to sit by me and said something that sobered my ass up real quick.

"Maine Sha, I don't know what the fuck you been up to but police been over here tough today looking for you. I heard one of them say it was a warrant out for you on a domestic violence charge before they suited up to go. You gotta lay low bruh cause I don't know what the fuck going on." Peaches said as I nodded at her and a million thoughts ran through my head.

I sat there silent and still for a while as I thought about going back to the cage. That was the last place I wanted to be so I knew I had to get my ass on that bus, but the problems was, I didn't want to leave Lydia. I got lost in thoughts of her for a while as I sat there and rolled another blunt and hoped I could regain the high Peaches had blew. As soon as I finished and had the blunt rolled up, a bunch of loud voices outside caught my attention. They were so loud they overpowered the music and caused Toon to run over to the stereo to cut it down.

"What the fuck going on?" Toon said as he looked around the room before he went over to the door. "SHA YOU LIL BITCH ASS NIGGA, BRING YO PUSSY ASS OUT. YOU SUCKER PUNCHED MY UNCLE AND BEAT HIM UP ON THAT RETARD SHIT, LET ME SEE YOU DO THAT TO ME. COME OUT SHA OLE BITCH ASS NIGGA. SHHHHAAAAAA, BRING YO HOE ASS OUT!" Some nigga yelled as I suddenly got up out my seat.

All of my niggas rushed towards the door as I followed and as soon as it opened we were on GO. We rushed out right into the crowd of niggas Shaheim had brought with him to get me, his son. It was just like he said, I was nothing to him and that was obvious when I saw him as he stood in the middle of 15 niggas all bandaged up with a bat in his hand. To see him as he stood there ready for war like I was some random nigga, gave me enough motivation to let the true beast out so rushed towards his ass without thought. When I moved my niggas moved and in minutes it was a huge brawl in the middle of the parking lot.

I ran straight into the tall light skinned nigga my dad called his nephew and who had called me out and knocked his fucking grill out with my first punch. I hit that bitch so hard he flew into a car and I was on him in a second as I kicked the bitch until his head caved in. I kicked that bitch until his bloody body slumped down the car then somebody hit me in the back of the head with a bat. That shit hit me so hard it made my teeth chatter and I felt like I would pass out for a second but my anger wouldn't let me do that.

Instead I turned around and football tackled my daddy and rammed his bitch ass into the ground. He dropped the bat as soon as I dropped him then I began to beat his ass. I delivered a series of forearm strikes and punches into his face as the fights around us raged on. I beat him until blood was up to my wrists then the gunshots started. The first shot came from behind me and whizzed through my shirt as I bent down over my father. I looked in the direction the bullet came from to see one of my daddy's goons as he pointed his 9MM right at me. I was frozen for a second as I saw my life flash before my eyes and decided I wasn't ready to give up yet. "Toon, aid and assist bruh." I yelled as the nigga cocked back and prepared to bust at my ass again and I sat there like a duck.

Before he could though my niggas were on him as he got hit multiple times with a 9MM and the AR15. After that Toon sprayed the crowd as I got my ass up and ran inside. I was in and out in a flash as I grabbed my bag and prepared to get the fuck out of town. Death had come so close again I could smell it, just like the first time and I had a feeling my luck would soon run out. When I got back outside all of the niggas that weren't hit in the gun fire had scattered, but there were multiple bodies on the ground and my father was one of them. I ran over to see that he had taken a bullet to both legs before I ran away and his pleas for help rang in my ears.

I ran fast and hard with no particular destination in mind as traffic whizzed by me and I felt like I was about to lose my mind. I didn't stop until I had made it to a Burger King, where I then sat on the sidewalk and dialed the only number I knew.

"I need you. Come get me. I'm at that Burger King by the apartments." I said into the phone as I got up, walked inside and sat at a table by the window.

I was paranoid as fuck as I sat there and watched every car that pulled on to the lot. "Okay, I'm here waiting and I love you too." I said to Lydia before I hung up and got up to walk to the counter and order. I ordered a whopper combo just so that I could sit inside the restaurant and wait on my ride then I sat back at my table by the window. I played with the fries on my tray and never even touched the burger before Lydia whipped on to the lot to rescue me. I kinda felt like a bitch who had to be saved as she left the car on and jumped out to come in and get me. I met her at the door as the concern in her eyes melted my heart once again and caused me to be soft, sensitive Sha.

"What happened baby? You bleeding all over! Oh my God what happened Sha?" She asked as I told her I was okay. Even though the cut in my head hurt like hell and I felt like my wrist was broken I didn't tell her as I escorted her back to her car. "Baby I'm okay. Let's just get the fuck out of here. Take me to the bus station. I gotta get out of here for a while." I told her before she kissed me quickly and we jumped in the car.

I watched her from the corner of my eye as we sped off the lot and the pain in my head intensified. Suddenly emotions and memories hit me like a ton of bricks and I felt tears run down my face. I dried that shit up quick with the back of my hand and hoped that Lydia hadn't seen me shed a tear. I knew she did though when she suddenly stopped three blocks from the bus station and turned to look at me.

"You don't have to hide anything from me Sha, I told you I love you for you. I already know what happened and I hate Shaheim for all the bullshit he has done and is still doing. So what's your next move now because it's not safe for you nowhere near Sacramento. You said take you to the bus station and I think that's a good idea. Why don't we just run away together?" She said as she took a first aid kit out from under her seat and began to clean and dress my wounds.

I thought about what she said as she bandaged my head and for a second I was ready to go. However, my logic kicked in quick and told me that wouldn't be wise until I got my shit together. I couldn't have the woman I loved on the run with me while I was still trying to deal with my demons. I would be able to get my shit together faster if I knew she was safe so I had to get that fantasy out of her mind.

"We can't do that Lydia, not now anyway. I don't have shit. I'm on the run, and you got school and shit. Let me get my shit together and build something for us then I promise I will come back for you. I love you girl, but you deserve better than I can give right now and I won't put you through that. Okay?" I said with tears in my eyes as she scooted closer to me and wrapped her arms around my neck.

"Baby I love you and I want to be with you Sha, but I understand. You have to do what you have to do. Just know that I will wait on you forever, no matter what. Let's just stay like this for a while so I will have something to hold on to." She whispered before she kissed me passionately and then laid her head on my chest.

We stayed like that for a long time as she cried and I kissed away her tears. By the time we pulled off and headed to the airport I felt anxious to get the sadness over and start a life with her. At the airport we kissed for ten minutes before I told her to leave or I wouldn't be able to let her go. I felt like a piece of me was stolen as I watched her walk away and disappear into the crowd. Once she was gone I made my way to the counter and found my ticket was there just like Tisha said it would be. I quickly made arrangements to get on the four a.m. bus instead of the one that left at seven and settled into a chair to sleep.

Slumber found me fast and my dream was filled with nothing but chaos from the moment I closed my eyes. I quickly found myself wrapped up in a series of nightmares that switched from memories to predictions of the future. I saw both of my tormentors and all they did to me and the dismal future I would have if I didn't change. I woke up in a cold sweat at about three thirty a.m. and found everyone in the room had their eyes on me. After I cursed a few of them out, I then went into the restaurant and got me a cup of coffee to wake me up.

I sat down at a table and pulled out the phone Lydia gave me with nothing but her on my mind. I started to call her but I changed my mind and went through the phone instead. I found that she had taken several pictures of herself along with videos and for a few minutes I got lost as I looked at her beautiful face. Her big gray eyes and copper colored skin with deep dimples made a mac really want to change his life. I saw a love I never knew, even different than the love from my sisters in Lydia's eyes. That's why it was so hard for me to go, but inside I was still eager to leave so we could move on to a better life together. When they called for my bus to board I quickly kissed the picture of her I still held and stared at, and put the phone away before I got up.

I got on the bus and settled into my seat before I pulled out my phone again. When I got it out I watched video after video of Lydia as I rode towards my sister and left the love of my life behind. I arrived in LA at 9 am and quickly found a bus to Tisha's plush neighborhood. I couldn't believe my fucking eyes as I walked up to the huge ass house all beat the fuck up with a tattered bag in hand. I felt nervous as fuck as I rung the bell and waited on my sister to answer. When Tisha opened the door I almost passed out from pure happiness when I saw her smile. Suddenly I was that ten-year-old boy again who just needed his big sister's love. I ran into Tisha's arms so fast she didn't know what hit her as she stood there astonished while she looked into my eyes.

"Sha, what are you doing here so early? How did you get here? And what happened to you?" She asked as she hugged me then helped me inside before she grabbed my bag off my shoulder. I said nothing as she led me into her plush ass house and we took a seat on the living room couch. As soon as we sat down and my sister looked at me with that loving, penetrating gaze broke the damn to my emotions and I let it all out. I told her the entire story from the time Alice came into the picture and didn't stop until I was finished. When I was done I fell back on to the couch emotionally drained and felt like I was about to lose it.

"Don't you worry about shit lil brother, I got you. You need to just go rest. We got some shit planned for today, but if you don't feel like it we can just stay home. In the meantime, let me show you to your room so you can rest your weary head. I got you lil brother and I always will. Everything gonna be okay now." Tisha told me as she kissed my forehead and wiped my tears away.

I trailed behind her to the huge bedroom with attached bathroom Tisha had set up for me. I couldn't believe how big and nice the muthafucka was, I had to take a second to stop and take it all in. "You made it Tisha. You made it out. It's hope for our cursed asses after all." I said to my sister as I plopped down on the king sized bed with Gucci covers and sunk into its softness.

"Nah, we made it bruh, you know what's mine will always be yours. Just wait you will see. I haven't forgot, I am my brother's keeper. Now rest lil nigga because today we have fun and leave all the sadness behind us." She said before she came over to kiss me again and then disappeared out the door.

I sat there and stared around at the beautiful furniture before my thoughts consumed me and I found myself lost in my memories again. That time my mind took me back farther, to an incident that happened when I was about eight and my mother beat me with a wet extension cord until I passed out. I could still feel the sting on my flesh as I sat there and cried when the most beautiful little girl I had ever seen walked in. She looked just like Tisha only smaller with the brightest eyes ever made.

"Hi, my name is A'Miracle and my mommy said I'm your niece. You're my uncle Sha huh?" She said as she came closer to wipe away my tears. "Yes, I'm your uncle. Nice to meet you. You haven't seen me in a while because your mommy always comes without you. I miss you though." I said as I reached out to hug her tight.

She hugged me back as I felt nothing but love overshadow all of my darkness. "Don't cry uncle, I missed you too. Everything is fine, you're here now and we all love you. Mommy said we're going out to celebrate so are you ready?" She asked me as I shook my head yes. "Well, let's go! We're taking you to the doctor first Killa Sha." Tisha yelled as she and Jerrod popped from around the corner and we all laughed.

I quickly broke my melancholy mood and got up to shake up Jerrod before I followed them down the hall. A'Miracle grabbed my hand so that I could walk with her and I gladly accepted the invitation. As we left the house to get in the car I looked up at the sky and it suddenly looked bluer than ever before. The happiness I felt inside at that moment seemed to help brighten the sky and I hoped my happiness would never end. It didn't think about it for the rest of that day either as me, Tisha, Jerrod, and A'Miracle got my sprained wrist and mild concussion treated first then went shopping, out to eat, and to the amusement park on the beach.

I laughed and played with my niece all night when I wasn't admiring the happy family my sister had. I loved the relationship she had with Jerrod and the happy family they were altogether. I wished for that same kind of happiness as we drove back home that evening and hoped I wouldn't have to lose anything else to get it. I wasn't so sure though because the thought of Terricka filled my mind as soon as I went downstairs to watch tv with Tisha after my shower. I knew that my sister was about to drown in the same despair our mother had and I felt I had to do all I could to save her. I couldn't take the loss of someone I loved so dear so I had to let Tisha know what I knew.

"Yo Tisha, I really think you need to go see Terricka. Maine its some real fucked up shit going on with her. I got word from my nigga in Memphis that CPS ready to take her kids after the youngest little girl went to daycare with a burn on her back. Maine Tisha, Terricka going crazy and we really gotta go help her. Please Tisha." I begged as I saw tears well up in her eyes.

Once I said that she was up on her feet before she even tried to respond. I watched as she rushed over to the phone. I watched her dial Terricka's number as my heart beat in my throat and I braced myself for the battle that was about to unfold.

"Hello Terricka, what the hell is going on?" Tisha yelled into the phone as I heard Terricka explode in rage.

Chapter 3

Terricka: I am; whatever you say I Am!

"Hell-to-da-fucking-lo!" I yelled into the phone after I ran all the way downstairs and waded through the piles of toys, clothes, and trash that was thrown all over my living room floor.

Tisha's voice echoed loud in my ear as soon as I answered and she yelled out for me to tell her what the hell was going on. I had to swallowed down the rage that was about to explode inside of me as I closed my eyes and sat down on my couch. I sat there for a few seconds as one voice in my head told me to calm down while another told me to curse Tisha the fuck out. The heavy footsteps of my kids as the ran over my head and Tisha's heavy breathing on the phone did nothing to help my internal battle between the voices that controlled me either as they both raged on. No, all that shit did was ignite my anger and cause me to give Tisha exactly what she expected.

"TERRICKA! Don't you hear me talking to you? What the fuck is going on in Memphis? Is Tania okay? I heard she got burned and CPS finna take your kids. What's going on sister? Talk to me damn!" Tisha yelled as I laughed in an eerie tone that made my flesh crawl because it was just like Denise's.

"Here we go again with yo bougie, messy ass. What the fuck do you want now Tisha? Bitch you ain't called me this much over the past four years. What the fuck is it you want from me SHARTISHA? WHAT? Bitch I don't want yo help. I don't want to talk to you. I don't fucking want to think about you Tisha. Every time I think about you, I think about what I did for you and what you gave me in return. You left me bitch that's what you gave. Yeah, I wanted the deed done more than you, but you are the one who had more to lose. I didn't give a fuck about anything then, much like now; nothing but you and Sha. I gave up my entire life for you both and what do I have Tisha? FUCK YOU TISHA! How dare you call now all concerned and shit when shit been fucked up. You listen to everything a muthafucka tell you cause it's so easy to believe Terricka bad. Well, guess what bitch? You're right! I am whatever you say I am Oprah. Bitch handle your house and yourself. Don't worry about what happened, her bad ass okay and ain't nobody taking my kids. I will kill us all before I let a muthafucka take them, including you sister! So WHAT TISHAAAAAAAA?" I yelled in Tisha's ear to the top of my voice as my body tingled and my mind felt fuzzy.

I must have sounded like a real fucking lunatic, which was often, because I suddenly heard my kid's footsteps stop overhead. I felt erratic and out of control as the voices in my mind suddenly burst through the fuzz and I could hear Tisha as she cursed at me and talked to someone in her background. I felt on the brink of insanity as I quickly stood up and paced the floor with the phone pressed to my ear as I bit the side of my index finger like I often did whenever I was angry, anxious, or sad. I growled into the phone as Tisha called my name and tried to bring me down from that blinding rage she had seen come over me before.

"Terricka. TERRICKA!! T, okay. It's okay T. Calm down. I'm sorry for leaving you Terricka. Please forgive me and let me help you. Let me help those kids because they don't deserve this Terricka. They don't deserve to relive our pain. They shouldn't have to pay for your sins like we paid for Denise's." Tisha said as I suddenly burst into tears and exploded again. "SHUT UP! SHUT THE FUCK UP YOU TRIFLING BITCH. SHUTTT UPPPP!!!" I yelled through my tears as the reality of what she said cut so deep I couldn't take it.

I stood there frozen as Tisha's words bounced off the graffiti covered, battered walls of my mind, and I tried to find that side of me that cared. I knew deep down my sister was right and I was a fucked up, little bipolar, thot just like my mama who needed to change. I knew I still hadn't dealt with so much pain that it had poisoned me from the inside out. I also knew that I had used that same poison to infect my kids and unleash my pain, heartache, and sins upon them. I knew all of that shit but something inside me just wouldn't let me give a fuck and my pride wouldn't let me allow Tisha to help, so I lashed out and used the only response I had.

"Didn't you hear me bitch? Why the fuck you still on the phone? Bye Tisha. Byeee!!" I yelled as my heart raced and I felt fed the fuck up with Tisha and all her bullshit. I could hear her sigh and sniffle as she said, "I give up", and I prepared to hang up the phone. Before I could though a familiar, warm voice filled my ears and my little brother quickly found that rational, sane part of me I had tried so desperately to find. "Terricka, it's me Sha. Wassup big sis?" Sha asked as I suddenly felt calm enough to stop the abuse on my finger and sit the fuck down.

I sat down on the dirty, torn green and blue loveseat by my living room door that was covered in clothes, toys, and trash and listened closely to the only person I really had. Sha had never left me. After it all he was always there. His dad sent letters to me he helped him write up until the day he was able to talk on his own. After that he had called me at least three times a week and talked for hours, unlike Tisha bougie ass. Sha didn't forget about me or all the love we shared when he moved on to a better life. He never left me by choice either, that's why I would always try to fight the madness in my mind to be close to him.

Only Sha could overpower the voices and bring back that Terricka I was before everything. Him and the drugs. When I was high it numbed the pain and the voices were a bit calmer and more rational, but when I was sober the dark side of me could not be stopped. Sha's love was different from that momentary high though. His love for me was pure and unconditional, which bred from pain, despair, and the need to hold on to the only people who loved instead of hurt. That love had created a bond that could not be broken because I loved my brother more than anything. It was a love I couldn't even find for my own kids; one I didn't even have for myself. Just the sound of his voice made me want to be me again. He brought back the

Terricka I missed, which was the Terricka I feared I would never be again.

"Hey lil bruh. Wassup big homie?" I asked Sha as my heart began to slow down and I felt the fuzz and voices in my mind fade away. "Maine, Terricka wassup with you? I'm worried about you for real sister. Now, you know I'm a real nigga so I ain't finna beat around the bush or shit with you. I gotta say this and I want you to just listen. You Losing it, flat out. I can't fucking believe all the shit Tisha had been saying was true. I can't believe you on the phone talking to her like that after all the shit we been through. We all the fuck we got Terricka! ITS JUST US. NOBODY ELSE! How can all we had turn into this? I can't and won't accept this shit." Sha yelled as he breathed hard into the phone and I felt my heart stop.

I had never heard my little, frail, soft spoken brother talk like that. Even though a lot of time had passed and he had changed into a man without me seeing him for years, I never imagined him as the stern, man he had become. The wise, bold man who would call me on my shit, but not tear me down. That's why I listened him and tried to process every word that he said.
"Now, I heard you telling Tisha she nosey and messy, and shit because she called you concerned about Tania. Well, be mad at me then because I'm the one who told her that shit. I told her cause I'm scared of what you may be going through alone, and what my nieces and nephews might be going through. Now Terricka, I know we all got our fucking dragons to slay and demons to confront, but we can't do this shit alone. We couldn't get out of hell alone so what makes you think this will be so easy? Come on now Terricka. We love you even if nobody else does. I just want us to be like we used to be. Can we Terricka? Talk to your sister Terricka!" Sha demanded as I felt that wall I had built around my heart begin to crumble.

Tears hit me quick and hard as I sat back and they rolled down my face and fell down on to the front of the tight, blue dress I had on. I wanted so bad to be who everyone expected me to be, but a part of me just couldn't care. I fought that part though as I let my brother coax me into yet another reconciliation with the sitter I always adored but grew to resent.

"Oaky Sha. Okay. I'll talk. For you, I'll talk." I said as I dried up my tears and prepared for whatever the conversation with Tisha would bring.

"Thank you sister. I love you maine." Sha said as I told him I loved him to before I dried up my tears. I listened to him call Tisha as I cleared my throat and sat up on the couch try and talk with more poise. I didn't know how long that would last though if Tisha got back on the phone with the shit, but I was willing to give it a try. When I heard her shaky voice on the other end I had a moment of clarity and all we had gone through flashed before my eyes. Somehow I was seventeen again and we were head to head in our bed with blood in our panties and tears in our eyes because our mother had sold us for drugs. Suddenly I felt that bond we once shared and I wanted to cry out for my sister to forgive me, but something inside just wouldn't let me do it. Instead I sucked up the tears that threatened to break forward again and held my breath while I listened.

"Umm Terricka, let me just start by saying how much I love you. Growing up you were all I had; my mother, role model, doctor, counselor, my best friend. You were and will always be the best sister in the world because just like you said, you gave up your life for me. I will forever be indebted to you for that sister. Let me pay you back. Please let me pay you back." Tisha whispered as a few tears trinkled from my eyes.

I quickly dried them up as I tried to keep my composure and keep further visions and memories of the past at bay.

"Terricka, I know I hurt you when I left. I also know that what happened di something to you I will never understand. I know that hearing me of all people chastise your actions now is what infuriates you the most. I know all of this sister and I'm sorry. I'm sorry for being a coward and leaving. I'm sorry you had to slay the dragon on your own and carry that cross with all the others. And I'm sorry for having to talk to you like this but, T something has to change. Your kids deserve to meet the real you.

Let me help you sister. PLEASE TERRICKA. LET ME HELP YOU!!!" Tisha cried as my tear burst forward like a river through a cracked damn.

"Ohh T, please don't cry. Just say I can help and I'm there. I know you're going through so much sister. You need my love. You need our song. That always helps right? You remember the words Terricka?" Tisha asked me as I continued to bawl, but managed to say yes through my tears. "Okay, let's sing it." Tisha said before she began to sing the song that almost brought me back.

"Nothing is forever what we're hoping for,

No more pain so don't you cry anymore.

Hold your head up high and dry yo tears,

Let me help you through and erase yo fears.

We'll overcome it all if we stick together,

We just gotta believe nothing lasts forever (nothing lasts forever)."

Tisha sang as I joined in and tried hard to grab a hold to her love and help. I tried but the voices in my head came back and my kids began to run, yell, and scream all at once. I could feel everything start to overcome me as Tisha began the song again, but it was far too late. A loud bang, followed by my son cursing then a loud shatter, pushed me right out of calmness back into the haze of insanity and anger I dwelled in. I quickly jumped up out of my seat and ran to the foot of the steps to yell at my kids with the phone still in my hand. One voice told me to calmly ask what happened but the other one said go the fuck off.

"WHAT THE FUCK IS YALL UGLY ASSES UP THERE DOING? I'M FINNA COME UP THERE AND BEAT THE SHIT OUT OF EVERY SINGLE ONE OF YOU BITCHES. IGNORANT MUTHAFUCKAS!" I yelled through my rage as I heard their footsteps stop, but my kids laugh as they imitated my voice. "Okay, you lil bitches wonna play. I'm show ya!" I yelled as I huffed and puffed while I walked back into the living room to find my big, leather belt. "Terricka calm down. What happened. Please sister, it's gonna be alright." Tisha said as I rolled my eyes and dug through the mountains of shit to find my weapon of choice.

I didn't hear shit she said as I concentrated on the voice in my mind that told me to beat their asses, lock them in their room, and then get the fuck out the house before I did something I would regret. I listened to that voice instead of Tisha's pleas as I continued to hunt for the belt. After a few seconds I found it under an empty pizza box and quickly grabbed it up before I wrapped it around my hand ready to go whoop ass.

"Look Tisha I gotta go." I yelled with irritation and rage in my voice as my sister protested. "No Terricka, I can't let you off the phone like this. Calm down and tell me what happened." Tisha said as I decided to just say what she wanted to hear.

I took a deep breath and pretended to calm myself as my sister hummed the words to our salvation song. More runs, jumps, and bangs over my head quickly ended that fake ass meditation and made me snap into pyscho mode. "I'm good Tisha, I am. I gotta go though. I'mma call you next week and tell you when to come. Bye." I yelled before I hung up the phone and threw it on the couch before I ran towards the stairs.

"OKAY YOU LIL BASTARDS HERE I COME NOW." I yelled through clenched teeth as I ran up the steps two at a time, ready to end their noise and get the fuck out of the house. As soon as I got halfway up the steps I could heard their footsteps as they scattered and ran for a hiding place. That shit didn't matter though because I was mad as fuck and their bad asses was gonna feel my rage.

"Where the fuck y'all at and what the fuck y'all do?" I asked as I got up on the landing and walked straight into my bedroom. It was filthy as usual because I didn't give a fuck about cleaning when the demon seeds from hell would mess it right the fuck back up, but on top of the usual trash and clothes on the floor of my room, there was glass everywhere. I quickly tiptoed through the glass deeper inside my room to see that the little fuckers had broken my mirror on my dresser along with the little glass heart filled with glitter my mother had bought me back when I wasn't even old enough to wipe myself. It was the only thing I had from the good times, the only thing I had kept to remember the good side of her. That was the one thing in the house I absolutely forbad them from touching and they had broken it.

I couldn't control my rage as I went over and bent down to pick up the shattered pieces of my broken heart. I couldn't control my rage as I stood up and threw the glass against the wall before I tore open my closet and pulled Rodney Jr. out of his hiding spot. I quickly yanked his 4'8", 110lb, 6-year-old body up by the collar of his dirty, blue t-shirt and drug him out as he cursed and told me to let him go. "Let me the fuck go. I didn't even do it. Don't hit me. Please damn." He yelled as I threw him on the bed and began to slice him everywhere with the belt that I could reach.

I hit him over and over again across the face as he cried and yelled out how much he hated me. "I hate yo ass too lil smart mouth fucker, damn trouble making snotty nose bastard." I yelled as I landed a pop to his right eye and he yelped like a scolded dog.

That meek, compassionate, tiny part of me that controlled a voice in my head stepped forward at that moment and for second I almost reacted like a real mother. I almost ran over to comfort and apologize to my child, but that side of me that didn't care wouldn't let me. Instead I left him there to cry while I went and found the others and delivered some of the same merciless ass whooping. I found my second son, Ryan, in him and his brother's room crouched down in their dirty clothes hamper and attacked. I yanked his little light weight, five-year-old ass up quick and unleashed a series of pops all the way up his back to his head before I drug him into the girl's room where I knew they always hid. Once inside I threw him on the bed as he cried and I glared down at the welts that had begun to pop up all over his body.

"I'm sorry mommy, I'm really sorry. Please don't whoop Tania and Talya. I broke it fighting with Rodney. Don't whoop my sisters." Ryan begged as he cried and stared up into my eyes. For a second, right there in that moment I saw my son as Sha while he sat and begged our psycho mom to spare us. Even though the fuzz in my mind and the voices that controlled me were strong at that moment, for some reason my son's words and that vision got through. For some reason I was able to hear and feel for him, and spare his sisters.

"Shut the fuck up. Don't tell me what the fuck to do. Tania, Talaya. Get y'all funky asses out here right now and I mean it. Rodney Jr get yo bad, smart mouth, blind, cry baby ass in here too." I yelled as my kids hurriedly ran out of their hiding spots right to me as they cried. "No, mama please I didn't do nothing. Neither did Talaya." My four-year-old daughter Tania said through her tears as she tried to defend her three-year-old sister as well as herself.

I watched her little lip quiver as she cried and reached over to hug her sister before Rodney stepped in front to shield them both. "Maine, I broke it mama. Leave them alone please." Rodney said as he continued to hold his eye and Ryan got up to stand beside him. For a second I felt outnumbered, unloved, and like a total disappointment to my kids, just like my mother must have felt many times before. Right then I kind of saw things from Denise's point of view and I hated that shit. That made me lash out again so I quickly began to swing the thick leather belt in the air and hit each of my kids in a different spot.

I left them all to cry as they laid on the bed and Rodney covered their welted up bodies with his. When I got to the door I turned around to stare at them and my son looked up to meet my gaze. It really was a sad sight to see them like that a sight that brought up old demons I should have learned from. However, it was too hard for me to feel what I was supposed to. It was hard for me to stand there and look at my son while I faced all the fucked up shit I did too, but that was all I could do.

"No matter what you do to us mama, I'll still always love you, but I hate living with you and seeing you every day. Let us go to live with aunt Tisha. Just let us GOOO!" Rodney cried as I rolled my eyes at him, walked out, and slammed and locked the door behind me. Once outside I took in several deep breaths as I fought the voices and tried to care while my son's words rang in my ears.

"I hate living with me too Rodney. I really do. Maybe one day soon it will all end." I said as I walked away and left my kids locked in their room to console each other just like the three kids who lived in hell before them.

Once out on the landing I walked down the hall and sat down on the top step exhausted and tired of feeling the way I did. I was so done being sad, guilty, and just down right miserable all the time but that was all I knew. I put my head in my hands and tried to take in deep breaths again so that I could think through the way I felt. Deep down I didn't like the way I treated my kids and I knew that shit was wrong. I just couldn't help it because I was always mad, broke, and disgusted, and had grown so used to pain. I wanted to be the mother mine never was to me, but I just didn't know how to. I didn't know how to be their mother; their protector and guidance because I couldn't even do that shit for myself. I figured I was still better than my mother though because I hadn't ever sold them or let anyone violate them in any kind of way. In my delusional, drugged out mind that was enough. I cared enough about them to shield them from that kind of pain but I still couldn't love them like I should have because I didn't love myself.

I sat there and worked through my thoughts as the fuzz in my mind came back and I felt out of control. I had to remember Sha's voice and Tisha's words to fight through that haze, but all that did was make my memories of my own hell take over my mind. Suddenly I was fourteen again, back in Denise's house free to feel her wrath. "Terricka, ShaTerricka!

Bring yo stanky ass here you lil hot bitch." My mother yelled as I quickly jumped up from the spot on the floor I was in as I read a magazine article about some celebrity kid's huge birthday party and we all dreamed it was our lives.

My mother's mayhem quickly ruined that dream though as I got up, sucked up the tears that had begun to build up in my heart and slowly walked towards the door. Once outside the room I turned to look at my brother and sister as they hugged and cried with tears in their eyes. "I love you Terricka." Tisha said. "I love you too T." Sha said right behind her as he cried and buried his head in her chest.

I put on a brave face and smiled at my siblings before I reassured them and tried to ease their fears. "I love y'all too, now stop crying. Everything gonna be okay." I lied as I turned to walk away and the knot in my gut told me it wouldn't be okay.

I closed the door behind me and walked on shaky legs until I got to the top of the steps. After I stood there for a few minutes and gave myself a pep talk I walked down the steps and into the living room to face my angry mother. She sat there in the dirty chair next to the window looking like a cracked out flamingo who had got ran through dirt with her friend Peggy sitting next to her and they both sucked on glass pipes.

I could feel my heart beat in my throat as I walked up to her and stood to wait on my punishment that was sure to come. Despite me being right in front of her my mother took hit after hit of crack before she blew huge clouds of smoke directly into my face. I coughed and choked on the thick, stinky clouds and tried to step away. I tried, but before I could my mother reached out and grabbed me by the arm to pull me close to her face. Her breath was so foul I felt my stomach churn and the skin on my face begin to peel.

"Soooo Terricka. Yo li freaky ass been outside being nasty and fucking with lil niggas for free huh?" My mother asked as I shook my head no and she began to smirk. I tried to think of something to get me out of the situation I was in but at that moment I could see no way out. It was obvious to me that

Mrs. Avery, the old lady who lived in the building behind us, had seen me and my almost boyfriend Tino kissing by her back porch and told my pyscho mama. I knew that if she told, my mama believed it and I was about to get fucked up. That's why I sucked that shit up and braced myself for what was to come. If I would have known what was to come though, I would have run for my life.

"No ma'am, I wasn't being nasty. I just gave my boyfriend Tino a kiss. That's all mama, I'm sorry." I said as she stared at me out of the side of her eye. I watched her as she looked over at her friend and smirked before she sucked her teeth and grabbed the jar of Icy Hot she had on the table.

"Oh so bitch you grown enough to be out here kissing niggas, and for FREE, but you didn't bring me shit. I don't give a fuck about shit else but that. Lil dumb hoe if I ain't taught you shit I would have thought you would know that. No cash no ass lil dumb bitch, but I guess I gotta teach you this the hard way huh?" Denise yelled as she quickly sat her pipe down, grabbed me up, and quickly lifted up my gown. "Mama, please stop. What are you doing?" I asked as I struggled in Denise's grip as she reached down to pull down my panties.

I tried to pull them back up as she pulled the down and that made her mad as fuck. She quickly stood up and punched me in my face, which caused me to grab my nose and mouth instead. I remember hard had she hit me and the warm blood that filled my mouth and dripped down the front of my gown. I remember it all like it was yesterday, every gory detail. "Now grab them muthafuckas again lil bitch and I'mma knock yo ass out. This will teach yo hot ass a lesson." My mother said as she crouched down in front of me with the open Icy Hot jar in hand and slathered a handful right into my vagina.

The sensation followed by intense burn the Icy Hot sent through my body was so intense I collapsed instantly. I can remember how I screamed for help while my mother sat back down and her and her friend laughed at me while they smoked the rest of their crack. I can still fell my heart race and the pain as my vagina hairs seemed to melt away. "Mama. Mama Please." I yelled.

Suddenly those words snapped me out of my memory and I was back at home on my steps. My daughter's Tania's voice helped me even more as she repeated the very same words I had just heard in my memory. "Mama. Mama please." She cried as tears ran down my face and I couldn't take it anymore.

I quickly got up and ran down the steps where I went into my kitchen to retrieve my canister of blunts out of the freezer along with my pint of E&J. I quickly took out one of the 20 pre-rolled kush blunts laced with cocaine I smoked on a regular, and fired it up to ease my mind. I inhaled the smoke deeply and held it until there was nothing to blow back out before I allowed my medicine to do what it did to me. After about three more hits and a swig of the beer I had opened I felt that calm I needed and grabbed my chair to go sit on my porch.

Once outside I sat down and stared directly at the place that haunted my dream. There I was in Breezy Point, right across, from the place I called hell all of my life. It was like life forced me to dwell in my pain when that was the only section-8 apartment in the city I could get in to. I was forced to look at that dungeon every day and see myself jump off that roof to escape death. That was hard as fuck and only added to my anger and clear disregard for life.

I finished the blunt I had lit in the house before I took out and lit another then got lost in another haze of memories and my voices as I stared at my childhood home. I sat there for a while just lost until my friend Tangie walked up. "Bitch what the fuck you doing? Let me hit that." Tangie said as her big six foot, 200lb ass walked in front of me and snatched my blunt before she sat down beside me. "Being stingy and shit. I'm the one with the problems." Tangie said as she imitated DaeDae from Next Friday and began to laugh.

I laughed too as the haze my memories brought on suddenly melted away and I looked at my friend. "What's up Terricka maine, you been in the house a few days." Tangie said as she hit my blunt so many times I had to snatch it out of her hand. "Dam ole greedy ass bitch. Ole big lung, Big Bird looking bitch." I said as Tangie laughed and elbowed me as I hit the blunt.

We both laughed for a minute as I continued to smoke and thought about what I would tell her. She was my best friend and all because we got high and sold pussy together or whatever, but I didn't trust nobody especially a bitch who shared no blood. Hell, I couldn't even trust all of my blood at that moment so I knew her gutta ass was no better, which is why I told her exactly what I wanted her to know.

"Maine bitch I'm just fucked up. Stamps got cut off because of some recertification bullshit so I ain't got no food. Lights just got back on but that made me fuck up the rent money. Then to top that off Vito bitch ass acting like he broke and shit. Bitch been missing two days ain't even answering the phone." I said as my friend shook her head and I thought about the real issues in front of me.

I thought about how my kids would be taken, we would be homeless, and I would possibly go to jail. I didn't tell her that though, that ratchet shit was more acceptable and relatable to bitch like her. Tangie sat there beside me in deep though for a few seconds as the sudden voices of her six kids as they walked up and my kids who were suddenly in the window, filled my ears. That shit tapped danced on my already frazzled nerves as I hit the blunt hard and my hands shook. Tangie noticed what I was going through fast so she jumped up to diffuse the situation. "Okay T, I know what you need and I'm gonna tell you soon as I do this. Let them damn kids out. All of them can play together and stay the fuck out of our hair for a while." Tangie said as she disappeared into my house before I could protest.

I sat there and stared at her dirty, snot nose kids and then the house of horrors before I shook my head and cursed the life I lived. In minutes my kids burst out of the door like they were freed from prison and ran right down to Tangie's kids to play. I sat there and watched them laugh and run as she sat back down beside me and took another blunt out of my box to light. I felt a glimmer of love in my heart as I watched my children act like kids who didn't have a care in the world, although they were forced to live their own hell. In that moment I got lost in my dreams of being a great mother to them, which was the hidden hope I held inside. I saw myself being everything Denise never was to me and deep down I wanted that.

"Bitch you need to get out tonight so that's what we will do. We gonna lock all of the kids in yo house and just leave. You know Vito bitch ass coming, he never stay away more than two days. Even if he don't Jermaine can watch them. Hell, my son 11, that's babysitter age. No matter what I'm getting you out. Okay?" Tangie asked as I stared at the door to the apartment, still wrapped up in my dream.

"Okay Terricka?" She asked again as she grabbed my shoulder and I finally heard what she said. "Hell yeah bitch, let's go. That's probably what I need for real. I know if you say party that mean money and dope so you know I'm game. Fuck Vito, whether he come or not and fuck them kids. It's gotta be about us sometimes." I said as I laughed and Tangie joined in, but I felt conflicted inside.

I fought the thoughts of how I was just like Denise as I hit my beer and stared around the apartments. Just as I looked at the driveway to come in I noticed the swagger of the double extra-large t-shirt wearing, fake chain having, no dope selling bitch I had two babies by. Right there in plain view of my house was Vito as he stood his tall, light-skinned lanky ass there and tied up his dreads before he leaned into a car. I had to stop smoking to stand up and see who the fuck he was in deep conversation with as my rage found its way home.

I walked off my porch and into the grass as Tangie called my name but I didn't stop until I was up on the hill and had a perfect view of what was going on. By that time Tangie was up on her feet too as she ran up the hill to stand beside me and I stared at Vito while he leaned into a green Volkswagen Beetle and kissed some white girl on her lips. That was enough to set crazy Terricka off as I took out across the parking lot at full speed while Tangie yelled my name and ran behind me.

"TERRICKA WAIT, Please stop!" Tangie yelled but I blocked that shit out as I continued to run with my eyes glued on the bitch.

Before Vito could even realize what was going on I was on his ass as I kicked him dead in the stomach. As soon as I did that he fell to his knees and I reached in the open car window to grab the white girl by her hair.

"Wait please stop. Who are you? What did I do? Antonio help." She yelled as she called Vito by a fake name and I yanked her face first to the ground.

As soon as her body hit the pavement I started to drag her face down while I kicked her in the head. All I saw was the color red and all I could hear was the voice in my head that said kill her as she cried and I continued to drag her. By the time Vito got to me and smacked me hard across the face to stop, I had pulled plugs out of the white girl's hair and there were strikes of her blood and skin all over the asphalt. "Terricka what the fuck wrong with you ole crazy ass bitch. Get yo ass the fuck home." Vito yelled as he pushed me down then hurried to help the girl up.

I quickly regain my composure and jumped up to rush the bitch again only to be met by Vito as he let her go to grab me. The next thing I knew I was being carried home as I screamed and kicked at Vito while my kids cried and looked on. When we got into the house Vito threw me down on the kitchen floor and I jumped up instantly with the shit. I picked up Rodney's Jr's metal scooter off the floor as I got up and swung that bitch with the intent to kill. Lucky for Vito he was still kind of fast to be 30 and I was slow because I was high, because I only missed him by an inch. When I missed he got the upper hand though and reached out to punch me with a weak ass jab. I shook that shit off in seconds and ran into his ass with a combo of punches and kicks. We jacked like that for five minutes until Tangie's voice filled our ears and I could feel her pull us apart.

"Vito, Terricka… STOP THIS SHIT." She yelled as he let go of my hair and I delivered one last punch to his face.

After I punched him I quickly pushed past my crying kids and grabbed my purse to retreat. "You right Tangie we should stop this. That's why I'm about to leave. FUCK YOU VITO. FUCK THIS HOUSE AND FUCK THEM BAD ASS KIDS!" I yelled as I left out of the door with his voice as he yelled and my kids as they cried in my ears.

Despite all of that I still walked out and didn't stop for a second to look back. As I walked I heard Tangie tell her kids to go into my house too before Vito slammed the door and she ran to catch up. We walked to her house in silence and once there she went straight into her room to get me clothes to clean up. I still said nothing as we smoked then I showered and we both dressed to leave.

"Maine Tangie. Something gotta give. I feel like I'm going crazy. Maybe I am just like my mama, just like Tisha said." I told her as I looked at her once we were in the car and on our way to the party. I really felt like I was about to lose my mind as I thought about my fucked up life and all I had done to contribute to it.

"Naw, fool you good. Just need to take care of YOU more. That's what this is, you time. Now, fuck all that bullshit. Take this tab and ease yo mind." Tangie said as she steered the car with one hand and handed me a pill that she took out of her purse with the other.

I quickly popped the pill in my mouth and swallowed it down with the Hennessey Tangie had brought with us. After that I sat back in my seat and let the Willie Hutch that blast through the speakers in her Impala, take me away. In no time I felt free and ready for what the night held. I was ready for a fast, fun night filled with dope, money and niggas and that's exactly what I got.

As soon as we got there we started our hoe game. We danced, drank, and consumed everything you could think of. By nine pm I was so high I couldn't see straight let alone know what I would do. The rest of my night went by like that too, it was just one big blur filled with dope, dicks, and a dull pain in my heart. I woke up the morning after the party with a wet ass, four hundred dollars in my purse, and a guilty feeling that nagged me to my core. I sat up in the bed I was in with two dudes who were as naked as I was and thought, how the fuck did I get there.

I quickly scooted to the end of the bed and retrieved my clothes before I quickly and quietly slipped them on. Once dressed with my shoes in hand, I stood up and prepared to go. When I walked by the mirror on the dresser I got a glimpse of my face and I recognized it, but not as my own. My rich chocolate skin that used to be so smooth, flawless, and full of life looked dirty, dingy, and pale. My hair was all disheveled, my eyes were yellow and I had tiny bits and bruises all over my face and neck. I looked just like my mother's after one of her dope parties or drug binges and that shit hurt my heart. Before I knew it tears ran from my eyes as I rushed out of the room to find Tangie. I searched the bedrooms of the dirty, three-bedroom trap house we were in until I found Tangie on the living room floor surrounded by three dudes. All of them were naked and there were beer bottles, cigar wrappers and a plate with cocaine still on it right beside them.

I felt sick to my stomach as I stood there and looked over that familiar scene and realized I was doing all the same things my mother had done. "Tangie. Tangie." I yelled as I kicked her foot and she jumped up quick.

I put my hand up to my lips to tell her be quiet as she jumped up found her clothes and quickly got dressed. I searched around the room while she did that and went through the pockets of the niggas still sleep on the floor. By the time she was done so was I and I had an additional $600 in my hand. "Let's go bitch." I said to Tangie as I flashed the money and noticed one of the dudes on the floor move.

As soon as Tangie saw that we both ran out of the house and to her car as the dude on the floor got up and yelled her name. Before he could realize what was gone we had sped out of the parking lot and were on our way home. I gave Tangie $300 of the loot I stole as we rode through south Memphis, headed back to The Bay. After a quick stop in North Memphis to get $150 worth of powder and $150 worth of loud we rolled up and smoked our way home.

By the time we got there is was 11 am on a Saturday in July and all the project kids were outside. As soon as I got out of the car I noticed our kids weren't out there though and a part of me got worried. When I stepped inside to a clean house and clean kids who were at the dining table I hadn't seen in years, I knew something was in fact wrong. "Terricka, where the hell have you been? These kid were here all night by themselves." My siddity friend Sky said as she came out of the kitchen with my clean, daughter Talya in her arms.

Tangie and I both sighed at the sight of Sky because we knew what her being there without notice meant. We knew that meant someone had called her and she was there to preach. I didn't want to hear that bullshit though the way my head pounded and the voices pushed their way back to the surface of my conscious. All I wanted to do was go to sleep and forget about my fucked up life. I could tell Tangie didn't want to hear that shit either as she sighed and then walked to the bottom of the steps to call her kids. I watched as they ran down to her and then she rolled her eyes at Sky who rolled hers back, and then walked to the door.

"I'll holler at you later T. I ain't got time for a sermon from preacher Sky when she was a bigger dope smoker and hoe than we are. Ha, look at the pot ready to call the kettle black, but that's none of my business though." Tangie said as we both laughed and she left out of the door.

I laughed so hard I almost fell off the couch as I watched Sky rolled her eyes at me. She didn't laugh though she just sat Talya down and told her, Tania, and Ryan to go upstairs. I laid back on the clean, Frebreezed couch and closed my eyes until

Sky finally took a deep breath. I knew the bullshit was about to begin so I just laid there and let Sky do her thing.

"Terricka I'm so fucking disappointed in you. I expect that shit from Tangie trifling ass, but not you. Yeah, I used to be worse but the point is I'm not now and you are. What happened to you Terricka? Maine you gotta get yo shit together and be better to these kids or CPS gonna take them. Hell, Ima take them if you keep doing this shit because nobody deserves to be treated this way. Do you hear me Terricka? I mean it." She yelled as I felt my friend harsh but true words.

Just like many times before she offered me insight that I should have listened to and took to heart but like times before it didn't stick. However, I did know deep down she was right. I knew all of that shit but it still did me no good when I was trying to figure out which way to go. "Maine Sky you, my sister, and nan other mutha fucka in this world know what I go through. Y'all come by or call with all this good ass advise on how I should change my life and be better. However, not one time did y'all stop to tell me how to change. Not one time did y'all actually give me the love I need to change. See that talk shit easy Sky but what I'm supposed to do when I feel like I'm all alone in the world and I'm drowning, huh? What do I do Sky?" I asked my friend as I broke down and she rushed over to hold me.

I let out all of my fears and secrets as I sat there in her arms before I handed her the $400 I had left in my purse. "Keep this for me. Just in case something happens or I get fucked up and stop taking care of the kids again. Take this and make sure shit get done. I'm fucked up Sky. I'm a fucking lost cause." I cried as I felt overwhelmed and my friend did her best to comfort me.

I let Sky hold me and tell me it would be okay for a while even though I knew it wouldn't. Even with that knowledge in my head I felt a little better as I pulled back from her embrace. "See you are gonna be aite pissy wissy." Sky said as she laughed and I joined in.

For a second I felt like everything would be alright as I laughed my tears away. That didn't last long though because in seconds Vito had burst through the door and brought all of my anger, sadness, and despair back with him. "Maine Terricka you an old dumb ass bitch, witcho thot ass. Bitch out here dragging folks and don't even know who they are. You fucked up this time though cause the bitch pressed charges and yo crazy ass going to jail." Vito yelled as he ran up on me and Sky held my arm as she yelled for him to stop. "STOP VITO, LEAVE HER ALONE! NO, TERRICKA!" Sky yelled as I broke out of her grip and got up to run up on Vito.

As soon as I stood up that bitch punched me straight in the eye. The impact made me stumble back some but I quickly recovered and kicked him in the dick. Once I landed that kick to the nuts it was over for him as I went to work and landed punch after punch to his face. He shook off the pain between his legs as I tried to grab him in his dreads and the fight was on. We fought our way into the kitchen where he pinned me up against the refrigerator and began to choke the life out of me as Sky yelled and punched him in the back.

"FUCK YOU OLE CRAZY BITCH. I HATE YO STUPID ASS. I SHOULD KILL YO BITCH ASS, SHOULDN'T I? SHOULDN'T I BITCH?" Vito asked as he stared hatefully into my eyes. I struggled in his grip and peered out of the corner of my eyes as I felt air slowly leave my body. Sky distracted him as she continued to beat him in the back and tried to pull us apart. That was enough for me to reach over and grab the butcher knife I saw on the counter and cut that bitch across the chest, just below his collar bone.

"Naw I should kill you, shouldn't I bitch?" I yelled as Vito dropped me and fell back as he held his chest. At that moment I was out of my mind as I jumped over him and swung the knife. He put his arms up to catch the blows as the knife cut through his flesh with precision. Blood flew everywhere as he cursed and tried to get me off of him and I went insane. Seconds later Sky's arms were around me as she dragged me off and wrestled the knife out of my hands. Everything in the room was red by the time I finished and Vito laid there in a puddle of his own blood as he cursed and moaned.

"That bitch tried to kill me. I think she hit an artery Sky. Call the police." He yelled with his bitch ass and I started to laugh. "Call the police? Call the police? After all them times you beat my ass you want her to call the police? Nigga fuck yo snitching ass." I yelled as I rushed towards him and Sky stood in the middle.

As soon as she did that the door to my apartment flew open and six, clothed officers rushed in. In minutes I was face down and in hand cuffs as I was arrested for domestic violence and assault with a deadly weapon while Vito cursed and Sky and my kids cried. I remained silent the entire ride to Jail East and remained that way the whole week I was in there before Sky posted bond. I lived in my head with the voices to keep me company the entire time while I dared a bitch to get wrong. No one did though, not even a glance. I guess them bitches could see I was out of my mind.

When Sky picked me up that following Friday I had a brand new state of mind. The voices in my head and haze in my brain had eased because that good side of me had grown stronger. That side of me wanted help and to change, and I knew it was that time. At my house I rushed in and hugged my kids before I planted kisses all over their puffy cheeks. My younger kids accepted the love I gave even though my love was sporadic at best and usually was just a part of one of my bipolar mood swings. Nevertheless, they wanted it and kissed me back before they told me they loved and missed me. All of them except my oldest who sat there with his arms folded and a mean mug on his face. I started to reach over and grab him when he pulled away and Sky grabbed my arm.

"Just give him time Terricka, just give him time." My friend said as I shook my head that I understood. "Go get yourself cleaned up and get some rest, I'll take care of the kids." Sky said before I hugged her and turned to leave the room.

I walked up the stairs in a daze as my kid's laughter and Sky's voice trailed behind me and I wished I could make them that happy. Tears fell from my eyes as I peeled my clothes off and went into my clean bathroom to shower. I let the hot water in the shower pour down on me and wash all of my tears away as I cried and yelled out for God to help me.

When I got out of the shower there was a feeling in my heart that told me I knew what to do. After I dressed I went over to my phone and dialed the number of the one person I knew would come to my rescue regardless of what I said or had done.

"I need you. Please help me. I can't do this on my own anymore. I'm sorry for all I said and did but I need your help. I'm going insane. I look at myself every day and I see Denise. I don't want to be her. HELP ME!" I yelled into the phone as my body shook out of control.

I cried like a baby as I heard the person on the other end cry too before they took the time to respond. "Say no more sister, I'll be on a plane in the morning. Just hold on T. HELP IS ON THE WAY!" Tisha said and I felt there just might be hope for me after all.

Part 2

Life As We Now Know It!

Chapter 4

My Worst Nightmare Come True

The entire plane ride back to Memphis I felt restless and sick to my stomach. I tried to curl up next to Jerrod and let the beautiful melody of A'Miracle's voice as she played with Sha in the seats in front of us calm my nerves, but no matter how hard I tried, I couldn't shake the ominous feeling that had taken over me. Somehow, I already knew that my worst nightmare was about to come true and I would have to face the shadow of an evil, deprived woman my sister had become. I tried to shake the visions of her all angry with Denise's face and lethal tongue as I sat up straight in my seat and stared out of the window, but it was her silhouette I saw in the clouds. I saw that same evil posture of a reckless, trifling mother I had seen my entire life. I saw all the pain her children had endured at her hands and those thoughts made me shudder.

"What's wrong Tisha?" Jerrod asked me as he awoke from his slumber and slipped his strong, athletic arms around my neck. I didn't know what to say as I sat there with tears in my eyes and wished that history was not on repeat. I wished that I could believe Terricka's plea to get help and change, but I knew she could quickly change her mind. I wished it with all of my might that this time would be different, but just like in the past wishes didn't apply to me or my siblings. We were dealt a bad hand from conception and that was a fate we simply couldn't escape. That was also a reality I knew I couldn't run from so I chose to tell my husband the truth instead of bottle up my feelings like I had done in the past.

"Jerrod, I'm just so fucking scared. I'm scared that everything everyone has said about Terricka is true. I'm scared that the feeling in my gut is right and my sister is another dragon that will have to be slayed. I'm scared that I won't be able to fix this baby." I ranted as my heart raced in my chest and Jerrod listened silently and intently.

"What if she goes crazy on me for coming even though she asked me to? I don't know if my heart can handle the pain I lived through in my childhood. The torture, the disappointment. I mean, what if it's worse than what we heard? What if we go there and find out Terricka is worse than Denise and totally unfit to care for her kids? What then? What will happen to them? Jerrod I just don't know." I said as I pulled myself together and then leaned in to whisper to him so that A'Miracle couldn't hear me.

Tears rolled down my cheeks as I contemplated the words I had just said and saw it all play out in my head. I shuddered in Jerrod's embrace as he hugged me tight before he held me out to look into my eyes. I melted when he poured his love down on me, lost in his loving gaze. "Baby there is no need to be scared." Jerrod said as he wiped away my tears with his thumbs then kissed me softly on the lips.

"Tisha, you know I'm by your side no matter what. Let's not make assumptions or even go on the he say, she say bullshit that made its way from Memphis all the way to us in L.A. Let's just go and see what happens and then act accordingly. If it comes down to it, you know we won't leave her kids alone or let them go to the state. Baby, we will take them all and love and raise them as our own. They're blood, they're family, and we don't give up on family unless we have no other choice. That's why we're not gonna jump to conclusions on Terricka. We're gonna stay hopeful. You know, hope for the best and let her prove us wrong. I know y'all SAY there's no hope or wishes come true for a Lewis kid, but I say that's bullshit. You're living your happy ending baby. And Terricka will too! Okay beautiful?" Jerrod said as he smiled and then kissed away the tears that lingered on my cheeks.

I smiled back at my love, my light and drunk his handsome ass up with my eyes while I wanted desperately to believe what he said. "Now, dry up those tears and give daddy some sugar with yo sexy ass." Jerrod said as he winked his eye then kissed me deeply and passionately.

I got lost in his love for a second as I forgot about the hurt in my heart and the worry that had taken over me. I allowed Jerrod to kiss me then wrap me in his arms again as my mind wondered off to Memphis. Vivid, violent scenes from my past danced in my mind along with horrible predictions of the future that struck like lightning as I listened to Jerrod breathe. I fought those memories and the pain they brought on until I closed my eyes and drifted off to sleep again. To my surprise, Denise came to me in my dream. Not the drugged out, always angry, ready to strike at any moment Denise, but that sweet, gentle, loving mother she once was and could be when she wanted something. I saw her clear as day as she walked through that same field of flowers my siblings and I used to dream about and held my hand. My dream felt so real I tossed and turned in my sleep and tried to grip the hand I felt in my palm.

"Tisha, I need you to be strong. I need you to be the caring, loving person I wish I was to you. Help your sister. She needs you. Everything she is going through is because of me and what I did to y'all so forgive her. I need you both to forgive yourselves as well. What y'all did to me was necessary no matter how cruel. Forgive yourself Tish and make your sister forgive herself so that y'all can let go of the pain and move on. I'm in a better place now Tisha, free of my own sins and demons. I need y'all to let go of my sins too. Okay? I love you Tisha. Promise me you will let it go. Okay Tisha? Tisha!" Denise's voice rang in my ears as I fought to wake up from my dream. "Tisha! Tisha baby, wake up!" Jerrod yelled and woke me up from my nightmare as I stared up into his handsome face.

I quickly fought through my anxiety and shook off the visions in my head as I smiled back and pretended to be okay.

"Tisha baby are you okay? I heard you yell Denise name in your sleep. Maybe coming back to Memphis wasn't such a great fucking idea." Jerrod whispered as he bent down to me.

I noticed Sha and A'Miracle as they stood behind him with their bags in hand and concerned looks on their faces, and that alone was enough to give me the courage to go on. I knew that I had to make things right and get my family back on track, if not for me or my sister's sake, but for the children we had brought into the world. That's why I was able to take what Denise said and run with it. I was able to see what she said was true and find the fight within me I needed to pull my sister out of her pain.

"I'm fine you guys, just a little tired. Let's get this family reunion started though. Mama got business to handle." I said as I looked past Jerrod to Sha and A'Miracle with a strong, confident smile on my face. That smile gave them the reassurance they needed so Sha grabbed A'Miracle's hand and they began to walk down the aisle. My half assed attempt to deflect my emotions and true fears was not effective enough to convince Jerrod though because he remained bent down in my face until I looked at him again.

"You know I'm not buying that shit right? I know wassup Tisha. I know the demons of your past are back to haunt you and you feel obligated to make shit right. I also know that what is happening to Terricka is eating you up. Just know that I won't let anything happen to YOU. If I feel like this trip is causing a greater toll on you than good I will end this shit, snatch up Terricka kids, and we will be going back to California on the first thing smoking. You hear me?" Jerrod asked me with a serious but loving expression on his face.

"I mean that Tisha. I love our family and all but you and A'Miracle are my first concern. You can't help anybody if you're fucking falling apart yourself so I won't let that shit happen. Now, I need you to tell me wassup. Do you think you are strong enough to get through this or should I just start plan b?" Jerrod asked as I thought about what I wanted to do.

Part of me did want to just go get the kids and go back home, far away from all of the pain and sorrow that awaited. That was the part of me that fled Memphis in the first place.

However, the stronger more determined part of me knew what had to be done. "No, baby I'm fine. I have to do this. She is my sister and my responsibility. I am my sister's keeper and I will not leave her when she needs me most. I can do it my king, as long as you are by my side." I said to Jerrod as I felt a tear well up in my right eye.

I watched Jerrod stand up straight through blurred vision before he grabbed my hand and pulled me up to stand. "Say no more then, we're on our way and I'm right beside you until our dying day." Jerrod said before he kissed me, grabbed our bags, and we walked off the plane hand in hand as we laughed.

We quickly found the rental car place after we waded through the crowds of people in the airport and settled into the 2015 Expedition Jerrod had reserved. I felt just like a kid who was being whisked back into their horrible, but sometimes happy memories as we rode down Winchester towards the expressway and to Terricka.

"So Sha, where does Terricka live now. I haven't been here in a long time and I know she moves around as much as I change panties so I have no idea where we are going." I said to my brother as I glanced in the rearview mirror and noticed he had a sad and uneasy expression on his face.

I continued to watch him in the rearview as he fidgeted in his seat and pulled at one of his dreads. I could see the nervousness in his face just like I did when he was a child and that made my heart race. "Uhhh Tish. I hate to say this, but she lives in Breezy Point now." Sha said as a lump developed in my throat and I suddenly felt flustered.

Jerrod quickly glanced over at me as my body shook and I closed my eyes and tried to block out all of the memories Breezy Point held. That was the place where most of our childhood torture happened. It was the one place I never wanted to see again and I was headed straight to it. I couldn't control myself as tears ran down my face, my throat began to close up. I felt like I was about to pass out as my memories rushed at me fast and hard like waves, and I looked over at Jerrod for help. As usual, he was right on point and pulled over to the side of the rode quickly before he jumped out and came around to my side.

"Tisha baby it's alright. Come here." Jerrod said as he pulled my shaky body up out of the seat and Sha and A' Miracle asked what was wrong.

"It's okay y'all. A'Miracle mommy is alright just a little hot. Sha, take care of your niece." Jerrod said as he winked and nodded at Sha to let him know it was exactly what he thought it was. I stood there beside Jerrod with his arm still around me as my body continued to shake and he closed the door behind us. As soon as the door closed all of my penned up emotions burst forward and I cried like a little baby.

"Jerrod I don't know if I can go there. I don't know if I can do it. That's where it all began. That's where I experienced the most hurt. How can I go there and pretend it's not tearing me apart? I don't know if I'm strong enough baby." I said as Jerrod wrapped me in his arms and kissed the top of my head. We stood there like that for a minute as I cried out all of my fear and Jerrod assured me that I would be fine.

"Baby, back on the plane you told me that this was what you had to do for your family. You said you had to save your sister and I know you meant that. That's why I'm not gonna let you run away right now, not because of some damn bricks and wood. Tisha, in yo life baby you have gone through some shit that would make a grown man crumble. I mean if I had to pick any female in the world to say I admire her the most for her strength, determination, and ability to love and give selflessly, I would have to say you. Tisha, you have beat everything that comes your way. Ain't no damn projects gonna win this baby. This a fear we gonna face together. I'm gonna be right there with you like I've been since day one and we're gonna slay this dragon too. You gonna do this for Terricka. For the kids. So, what you gonna do Mrs. Lewis - Hill?" Jerrod said before held me out at arm's length to stare into my eyes.

I could do nothing but suck up my tears and feel the strength he transferred to me as I noticed the tears on his cheeks too. My husband, the young boy who taught me how to smoke weed, be confident in myself, and love even when it hurts was still right by my side, and he made me stronger. I hugged Jerrod tightly to me and inhaled the scent of his Gucci cologne as he gently rubbed the center of my back. "I'm gonna be alright baby. I can do this. I can do this." I whispered in Jerrod's ear before I stood back and wiped away the tears that lingered on my cheeks with my palms.

Jerrod smiled slyly at me as he stepped back in closer and wrapped his arms around me with my arms folded in front of me. "You know I'm not about to et yo beautiful ass be sad sooooooooo, let's lighten this mood with a song. How about a song of salvation? Ummmm What about Tisha and Terricka's Lewis's Salvation Song!" Jerrod said as he squeezed and shook me while he laughed and I tried to squirm out of his embrace. "NOOOOO don't sing it. Shut up Jerrod!" I yelled as Sha and A'Miracle noticed what was going on and let down the window.

"Okay, younger people." Jerrod said as he laughed and I stretched my arms down far enough to tickle him. "Oh you're not getting out Tisha. Just be still and let the melody soothe you." Jerrod said to me before he kissed my forehead and I attempted to bite him before I laughed. "Ohhhh feisty huh? Okay let's see if you like that tonight." Jerrod whispered before he leaned down to kiss my neck and then turn back towards the truck.

"Okay, Sha and A'Miracle joining me in singing, THE SALVATION SONG!! 1-2-3 Hit it!"

"Nothing lasts forever, what we're hoping for. No more pain so don't you cry anymore."

My family sang as I hummed over their voices until Jerrod called it all off.

"Okay, okay you guys, we got a bad ass. Now baby, shall we go?" Jerrod asked me asked held my hand out like I was a queen.

"Yes we shall." I said as we both giggled and I let him put me back into the car. Sha gripped my shoulder as I got settled in my seat and I looked back into his concerned eyes before I nodded and whispered I was okay.

"Now, we're on the road again, so let me provide the entertainment. Nothing lasts forever…" Jerrod began as soon as his ass was back in his seat and I reached over to chop him before we all laughed.

I laughed from my heart and forgot my pain and the trouble that awaited me as we continued on to the expressway and I rode down I-240 towards The Bay with my family's laughter in my ears. We drove for what seemed to be an eternity as I contemplated what I would feel when I actually saw the hell hole I was once forced to live in. I couldn't predict the range of emotions that would take over me or my reaction to them, but I knew I had to face that fear regardless of the outcome.

For the rest of the ride I concentrated on the strength I had at a time in my life when I should have fallen short. I thought about how Terricka and I had to jump out of a window to escape what could have been our death. Along with how I lived through torture while I looked into the eyes of my tormentor. The tormentor with the same eyes as mine. I knew in my heart that Jerrod was right and I had lived through too much to let a building, an apartment, or a memory defeat me. I had come too far to turn back, so to give up was forbidden.

That is why I channeled that strength I remembered and forced my heart to move past the thought of seeing the one place I vowed to never returned to. I let go of all of the fear I had to relive the pain and embraced it instead. Pain was all I knew anyway. That's why I decided to use that pain to motivate me to end it once and for all. I knew I had to be strong enough for everyone one more time and make things right once in for all.

"Off to my childhood home. A'Miracle, you can finally see where mommy grew u. This is where I learned all about life, conquered some demons and learned to fly." I said to my daughter as I turned around and nudged her nose while she giggled and I smiled back at her. "This was also the place that really made us realize who we were too. Huh, Sha?" I said as I looked at my brother in the rearview mirror and he stared back at me with that same, strong, determined, wise look in his eyes he had as a kid.

"The place where we found out fairytales don't always come true and sometimes you have to slay more than one dragon." I said as my brother nodded and looked down before Jerrod reached over to grip my thigh and then turn the radio up.

We rode the rest of the way to Breezy Point almost in silence as the slow jams on the radio and the sound of the game A'Miracle was engrossed in on her IPod calmed our moods. When we pulled into the big, black, wrought iron gate that surrounded the place I called home most of my life, to my surprise I felt nothing. None of the emotions I felt when I first learned Terricka stayed there rushed over me like they had done before, instead I felt numb.

I sat up in my seat and pressed my head against the glass as we turned right and headed up the driveway directly towards our old apartment. I closed my eyes and saw the dingy, beautiful spirited little girl I used to be, run across the grass as the cool air conditioner air of the new truck caressed the skin on my cheek. When I opened my eyes I stared directly at the front door of my hell hole and I felt void of any fear or hurt. Instead I felt angry as fuck and ready to get it all over with. I just wanted to say fuck that ugly chapter in my life and move on, with all of my family with me. I made it up in my mind right then that Terricka was going to listen to reason or I was going to whoop her ass until she did.

"Okay my loves, we're here." I said as we pulled into the parking lot of the building across from where I used to live and Jerrod turned off the car. I hid the anger that continued to grow inside of me as I smiled at Jerrod then turned to smile at my daughter. "Now A'Miracle baby I realize you have never been here before and you may not be used to how other people live. It may be different from at home, but be polite and if anything scares you let us know. Okay?" I asked my daughter as she looked out of the window and scanned the apartments before she turned back to me, smiled, and then replied. "Let's go mommy. I want to see my cousins." My baby said as she hopped out of the truck and we all hopped out behind her.

I quickly caught up to A'Miracle as she skipped up on to the curb in front of the apartments and Jerrod and Sha trailed behind us. I let A'Miracle pull me along quickly until we go to the door, then I stopped abruptly before I pulled her back close to me. I stood there with my arms wrapped around her neck and my eyes glued on the door as the loud music and voices inside filled my ears and the strong smoke creeped from under the door and into every crevice of my lungs.

I instantly got a vivid, full-color, Quentin-Fucking-Tarantino type of movie flashback at that moment and saw history come to life right before my eyes. I couldn't move or talk as the anger I had found beyond my pain and hurt sent a whirlwind of evil thoughts through my head. I just wanted to go into the apartment and beat the shit out of Terricka. I wanted to drag her to rehab, face down by her hair, and then take her babies and love on them. I wanted it so bad, but my body just wouldn't let me move.

"It's okay baby." Jerrod said as he walked up to hug me from the back before he reached around to take A'Miracle out of my embrace. When he stepped back Sha stepped forward and leaned in over my shoulder so that he could whisper in my ear. "I got you big sis. We can do this Tish. We slayed the dragon. This is nothing!" Sha said as he reached over my shoulder and pounded on the door like the Police.

The second he did that my heart began to race in my chest like a pack of project dogs when the free lunch truck comes around. I didn't know what to expect when that door opened and that no knowing is what worried me. "I got you I told you." Sha said as he laid his strong, massive hand on my shoulder and I turned to nod and smile at him.

After about three heavy knocks on the door I could hear the music inside go down and hear people scurry away. Seconds later the front door flew open and I was greeted by the biggest, ugliest, ghetto, hood booger I had ever seen. She was about six feet tall and 250 lbs. with dirty, shit colored skin, gaped, dingy yellow teeth with a nappy red weave that looked matted to her scalp. I almost threw up in my mouth as I scanned her from head to toe and noticed the hot pink booty shorts and matching bra top she had on. She looked a hot mess as she sucked on the Newport in her hand and eyed me as intently as I eyed her. Her eyes were a swirl of yellow and red from the dope she had smoked and the expected shot of hepatitis she undoubtedly carried. Just the sight of her made me itch and feel uneasy so I wanted to get the greetings over as soon as possible.

"Yeah, wassup?" The woman said as she blew the smoke from her cigarette directly into my face. That was enough to push that pussy, all in her feelings Tisha deep inside of me and let that Frayser Wild Girl out! I jumped back with the shit before I knew it and my not so little anymore brother Sha was right there with me.

"Hold the fuck up! First of all, hoe, how dare you blow smoke in my muthafucking face. You ole big, back, based out bear looking bitch. I will drag yo big ass. As a matter of fact," I screamed, just at the point of murder, as I reached out and knocked the cigarette out of the bitch's hand before I snatched her up in the collar of her dirty ass t-shirt.

"Bitch you really don't know who the fuck you fucking with. This my muthafucking sister's house. I'm Tisha. Yeah, hoe I know you heard of me. Now get yo big lame ass on before I kick a patch of skin off yo fucking face." I yelled as I drug the big bitch out on to the porch, past my family as she cursed and tried to hit me.

"Bitch let me go. I don't give a fuck who you are. I'm muthafucking Tangie bitch!" She yelled as I wrapped my hands in her hair before I kneed her in the face and broke her down to her knees.

I shook her like a mad dog with a weaker dog between its teeth as she flapped around like a fish out of water. I didn't care what she did though I just kept my grip on her hair and whipped her head from side-to-side. Even with Jerrod's hands on my shoulder I still continued to shake and curse at Tangie.

"And I don't give a fuck that your name Tangie. ANNDDDD hoe. Who the fuck are you? I will murder yo bitch ass so you better just listen closely big bitch before this becomes yo last day to suck dick and eat burgers. Big Winnie the Pooh belly bitch. Stop squirming!" I yelled as the bitch finally began to calm down.

"Now, it's about to be a new program around here so I don't want to see you on these steps no more. You understand that bitch? I don't want yo maggot ass around my sister or her kids again. If you think I'm playing bitch, try me. You better ask somebody." I said before I quickly stood up and walked around behind the big bitch with her hair still in my hands. "NOW GO!" I said as I Sparta kicked the skank in her ass and she rolled off the porch like a sack of dirty laundry.

After that I didn't even wait for my anger to subside or to hear the curses and insults the bitch on the ground behind me hurdled my way. Instead I turned around instantly and sprinted inside the apartment. When I stormed into Terricka's apartment a day after our heartfelt conversation I was instantly astonished by what I saw. The de ja vue was so strong and so real it was intoxicating as I stood inside of the nasty, smoke filled room. Beer bottles, cigar dumping, plastic baggies, clothes, and just plain filth meet me at the door and stretched across the floor for as far as the eye could see.

I quickly scanned the room as my family entered behind me and I knew that my worst nightmare had definitely come true. Everywhere I looked was a drugged out face of a female half naked or a nasty ass nigga who wanted a way to spend his money or dope. It was like a project whore house on some of that Biblical Sodom and Gomorrah shit, all sick and twisted. Like a two-dollar bunny ranch that had just opened for the day with everyone laid back and enjoying their drug of choice before the main event began.

Everybody in the room was so wrapped up in their own shit they didn't even hear the whole ass kicking I gave out at the door or notice my entire family as we stood in their faces. They didn't have to notice me though because as soon as I scanned the room and got a glimpse of one of Terricka's babies, all scared and dirty as she peered down the stairs, my anger made sure everyone in the entire 171-unit apartment complex knew I was there.

"OKAY, I NEED EVERY LAST ONE OF YOU NASTY, JUNKY, LOW-LIFE MUTHAFUCKAS UP OUT OF HERE RIGHT NOW BEFORE IT GET REAL UGLY UP IN HERE." I yelled as Sha stepped up next to me and folded his massive arms in front of him.

A few of the junkies with sense hurriedly scurried to the door and out on the porch as I turned to see Jerrod sit A'Miracle in a char by the window before he put her earphone over her ears and kissed her on the head. As soon as he did that I knew it was on because Sha was already with the sit as he grabbed niggas and females up and pushed them out the door.

"Get the fuck out!" Sha yelled as he came back for another group and a dude just as tall and buff as Sha who had to be a drug dealer and not a junkie stood up and stared him down. "Nigga, I ain't going nowhere until I get paid. Who the fuck gonna make me go?" He yelled in my brother's face as I watched Sha's always calm demeanor turn into that of a beast.

I watched as veins popped out of his neck and he clenched his fists so tightly that they turned white. I could see the murder of the lanky, stupid ass nigga with a big mouth in my mind as I called my brother's name. It was too late to stop that runaway train though and I learned that when I saw Jerrod come from around me with the Mark XIX Desert Eagle in his hand. I watched him for a second as he stalked up behind the dude and put the barrel of his gun to the back of his head.

"Now who ain't gonna leave ole pussy ass nigga? Now from what I can see you can have this one or two way. You can either leave quietly and get you money at a later time and date.

Or you can get yo muthafucking head stomped in to the brink of death, be revived then be tortured for hours before I shoot you in the fucking face? Which one ole tough ass nigga? Huh, which one nigga?" Jerrod yelled as he slapped the dude across the back of the head with the gun just as Sha punched him and I turned around.

I quickly went over to the chair by the window A'Miracle sat in with her back turned and headphones on as I put my hands on her shoulder and stared out right along with her. I looked directly at the big, picture window I used to stare out of and wish for someone to come rescue me. I saw myself as I stood in the window like I did countless times as a child, hungry, beaten, and just worn the fuck out. I closed my eyes and felt the pain I felt as a child who was sexually, mentally, and physically abused for as long as I could remember and I didn't want that for my nieces and nephews. I didn't want that for them because I knew they deserved better than that and that maybe that better was more than Terricka could give.

I continued to relive my decades of despair through my memories as my brother and Jerrod finished whooping the dude's ass and threw him out along with everyone else. When they were done and the room was clear I looked over at Sha before I turned to Jerrod and held my hands up in the air. "OMG, ITS JUST LIKE I THOUGHT! FUCKING HOPELESS!" I cried as tears poured down my cheeks and I walked over to the steps.

I stared up the stairs and looked for the little, dirty scared face I had seen before, but there was no one in sight. "Children, you can come down. This is your aunt Tisha and uncle Sha. It's okay now." I said in the gentlest, most sensitive, kind voice I could muster through my anger and tears.

I waited at the bottom of the steps as I heard their little footsteps overhead, but no one came down to see what I wanted. "Come down children, it's okay." I said through my tears as I imagined them running to hide like we had done. "It's okay baby give them a little time." Jerrod said as he came over to hug me just as the front door swung open behind me.

I couldn't see who had come in as I held on to my husband, but I instantly knew it was Terricka when Jerrod's whole body stiffened up and he tried to keep me from seeing who was behind me. I quickly squirmed out of his embrace and turned around to see my sister as she stood there all drunk, and high in skank gear, an exact twin of Denise. She had the same ashy pale skin, and dirty, nappy, long hair that was pulled into a raggedy ponytail that Denise often wore when she staggered home after one of her binges. I looked at her from top to bottom dressed like a prostitute in black tights, a white studded bra top and six-inch stiletto heels. Her face looked distorted and her eyes wild like a wolf with rabbies as she smirked at me before she turned up the bottle of Hennessy in her hand. I almost didn't recognize the sister who I once admired as she stood there dressed like the whore Denise tried to make us become.

I stared at her and right through her to that hurt little girl she still was inside as she tried to put on that tough girl routine and sucked her teeth while she shifted from one leg to the other. I wanted her to know at that moment I was tired of her bullshit and I would not bow down to big sister know-it-all anymore. I was going to show her that I was right in that situation and she was going to have to listen or else.

I folded my arms in front of me and leaned on my right side with my mean mug on, heated as I continued to watch her from across the room. Sha, Jerrod, and A'Miracle stood there silently and watched us as they waited for the war to begin. Minutes crept by like hours as Terricka and I stood there in front of each other, less than three feet away and exchanged angry glares that could melt a glacier. Finally, I had enough of the stare off bullshit as my sister rolled her eyes at me before she smirked and my anger erupted like a bottle of soda that had been shaken up and opened. I rushed forward right at my sister as I caught her off guard when I quickly wrapped my hands around her neck as I cursed.

"TERRICKA WHAT THE FUCK WRONG WITH YOU? HAVE YOU LOST YO FUCKING MIND? YOU STANDING HERE LOOKING JUST LIKE YO MAMA. LIKE A SORRY, CRACK HEAD BITCH. WHAT THE FUCK HAPPENED TO YOU T?" I yelled as my sister slowly regained her composure and wrapped her hands around my neck in return.

We both stood there and struggled with our hands wrapped around each other's throats and stared at the similar rage in our eyes. "Tisha you silly, green bitch." My sister said as she began to laugh this eerie, deep laugh that made the air on my arms stand up. She sounded just like a demon on a horror movie and looked like one too as the red and yellow in her eyes blazed like fire and she changed from psychotic happy to insanely mad in a second.

"WHAT THE FUCK ARE YOU DOING HERE? I DON'T NEED YO FUCKING HELP ANYMORE BITCH. I'M GOOD SO GET YO BOUSHIE ASS OUT AND TAKE YO LITTLE GREETING CARD LOOKING ASS FAMILY RIGHT WITH YOU. YOU THINK YOU CAN SAVE ME TISHA? BITCH YOU COULDN'T EVEN SAVE YOURSELF OR YO BABY, BUT YOU HERE TO RESCUE MINE? BITCH GET YOUR LIFE QUICKLY!" Terricka said as her words cut deep and pushed me to the point of no return.

Before I knew it I had released my grip on her neck and punched Terricka dead in her face before I wrapped my hands in her hair. I was prepared to take her down then beat her face in, but I forgot she was still the big sister who had taught me all of my moves. As soon as my fist touched her face, Terricka gave that shit right back to me in the form of two jabs straight to the nose. I quickly learned that the drugs had done nothing to my sister's fighting skills because she still had them hands. Those jabs hit me so hard and so fast I had to stagger back and let the room stop spinning before I gave her two, extra hard jabs of my own. After that the tussle part of our fight was over as we threw blow after blow at each other while we yelled and cursed as loud as we could.

After a few minutes to let us get it out of our systems, Jerrod and Sha stepped in between us and pulled us apart. "Fuck you Terricka, you junky bitch. I should beat your ass again." I yelled as Jerrod pulled me towards the steps and begged me to calm down. I tried to hear him as he yelled my name, but I was so mad all I could hear was the curses and insults my sister continued to shoot at me while I tried to wiggle out of my husband's grip.

"No fuck you Tisha, you little spoiled bitch. You ain't beat shit lil weak ass hoe. Run up now. RUN UP PUNK BITCH!" Terricka raged as Sha picked her up and carried her out of the door. I held in the curses I wanted to yell back as Jerrod held me around the waist and turned me away from the door so that I was pointed towards the stairs. When he did that I instantly went limp as I stared at the four, beautiful, traumatized babies that sat on the steps and stared down at me with tears in their eyes. I regretted them and my daughter having to see me act that way, but I felt it was necessary to get my point across. I just wished that I could have contained myself until I got Terricka away from them, but what was done was already done.

All I could do was cry as I looked at them and then broke away from Jerrod's embrace to walk closer. Jerrod yelled that he was going outside to help Sha with Terricka as I waved him off and he ran towards my sister's loud curses and threats. I paid that shit know mind as I stepped up on the first step as A'Miracle walked up beside me and reached out to grab my hand. I looked down at her beautiful face as tears fell from my eyes and she smiled at me so sweetly. I saw the innocence and right to be loved in her eyes that all children had and all I wanted to do was protect them. I wanted to protect them because no one had managed to protect me.

"Hey Rodney Jr, it's your aunt Tisha. You remember me?" I asked as A'Miracle and I stepped up another step and the kids continued to sit there and stare. I stopped within inches from his little grimy, handsome face as he stared up at me and squinted his eyes like he was trying to remember my face. For a few minutes he couldn't place my face then suddenly I saw something sparkle in his eyes. In seconds he was up on his feet and in my arms as I held him tightly to me and kissed his head.

"Yes aunt Tisha, thank you. Thank you for saving us. Mama crazy." He cried. "Yeah. Take us wit chu." The smallest girl with long pigtails said as she grabbed the hand of the bigger girl with a cast on her arm, and the little curly haired boy with big brown eyes followed them as they all ran to me too.

In seconds I had all four of their tiny bodies along with the body of my own baby wrapped in my arms as I cried and vowed to always protect them. I quickly forgot all of the anger and hate I felt before even though I could still hear Terricka rage outside. Just to feel their love and need to be loved in return was enough to snap me back into the Tisha I had grown to be. "Go get my bag off the floor A'Miracle." I said to my daughter as I carried the kids upstairs and to the little bathroom at the end of the hall.

A'Miracle was back at my side in seconds with the bag of clothes and underwear I had brought with me for the kids because I knew they would need them. We walked into the bathroom together and the horrible stench almost took my breath away. I quickly sat the two girls I still held in my arms down on the floor before I ordered A'Miracle and Rodney Jr. to take them to their room. "You guys go play for a while and let me clean up this bathroom. After that I will clean you all up then we will get out of here. Okay?" I said to the kids as I smiled and all of their faces lit up.

I watched them giggle and jump for a minute before they agreed and then ran off to the room. As soon as they were gone I lost that fake smile and began to cry again. I felt like I was in the Twilight Zone as I looked around the tiny bathroom with the same filth I was forced to clean all of my life. "Well, you know the drill Tisha." I said to myself as I opened the linen closet behind the door and took out the unopened cleaning supplies.

I quickly fell into that clean and get it over with haze I used to have often as a kid whenever my mama would beat my ass or threaten me into cleaning up after her drug parties. I felt just like the ghetto Cinderella as I put on the yellow gloves I found and began to throw away the used condoms, maxi pads, and cigarette butts that littered the counter and floor.

"How can any mother let her children live this way." I said out loud as I picked up razor blades and a loaded needle off the counter right next to my nephew's Batman toothbrush. "I don't know baby, but we will find out." Jerrod said as he stepped into the bathroom behind me. In seconds Jerrod had on gloves and was elbow deep in filth as he helped me to clean the floor. "Tisha me and Sha about to take Terricka away for a while and let her get her head together. Maine she really fucked up right now and I don't think her kids should see her like this. I don't think her crazy ass needs to be alone either so we just gonna go with her, get her sober and bring her ass back. She said something about going over her friend Sky house so that's where we gonna take her. Okay?" Jerrod said as he swept up the last bit of trash on the floor and began to mop. I stepped back into the hallway and let him finish before I replied.

"Thank you baby, for all of this. Bring her back in one piece and sober because we gotta find a solution to this." I said to my husband as he took off his gloves and pulled me into his embrace. "I got you baby, don't worry. Just enjoy your time with the kids." Jerrod said before he kissed my forehead, grabbed the trash, and disappeared down the hall.

Once he was gone I finished cleaning the bathroom before I ran a nice hot bath to put the girls in. I called them in and put them in the tub and was instantly taken aback but the amount of bruises and dirt that was on their bodies. I cried as I rang a rag over their old and fresh wounds and they told me how nice I was. After I bathed them, I got them dressed, and ran the boys water as I cursed Terricka for being so awful as a mother. Once their tub was filled I wondered out into the hall and walked into the boy's room on my way to the girl's to get them.

Their room was even worse than the pits of torture I lived in all of my life and that was really hard to beat. None of them had beds or even a dresser to put their clothes in, just mattresses on the floor and plastic bins. The little clothes they did have that looked like something were sprawled across the floor dirty and covered in stains, along with trash and what appeared to be human feces. I had to close my eyes and quickly leave the room before I went off again just seeing how my sister had let her kids live in deplorable conditions.

I held my breath and thought about how happy they would be once I got everything figured out as I went into the bathroom to get the boys out of the tub. Rodney quickly covered his privates with one hand when I walked in and used the other to grab his chest right below his collar bone. That made my heart flutter instantly so I walked over and removed his hand. He had a long, deep, red bruise on his chest like someone had burned him with something metal. I cried as I dried him off and put cream on the burn and he told me thank you.

"You don't have to thank me baby, I'm your Te Te and I will love and protect you forever and ever." I said as I whisked his frail body up into my arms and kissed him as I carried him into the girl's room.

I stood there and watched them all play together like the had been around each other the entire time before I slipped off into Terricka's room. Her room was no better than the kids but I did notice off the back that she had a bed, dresser, and TV in her room unlike the kids. I wanted to whoop her ass at that moment but I fought through my feelings as I waded deeper into the three inches of trash on the floor with my eyes fixated on a picture stuck to the mirror.

When I got closer I snatched the picture down and looked at the happy family we once were. It was a picture of us all when I was about seven and Sha was first born. We were all sitting in my grandma's living room and my mother held Sha in her arms while she kissed him and looked as if she loved him more than anything in the world. I ran my fingers across the picture and touch me and Terricka's happy faces and wished we could have that happiness again. "One day we will be happy again sister, I promise you. And I won't give up until we do!" I said out loud to the Terricka in the picture before I stuck the it back where I found it and left the room.

On my way down the hall a red box in the toy bin in the corner caught my eye and I stopped to take it out. I plucked it up into my hands and walked towards the kid's rooms as I opened it and looked inside. Inside was all of the works a junky might have from needles, to crack pipes, and a straw for snorting cocaine. I felt completely disgusted and scared for the kids as I sifted through the shit and thought about how tragic things could have been if one of the kids had found the box amongst their toys. Just the thought of one of my beautiful nieces or handsome nephews with that junk in their hands sent me into a rage and I rushed to the bathroom to dispose of the shit.

Inside the bathroom I crushed needles and crack pipes beneath my feet and flushed everything else in the box as I cried and saw resemblances of my own life. There I was, once again forced to clean up the mess of a dysfunctional mother not fit to care for a dog. I felt sick to my stomach as I watched all of the drugs go down the bowel then my anger sent me on a tirade again. I stormed out of the bathroom and down the hall towards the stairs ready to run down and call Jerrod to bring that bitch back so that I could fuck her up. However, as soon as I stepped close to the girl's doorway the uncandid, fearful pleas of my sister's kids filled my ears.

"I wonna go home wit chu Miracle. I like your mommy." Talaya, the youngest said as her sisters and brothers joined in. "Yeah me too." Tania said. "Me three." Ryan repeated." As A'Miracle laughed. "We all wonna go A'Miracle because our mommy mean and not clean like your mommy. She hit us all the time and do all kids of nasty stuff. Sometimes she won't let us out the room and we never really eat. I'm so hungry right now I might die. I just wonna go with y'all." Rodney Jr. said as my heart melted and they all agreed.

I stood there for a few more minutes as they continued to talk and my heart went from cold to warm as they explained the ups and downs of life with their mom. "Sometime her can be sooo nice though R.J." Ryan said to his big brother. "Sometimes her reads to us, take us to the park, and makes cheesy spaghetti we can eat with chips. Sometimes. But the sometimes she being mean happens most. I just wish it would stop so I could stay with mama cause I love her. Her just mean." Ryan repeated as the other kids agreed and A'Miracle offered them all comfort.

After I heard Ryan talk about how much he loved his mom despite the fact that she was mean and how she would change between mean, and nice, my anger began to melt away as I thought about the inheritable disease Terricka clearly had. Once again Denise's sins were our burdens to bear and I felt it was unfair if I punished Terricka for that. "Help your sister." I heard Denise's voice say as it rang in my ears and I looked around the dirty hallway then down the steps.

I knew right then that I was no better than the people who had failed us as kids, or those who had failed our mother for that matter if I got mad at Terricka, lashed out, or left. I knew that my sister was in fact possessed by something much stronger than her and that it was my duty to help. "I'm gonna help her Denise. I'm gonna do what you should have done when she was a little girl. I'm gonna love her unconditionally and never give up on her." I said through my tears as I looked up at the ceiling.

I cried as I made my way back to the bathroom and grabbed up the cleaning supplies I had left behind. I decided I would clean the downstairs and then order in for me and the kids to get my mind off things. Once downstairs I got to work and zoned out to the Erykah Badu I had put on the radio. Before long I had cleaned the living room and kitchen from top to bottom and the pizza, wings, fries, and milkshakes I ordered were delivered.

After I called the kids down I sat all the food on the coffee table and put on a Despicable Me DVD. I plopped down on the now cleaner couch and waited on the kids as my phone vibrated and I looked at it to see a text from Jerrod.

We're good baby be there soon. I love you.

Was the text I read before I replied and told him I loved him back. I sat my phone down just as the clean, happy kids ran downstairs and was blown away by the clean living room. "Everything clean." Tania said as she came over to the couch and plopped down beside me. "And she bought all this food. This must be our lucky day." Rodney Jr. said as a tear fell from my eye.

"Can we eat some now?" Ryan asked me as he kneeled down at the table next to me and stared up at me with his big, beautiful, but sad eyes. I couldn't hide my emotions as a tear fell from my eye and I got choked up as I tried to talk. I had to clear my throat and breathe deeply to keep my emotions at bay. "Of course you can eat baby. All of you can eat, and eat as much as you want." I said as I watched them all dig in with their hands like they hadn't eaten in months.

I sat there and watched them eat and smile at me the entire time as they joked and played like me and my siblings used to. Once dinner was over we all cuddled on the couch and watched movie after movie. Before long there was five sleeping babies all over me and I was covered in love. I felt at peace as I laid beneath them, but that all ended as soon as I heard the door knob turn.

My heart raced in my chest as I sat up and gently moved little bodies to the side. Part of me was afraid of the chaos that could ensue if Terricka still hadn't snapped back into her right mind. Another part of me was anxious to get whatever was going to happen over with and move on to the next phase. I stood up on wobbly legs as someone put the key into the door and I watched the door knob began to turn again. As soon the door was unlocked it then flew open and I felt no anger, disappointment or fear. All I could feel was love and compassion as I stared into my sister's sympathy and sober face.

Chapter 5

Never Ending Hurt

Terricka and I stood feet apart locked in our twin-like haze as Jerrod and Sha walked deeper into the apartment. I paid them no attention as they commented on the cleanliness of the apartment, kids, and how they were about to eat the rest of the food. Instead of making their greedy asses step away from the food like I normally would have, I kept my eyes locked on my sister as we talked to each other without words. I told her how much I loved her as tears fell from both of our eyes and I vowed to never give up on her. In those few moments of silence I looked into my sister's heart and saw how desperately she wanted to break free. I saw something in Terricka's eyes that I never saw in our mother's and that was the genuine desire to change, which was all I needed to see.

"Come take a ride with me." I said to my sister as I wiped away my tears and walked over to get the car keys from Jerrod. He smiled at me and then stood up to kiss my lips before he slipped the keys into my hand. "I admired you Mrs. Hill. And I love you!" Jerrod said before he kissed me again and I told him that I loved him too.

I nodded and smiled at Sha as he sat down on the floor and then winked his eye at me. When I turned back towards the door Terricka was gone so I walked out behind her. As soon as I walked out and closed the door my sister wrapped her arms around my neck and both of our emotions exploded.

"I'm so sorry TISHAAA. I'M SO SORRY. I don't know sometimes sister; I just need help. I love my kids and I love you. Please don't stop trying to help me. Don't give up on me sister because without you I don't know where I would be. Please Tisha. I just be so angry." Terricka said as she cried like a baby and I matched her tears.

I wrapped my arms around her like she had done me all of our lives as we both stood out on the porch and cried. "I love you too sister, you know I do, Terricka we all we got. I'm sorry for leaving you and then coming back like I can save the world. I'm sorry sister. I just want you to be alright Terricka. You always been so strong sister, but I need you to know that it's okay to be weak sometimes too. All of us need help sometimes sister and I promise I will be your help. I will do whatever I have to in order to make things right. I LOVE YOU TERRICKA." I said as we both cried harder and swayed from side -to-side.

I closed my eyes and savored the moment as my sister clung on to me for dear life. I wasn't sure how long her moment of clarity would last so I wasn't ready to let her go. "Terricka, I saw Denise in a dream and she told me to help you. She told me that we had to let go of what happened because it had to be done. She forgives us sister so we have to forgive ourselves and let all of our pain go. Lord knows we've lived through hell, RIGHT HERE."" I said through my tears as I stared at our childhood apartment over her shoulder. "But you know what sister? Right here has to be where we let go of this pain and start anew." I said to Terricka as I held her out at arm's length before I turned her towards the apartment.

"This is where we must leave everything that weighs us down T and start a new, better life. Our kids deserve that. Let me help you get into rehab and get some mental health T, because you suffer from bipolar disorder just like mama. Let's be real Terricka. Let's face this together and move on. Okay?" I said to my sister as she cried and I reached over to wipe away her tears.

"Okay Tisha, help me. Help me let this shit go and be alright again. Fuck this apartment where we lost so much. Fuck our pain. Our guilt. Fuck it all. I just want to end it all sister and finally be happy and free enough to run bare foot through a field of flowers with me some fine ass Mandingo." Terricka said through her tears as she laughed and I joined in.

I felt my heart swell when my sister looked at me and her eyes twinkled. For a second I saw the old Terricka again and I had hope everything would be okay. "Alright nah. Talking about a damn Mandingo. Girrrllll. If he gives it to you, what you gonna do wit it?" I asked my sister as both laughed away our tears on our walk to my car.

Once we got inside of my car and pulled out of the lot I felt all of the tension and animosity that was a barrier between my sister and I disappear as she complimented me on the rental truck choice before she found a song on the radio. "Yeah, this is HOTT Tisha! I can't wait to get myself together, get my kids on track, and then find me a man so we can rent fye ass whips like this whenever the fuck we want to. You living the life for real little sister. That's part of why I'm always so angry at you. Despite us both coming from the same fucked up place, you got everything." My sister said as she looked at me with tears in her eyes and I glanced at her quickly before I looked back at the road.

"You got the education, the money, the beautiful, respectful daughter, and the devoted man. I guess I've been slick jealous that you have it all and I have nothing. You have everything I have ever wanted, but just couldn't admit because I knew I would never get it. I mean, it's not like a happy ending waiting around the corner for me. What nigga would want me all crazy and shit? What good nigga worth who's worth something anyway? Nah, a bitch like me gonna be alone and miserable forever or have some nothing ass nigga like Vito." Terricka said to me as she turned to look out at the sunset as it disappeared into the clouds.

I felt my sister's pain at that moment because I knew that someone she wanted to run through a field of flowers with was Rodney Sr. Aka Buddy. I also knew the pain that comes along with love for someone you simply couldn't be with. That's the same pain I felt every day when Jerrod was gone. That was the same pain that I saw in my sister's eyes and all I wanted to do was help her. I knew the turmoil losing Buddy had caused and I knew that all of that hurt had done nothing but exacerbate her condition and push her further over the edge. I also knew that I was the one who had to pull her back up.

I reached over and rubbed my sister's arm as she turned around to stare at me with tears in her big brown eyes. I opened my mouth to offer her comfort, but as soon as I did my text notification went off and I grabbed my phone off the dash instead. As soon as I hit the message icon a long text from Jerrod came through and I quickly read it as I drove.

Tisha. I don't know where y'all at or where y'all going, but just be careful because I heard Memphis is a war zone right now. And another thing, don't mention Buddy at all to her cause she gonna go crazy. She tried to fight Sha when he asked about Buddy in the truck, then she made us drive around for an hour to look for him and when we couldn't find him she wanted to fight Sha again. We finally got her to calm down when we got to her friend Sky house, that's where she ate and got cleaned up. Maine she was crazy as fuck Tisha. More than usual. Anyway, just don't mention the nigga at all to her. Don't say Buddy, Rodney, or any names that begin with a B or R. lbvs!! In the meantime, I got my ear to the streets looking for the nigga. Love you BABY!

I read the message, replied to Jerrod that I loved him too, and contemplated the words before I sat my IPhone back into its dock on the dash and looked over at my sister who had a calm, serene expression on her face. "You will have all of that and more someday big sis, I promise you. You just have to trust me and the other people in your life who want to help. You are a beautiful person inside and out Terricka, and you know that you are. Somehow, you just lost your way and I'm gonna help you find it. You deserve happiness big sis, we all do, but happiness starts within. You gotta learn to love Terricka first, flaws and all. Your happiness is just around the corner sister and soon we will all run through a field of flowers together." I said to my sister as she smiled and I did too because I had avoided a potential disaster if I had mentioned Rodney. "Running through a field of flowers with a Mandingo bih. Don't try to leave that out!" Terricka said as we both burst out in hysterical laughter once again and continued to laugh all the way to the grocery store.

Terricka chattered on and on as we rode down Whitney and then turned on Thomas to enter Kroger's parking lot. I hadn't heard my sister talk so willingly about change in a long time or look as happy as she did at that moment while she talked about going to school to become a counselor.

"I figure after all the hell I have put people through the past few years and all of the hell we had to live through at the hands of someone with mental illness and substance abuse, the least I can do is give back to the same type of people when I get my shit together. That's why next week I'm gonna go ahead and do whatever it is you think I should do to get on track. If that means psychiatric help, in-patient rehab or out patient. No matter what it is I'm willing to do it sis because I'm tired of being a prisoner in my own fucking body and mind. I'm ready Tisha. I promise!" Terricka said to me with tears in her eyes as I parked the car before I reached over to hug her.

"No matter what, I will be here to help too sister. No matter what or how long it takes. I love you Terricka." I said to my sister as I tried to hold on to her promises although there was a feeling in the pit of my stomach that told me otherwise. I didn't want to listen to that voice in my head or that feeling in my stomach though, just like many times before. Like all those other times I wanted and needed to believe in my sister because that was all I had; her word. Her word and a little hidden hope that one day, one of her promises would be genuine and she would in fact change for the better. After I looked into her eyes when we pulled away from our embrace, I really felt that was one of those times. I saw clarity in Terricka's eyes I hadn't seen in years and that made my heart smile.

"Aww, what the fuck happened to us? We a couple of pussies now lil sis always crying and shit." Terricka said as she reached over to wipe the tears I didn't even know had fallen from my eyes. "Oh speak for yourself old Charmin ass lil girl. You know I'm gangsta." I said to my sister as I wiped away her tears in return and then threw up the GD pitchfork I had seen her, Jerrod, and Buddy throw up all of our lives.

"Oh shit. Now I know banging has went out of style when they got the nerds doing it. Stick to your day job sis. You better write about some gangsta shit and leave the real banging to the professionals." My sister said as she popped the collar on her imaginary collar shirt and we both laughed.

It felt just like old times as my sister and I got out of the truck and walked into the grocery store we would walk to as kids. Our hearts were filled with laughter as we pushed and checked each other the entire time. We quickly filled the basket with things for the kids and steaks for the men along with chicken for the cookout we had suddenly planned. It was almost perfect as my sister gave me the recipe for her famous lasagna and we laughed about which sauce to get. "Girl you better get that cheap shit. We gonna spice it up anyway. Don't be bougie Tisha." Terricka said as we continued to laugh, but I could feel slight irritation in her voice.

I walked behind her and held my breath as we continued to shop and I could see her mood become volatile and irritable with each minute that passed. "Anyway, just get the expensive sauce since yo rich as paying for it and hurry the fuck up so we can get out of here. All these bitches looking at me starting to work my nerves." Terricka said as she turned around to me and grabbed the sauce out of the cart and slammed it back on the shelf.

I watched her in awe, amazed at how quickly her moods had changed as she grabbed up an expensive brand and threw it in the cart before she turned to look at the woman who stood next to her. "Uhh BOO BITCH! What Dafuq are you staring at? Ole swoll neck bitch mind yo business. Ugggghhhh Tisha, see that's the shit I'm talking about!" Terricka said as she bumped past the woman and almost took her shoulder off while I stood there like a deer in the headlights for a second.

I just couldn't believe how fast Terricka had flipped. She looked just like Denise; all crazy and out of control and I knew I had to stop her before things escalated even more. "I'm so sorry ma'am!" I said to the 40-something-year-old woman with cat woman glasses on as I scurried past her to catch up with Terricka and she stood in the aisle with a pained expression on her face while she held her shoulder.

I caught up with Terricka just as she turned the corner and walked down the ice cream aisle. I swallowed down the lump that had formed in my throat as I thought about what I could say to diffuse the situation and not set her off. "Terricka? What the fuck going on? You have to calm down sis. It's like you just clicked for nothing. What we just say about changing and shit? Well, all of that starts here, okay? I'm here to help." I said as I walked over to my sister and rubbed her shoulder.

I felt some of the tension in her begin to evaporate with my touch and words as her shoulders relaxed and she tried to force a smile at me. "Now how about some Rocky Road ice cream? I know that will make you feel better." I said as I elbowed my sister and I saw a little sanity return to her eyes.

I did a goofy dance as I reached into the freezer and got a container of Terricka's favorite. I saw a slight smile cross her lips as I danced and put the container in her face. You still know how to bribe yo big sis huh? Rocky Road does it every time." Terricka said as she did a flat laugh close to her regular one.

That told me she was willing to fight whatever was happening to her, but that didn't mean she would win, which is why I decided to wrap up out grocery store, sister bonding moment as soon as possible. "Okay T, I think that's about it for now. You ready to go?" I asked my sister as she nodded her head and put her head down.

I walked ahead of her as I crossed paths with a tall girl with blonde hair and a cat suit on as she walked up the aisle. She caught my attention because she was so colorful in the bright orange cat suit with bright blonde hair. The fact that she talked loud enough on her phone for the entire store to hear also drew my eyes to her. I rolled my eyes at her ratchetness as she popped her gum and talked to some dude about how she was gonna fuck his socks off. I turned back for a second to see Terricka right behind we as she eyed the girl with the same irritation.

By the time we got to the end of the aisle we were at the end of one of the shortest check-out lines so I decided to just stay there. I turned around to Terricka as she leaned on the ice cream box and the ratchet girl began to rummage through the box right next to her, still engrossed in her conversation. I started to say something to Terricka because I could see the irritation in her face, but my phone rang before I could and I noticed it was my assistant. Against my better judgement I answered the call and turned my back on my on-the-edge sister.

As soon as I answered I quickly got wrapped up in a conversation with my assistant about my top author's release date and blocked out everything that went on around me. I only noticed something was wrong when I suddenly felt the hair on the back of my neck stand up. In that moment I took the phone away from my ear and tuned back into the world around me as Terricka told the loud girl off. "Damn that's rude. Right here all loud and in my ear. Step the fuck back." I heard by sister say before the girl laughed and sucked her teeth.

I knew that was a mistake as soon as it happened so I turned around ready to intervene when my sister snatched her ass up. To my surprise Terricka didn't say another word, she just closed her eyes and stood there as the girl came to the case directly behind her while she still talked on her phone. I don't know if it was the fact that my sister remained silent with her eyes closed as her body shook, or because the girl opened the freezer and bumped my sister's back, but one of those things had me frantic as fuck on the inside.

"Maine baby, I'm in the grocery store and some female trying to beef with me over nothing. Talking about I'm rude cause I'm loud. Hell, I'm always loud. She better ask somebody." The girl said as I watched Terricka's body tremble a little more. "I know right bae. She don't know a bitch can get LOUDER, especially when she taking the dick." The nasty girl said as she laughed into the phone. "Oh Rodney, you so nasty daddy. I'mma show you how loud I can get tonight." The girl suddenly said and my fucking heart stopped.

Unknowingly that bitch had said the trigger word and reignited my sister's insane rage in an already volatile situation. In my grandmother's words, that bitch had stepped on a hornet's nest with flip-flops on and wasn't shit anyone could do about it. Before I could get my body to react to the warnings that came from my brain, my sister's eyes had popped open and she had grabbed the handle of the freezer door in her hand as the girl bent inside and looked for something.

"NOOOOO TERRICKA!" I yelled as my sister slammed the freezer door on the girl's neck and then her head three or four times before I could even move. "OH THAT'S RODNEY HUH HOE? YOU CAN GET LOUDER HUH HOE? WELL, I CAN TOO BITCH WHILE I DRAG YO FUNKY ASS!" My sister yelled as she drug the dizzy, bleeding girl out of the freezer by her hair.

My moment of paralysis was over as I watched her slam the girl to floor and prepared to stomp her while people yelled out, "World Starrr" and recorded the massacre. I grabbed Terricka in her shoulders and hit the pressure points I knew would break her down as someone called for security over the intercom.

"Terricka what the fuck you doing? Yo ass gonna go to jail. Come on T, RIGHT NOW!" I yelled as I reached down and picked her frail ass up before I rushed out of the store and she fought every step of the way. We barely made it to the car and got in it before store security and cashiers rushed outside to find us or at least get a glimpse of our license plate so that they could turn us in. I instantly crouched down when I saw the snitching bastards come out, but Trricka just continued to sit upright in her seat and curse.

"T, what the fuck you doing, trying to get us flapped?" I whispered as I quickly grabbed Terricka and pulled her down in her seat along with me. I covered her mouth with my hand and hid from the two rent-a-cops who followed us and what would surely be a mean ass assault charge for my sister. I held on to Terricka's mouth as we laid half way on the seat and half way on the floor for nearly three minutes before the security guards and store manager gave up right at the hood of the rental.

"Them bitches gone maine. Damn they were fast. Good we got the security footage." One of them said as the other interjected. "No the fuck we don't. DAMN! The camera been out for a week and I keep forgetting to get the shit fixed. The interior and exterior cameras broke too so we can't even find out what the car look like. SHIT! If both of them ratchet hoes would have just swiped they cards and got the fuck out of here none of this would have happened. Who gonna be the blame in this shit now, huh? I'll tell you. Me, Ricky, the fucking manager. Let's go nigga that big wig bitch better just go home and mend her wounds and hope she never cross lil mama path again." Ricky said as they both laughed and I listened to their footsteps and laughter fade away.

My heart raced as I waited a few more minutes after their laughter faded just to be sure they were gone. When I felt it was cool and I could catch my breath, I quickly sat up, glanced around, and then laid back down on the seat. I did that shit so fast I was like one of those little toys at Chuck E Cheese that pops up and you have to hit it with the little hammer.

I guess the sight of me all scared and shit hit Terricka's funny bone because she suddenly began to laugh hysterically behind my hand as I sat back up. My heart raced as I frantically searched the lot then turned around and eyed Terricka with malice as she continued to lay there and laugh her ass off. She was a mused as fuck at the fact she had beat up a girl for shit and almost got our black asses arrested. She found that shit funny but I didn't and at that moment I could do nothing but tell her that.

"Oh that shit funny huh? It's funny Terricka? I bet it wouldn't have been funny if the police would have gotten us. I mean really? What the fuck you on?" I yelled as I crunk up the truck and quickly pulled off the lot.

I was hot as fuck and I sped off and flung the big truck and Terricka's bitch ass while she continued to laugh. "T, aint shit funny. Ole stupid head ass hoe. Bitch I hope you choke!" I yelled as she continued to laughed so hard she coughed then slobbed and I couldn't help but to laugh too. I laughed so hard I almost wrecked as we sped towards Terricka's apartment. I was mad as fuck at the situation my sister had almost put me in, but at the same time I knew that was the most excitement I had in years. I hadn't felt my heart race like that since Terricka in I had chased our mother down.

"Maine Tish, I'm sorry. I know I was completely wrong for that shit, but shit just get too much for me sometimes. ANDDDDDD you have to admit that hoe was annoying as fuck and disrespectful." My sister said as I turned to look at her. "Yea, you right T that hoe needed a slap, but you need to learn to NOT do what you feel needs to be done all the time. I held my peace you gotta learn too because you got too much to lose. You got four reasons why shit like that shouldn't take you there anymore. Okay? You understand sis?" I asked my sister as we pulled into the apartments.

I waited on her to respond as she sat there with a serious look on her face and I pulled into a space right in front of her door before I turned off the truck. After I turned off the truck I turned to my sister just as she turned to look at me. "I feel you Tisha, I do and I'm gonna try. I tried in the store, you saw me close my eyes and count. I tried but that bitch wouldn't let me. Her mouth set me off." Terricka said as the real cause poppe in my head.

I knew just like she did that the name Rodney was what made her click and I was tired of the dance we had to do in order to avoid the subject. "Okay T, yea the bitch had mouth, but you and I both now that is not why you went off. Tell the truth T. You went off cause she said Rodney, right?" I asked my sister as I watched her eyes get big and she quickly jumped out of the truck.

She reacted so fast she totally caught me off guard and I couldn't get my seatbelt off fast enough to catch her before she ran to the porch. "TERRICKA!! TERRICKAA! STOP, PLEASE!" I yelled as my sister suddenly stopped and turned back to face me. I watched her and paid close attention to the hurt in her eyes as she walked towards me to talk.

"Tish, I love you so I'll just say I can't talk to you about this right now. I definitely want to talk to you but I can't talk about it at all right now. I want to be well and get my shit together like you said and talking about that won't help me do it. SO let's just leave it alone for now okay? When I feel comfortable, you're the only one I will come to. Alright?" My sister said to me with tears in her eyes as I nodded my head and she turned to walk away.

I watched her walk inside and close the door and then the door suddenly popped open again as Jerrod came out. I remained in my seat still in a semi trance as he jumped in and kissed me gently on the lips. "What's up baby? Why you sitting here looking like you seen a fucking ghost?" My husband asked me as he giggled and I snapped out of the trance I was in.

I looked at Jerrod, at Terricka's door, and then at the door of the hell we lived in all of our lives before I suddenly crunk up the truck and replied. "I did see a fucking ghost. The ghost of Denise past, but I hope her ass gone." I said to my husband as I pulled of the lot and began to tell him what happened.

I told Jerrod all about how Terricka beat the girl up in the store, how her moods changed every second, and how I feared she was on the path to being worse than Denise. Jerrod listened intently until we got to the other Kroger on Frayser Blvd., then he told me to just give everything time.

"Give her a little time Tisha. See if she will get in counseling and treatment, then you will know if she really wants help and to change. That shit that happened today was just her ratchet side. I don't think that was bipolar, just bi-thottish." Jerrod said as he laughed and we got into the checkout line with a basket full of food.

I laughed and agreed with my husband before we paid for the groceries and then went back to Terricka's. As soon as we stepped in the door I had de ja vue as I walked in to find Terricka up on her feet as she danced and laughed with the children. I watched as she laughed and kissed each of them while she told them she loved them. It was Dr. Jerkel, Mr. Hyde all over again, except it wasn't Denise it was Terricka. I almost screamed out for her to stop her shit, but Sha could see it on my face as he walked to the door to help with groceries and stopped me.

"She not mama Tisha, or at least I don't want to believe it. Give her a chance and see how long it lasts, then we will know." My brother said as she squeezed my shoulder and I thought about what he said. I decided he was right as my sister looked up and smiled at me and I saw the T that I missed so much in her eyes. I believed she would change and everything would be good, and after that it did. For three days everything went perfect with us all in the house like a family. Terricka talked to a specialist in bipolar about an appointment the next week and she and I became even closer. On that third night Terricka finally told me what happened with her and Rodney and I knew that her mental health was really in trouble.

"Tisha, I'm ready to tell you what happened with me and Rodney. Better yet Buddy. I met him as Buddy and that's what I will call him. I don't care about that other shit anyway." My sister said as she exhaled deeply and walked into the living room to sit beside me on the couch.

"Buddy left me because I'm crazy sis. I know you heard me say that shit before, but I really mean it this time. You'll think so too after I tell you this. One night after we fucked, Buddy laid in my bed as I sat up and smoked a few blunts and blew a few lines. As I sat there and got higher and higher these voices got louder and louder in my head. I could hear bitches like they were playing on an answering machine, talking about how they missed him and wanted to fuck."

"Now as I'm hearing this shit, his fine ass laying there smiling with his massive dick in his hand like he could hear the bitches too. As soon as I saw that I lost it and reached over for my box cutter on the nightstand. Without thinking I popped that bitch open and pulled down the front of his boxers. He opened his eyes instantly as I pushed his hand to the side and grabbed his meat in my palm ready to cut a chunk of flesh off. When his eyes focused and he saw what I was about to do he kicked my ass so hard I almost flew into the hall. After that it was over because he was dressed and out of our lives before I could blink. He tried to call for the boys after that, but I told him if we weren't together he couldn't see them. I know I was wrong for that and every fucking thing else sis, but I just can't stop it. I can't stop it T. He told me I was rotten and he didn't want nothing else to do with me unless I got help. I want help Tisha, but I don't know how. I fucked up. I want him back. Help me TISHA!" My sister cried on my shoulder as I vowed to help her and I did.

The next morning, I sent Jerrod, Sha, and A'Miracle back home to California because it was August 1st and school was about to start. I told my husband I would be back home the following week and that I would be careful as I kissed him goodbye at the airport. It was hard to pull off and know my family were on their way home without me, but I knew I had to finish what I had started in Memphis. That is exactly what I did too because when I got back to the apartment Terricka and I began to work on the plan. I quickly created her a resume and sent them out before I helped her get dressed and we went to her first counseling appointment. By the time her appointment was over she had received two interview letters and everything started to look up. We drove home that night happy, so we celebrated by smoking a blunt and watching old movies once the kids went to bed. I felt hopeful as I watched my sister smile when I told her I was proud.

"Everything about to turn around sis, I can feel it. You just gotta keep going. You gotta stay optimist no matter what happen. I'm right here to help okay? I got you!" I said to my sister as she nodded and we tuned back in to the movie. For four days everything did start to look up as my sister went on interviews and visited a new therapist. By day five all of that shit crashed when Terricka came home to say her five interviews were followed by five rejections. That alone was not enough to disappoint me because I knew the job market in Memphis and I knew she had to just keep trying. What hurt was the fact that she was drunk and high as hell as she walked in the house loud and rude how she usually was.

"Well, bougie, know-it-all sister of mine, I guess you can put up yo psychic hat cause bitch five interviews made five rejections. Bitch you don't know shit. Ain't nobody gonna hire my ass. You might as well gone slide yo bougie ass back to Cali cause you ain't helping shit here." Terricka yelled as I sat there on the couch and just stared up at her.

That was one of her other personalities, as rude and belligerent as usual, but I wasn't gonna listen or let the kids be subjected to it. I jumped up just as Terricka walked over to the couch Tania and Talaya were sitting on and pushed Talaya on the floor so that she could sit down. "Move yo lil ass out the way then. Mrs. Bougie finna go home soon so y'all can go back to the way y'all was…OUT MY FUCKING FACE!" Terricka yelled as she laid down on the couch and closed her eyes while Tania jumped up and Talaya cried at her feet.

I quickly rushed over and picked her up before I whispered for Tania to get her brothers. By the time they all came down the steps I was at the door with it open. I didn't even stop as I snatched up my purse and guided the kids out and down to the truck. As soon as I put Talaya in the truck and strapped her in, Terricka finally realized we were gone and ran out on the porch.

"Where the fuck you think you're going with my kids TISHA!'" My sister yelled as I jumped in the truck and she jumped off the porch like a cracked out cat woman. She caught me so off guard with that shit so I forgot to lock the doors and she almost got in. I was slipping but Rodney Jr, wasn't as he quickly hit the locks from the passenger seat. "I'mma fuck you up bitch." Terricka yelled in my face as she pressed her distorted face up against the window.

I didn't want to hear that shit though so I crunk up and pulled back as she ran alongside the truck. I didn't even look in her direction as she yelled she would call the police and I sped out of the parking lot. I could still here her voice ring in my ears as I rode towards the Robinsons' and the kids chatted about how crazy their mother was. Once at home with the Robinson's I got the kids something to eat and fixed them a spot in the family room to lay down and watch movies while I talked to Tania. I told her about everything I had gone through with Terricka and how I saw so much of our mother in her. I told her how I feared for the kids and asked what I should do.

"I don't have to tell you what to do Tisha, you know what to do. Save your nieces and nephews the same way we did you. Their safety is what's most important. Your sister is grown and has to work through her own demons. Those kids can't. Do what you know is right Tisha." Tania said to me before she left me to sit alone in the dark in the living room.

I sat there and thought about that for a while as I went over all of the possible outcomes in my mind. I thought so long and so hard that I had to lay down and before I knew it I was asleep. When I woke up it was after midnight and the Robinson household was quiet as usual. I tiptoed into the family room to find the kids fast asleep before I creeped up to my adoptive parents' room to find Tania up reading.

"I'm going to talk to Terricka about taking the kids." I whispered to Tania before she nodded her head and whispered back that she knew I would do the right thing. I left there with an eerie feeling and drove all the way tense as fuck with the words that I would say to my sister on my mind. When I pulled up in front of the apartment and saw all the junkies and others outside of the apartment I instantly forgot all of that shit as I jumped out and went inside. I had to punch a few fuckers on my way in as one groped me and the other kissed my hair. Their laughter trailed me inside the house, but was quickly overpowered by the loud ass music that played on the radio. I almost passed out when I stepped in and the thick, mixed weed and crack smoke filled my lungs and caused me to cough and gag. I bent down and tried to catch my breath as I looked around for Terricka. I didn't see her anywhere as I stood back up and was approached by a tall, dark skinned dude with gold teeth.

"Damn lil mama, what's yo name and yo poison. Big Daddy got you girl!" The boy said as his stank ass breath choked me harder than the drugs in the air. "Boy please, get yo life. My poison is nothing ass niggas so get yo bitch ass back." I yelled as I pushed past him and searched the kitchen.

After I didn't find Terricka I damn near threw up everywhere after I caught a fat lady eating a skinny lady's dirty, nappy pussy on the kitchen table. I rushed out that bitch so fast my head spent. I quickly jumped back in my truck and decided I was tired of trying to reason with Terricka or even seeing that nasty, ghetto shit she was in to. That was the final straw because I knew deep down she was everything Denise had been to us in my eyes and I couldn't help but to think that the sexual abuse would come next. I just couldn't let that happen to her babies.

I sped off the lot quickly as I got my phone out of my purse and dialed Terricka's friend Sky's number. I knew that Sky was logical, had her shit together, and could help me if I needed it. That was a moment I needed it so I reached out. "Sky, this is Tisha. I really need your help. Terricka is really out of control and the kids are in danger. Meet me at the apartment at 9 am. We're doing an intervention and I'm going to take the kids. "I said to her answering machine before I hung up and sped towards home at the Robinson's.

Once I was back at the house I went straight to bed and tossed and turned all night as I dreamed about what would happen when I told Terricka my plan. My phone rung for a half second at about 4:45 am and jolted me out of my restless sleep. When I flicked on the light and looked at the ID no number showed up because it didn't ring a complete ring so I threw the phone back on the nightstand before I laid back down. I laid there for about an hour with the light on as I worried about my sister and that mysterious phone call parked another separate, but deep fear within me. I had to make myself close my eyes at six am as I finally fell back to sleep. I could barely keep my eyes open or even eat breakfast for that matter the next morning as I mentally prepared for the battle ahead. After I got the kids dressed in clothes I ran out to buy that morning from Walmart we all loaded in the car and headed to the apartment.

"TeTe Tisha, I don't want to stay with mama. Can we stay with you for a while?" Rodney Jr. asked me as we pulled into the parking lot of their apartments right next to Sky. I turned off the engine and then turned to look at him as tears welled up in my eyes. "That's what we're here to do boo so let's stay hopeful. TeTe would love to take care of you all until mommy gets better. Now let's go get some stuff. When we get inside you all go upstairs and pick yo favorite things and put them in a bag. After that hurry back downstairs so we can go. Okay?" I asked them as they all shook their little heads with excitement in their eyes.

"And give mommy kisses and tell her you love her and to get better before you walk out the door. Now, let's go." I said as I tried to pump myself up. The truth is my heart raced in my chest and I felt like I couldn't breath as I walked on the porch behind the kids and Rodney, Jr. opened the door. As soon as he did the cursing inside hit my ears and Terricka flew at me like a possessed cat.

"Where the fuck you been with my kids bougie bitch? You ain't getting them and I ain't going no fucking where unless it's to jail for whooping yo ass." Terricka yelled as she tried to hit me and I side-stepped her as Sky stepped in the middle of us. I didn't even say a word, I just stared at Terricka with a smug expression before I nodded to the kids to go upstairs and Sky tried to calm Terricka down.

"Stop it Terricka this is for your own good. You need help. Let Tisha take the kids for a while and I will be here to help you through rehab. You need this." Sky said with tears in her eyes as she hugged Terricka. I stood back on guard as I watched Terricka flap around in Sky's arms and curse as she stared at me. I couldn't believe how different that Terricka was from the one I had seen days earlier, but I knew I didn't want to be around long.

"Yes T, you know you need this. Now, it's time for tough love so either you get help now or you won't see the kids again. Either way, I'm taking them." I yelled as I ran up the steps to help the kids and Terricka went crazy behind me. "That's what you think bitch. I'll call the police or kill yo bitch ass first." Terricka threatened but I didn't stop until I was in the girl's room.

Within four minutes I had them all packed and Talaya in my arms as I ran down the steps with the others behind me. "Bitch, I bet you ain't going nowhere." Terricka yelled as I ran to the door with the kids right with me. I opened the door and ran out right into the hands of four clothed police officers. "That's her police, the crazy stalker, and she trying to take my kids." Terricka yelled from the door as a female officer stopped me and took Talaya out of my arms.

I stood there shocked as another one put me in cuffs and Sky told Terricka she was wrong. "Terricka you know that's your sister and she is just trying to help. You're wrong for doing this Terricka. Let her take the kids before the truth come out and they go to the state. Come on now Terricka." Sky yelled as Terricka cursed at her and I thought about whether or not I should tell the truth.

I wanted to yell out every horrible thing she was and have her ass arrested, but I knew what would happen to the kids. I was just a sister, not the parent so they would surely go to the state first. I didn't want that for them so I decided to say just enough to keep them safe until I could get them for good.

"Please don't take me to jail. I'll leave the kids. However, my sister is drunk and I feel the kids shouldn't be with her like she is. Let me or Sky take the kids for the night and then everything will be fine." I suggested as one of the officers nodded his head.

I watched Sky whisper in Terricka's ear as an officer told her to calm down or she would go to jail, then she turned to look at me. "Okay the bitch is my sister and she wasn't kidnapping them, but I don't want her to take them. Sky can keep them until I sober up." Terricka said as my heart broke but I felt relieved.

I stared at her and shot a million daggers her way as the officers lectured her on false accusations and being drunk in front of her kids. I stood there mad as fuck and listened as tears ran down my face and the female officer released me from the handcuffs before she pulled me to the side.

"What you were trying to do is right Mrs. Hill, but you did it the wrong way. I know all about your sister but can never prove anything. Go fill out the proper paperwork to take those kids and I promise I will help. Here's my card." The woman officer said as she handed me her card and I noticed her last name was Black just like the police woman who had helped me.

After that we had to sign some papers before the police went to talk to Terricka again and I hugged and kissed the kids. Just as I walked on to the porch to grab my purse which had fell off my arm when I was handcuffed my phone rang inside and I quickly took it out. I recognized Sha's number to the cellphone I got him instantly and answered it to hear a girl's voice. "Mrs. Hill, this is Lydia, Sha's girlfriend. You have to come quick because he's in the hospital and they think he won't make it." Was the last thing I heard before I passed out.

Chapter 6

Sometimes to Love, Is to Let GO!

I woke up on the cold, hard, concrete of Terricka's porch as she frantically called my name and an EMT worker put an oxygen mask over my face. I felt dizzy and confused for a second as my eyes fluttered open and I tried to focus them despite the intense throb in the back of my head. When I was finally able to see I looked up at my worried sister as tears streamed down her face. I could see nothing but concern and love written all over her, but it was too bad because I didn't feel that way back.

Suddenly all that had happened flashed in my mind and I couldn't feel anything but hate for my sister. It was her fault I was even in that situation, even in Memphis in the first place, and I wasn't going to let her forget that. I yanked at the mask and sat up despite the pleas of the emergency personnel around me.

"Ma'am, you have to lay down. You might have a concussion because you hit the porch pretty hard." A female EMT yelled as I sat up and waited for the world to stop spinning.

"Tisha please you have to lay down and let them make sure you're okay." Sky said as she stepped forward and grabbed my right shoulder while Terricka grabbed the other. "What happened anyway Tish? Who was that on the phone and what did they say?" Terricka asked as I realized she had her hand on me and I violently jerked away.

I disregarded everything that everyone said as I slowly got up on my feet and grabbed my purse off the ground. I quickly found my phone with a now cracked screen that someone had put back into my purse and called back the last number that had called me. I walked over to the kids as everyone continued to beg me to lay down but their words were nothing but a jumble of mixed match sounds.

After I kissed each of the kids and promised to come back for them, I slowly walked back over to my sister with the phone still up to my ear. I stared at Terricka as she stood there ashamed and struggled to meet my gaze. I knew that she could tell by the look in my eyes that I was done with her and that was a reality she didn't want to face. I really didn't want to feel that way, but I couldn't help it as my heart broke over all she had done and what I was potentially about to face.

"Terricka, I'm..." I began when someone suddenly answered Sha's phone and I turned my attention to that crisis instead. "Hello. Who is this and where is my brother?" I yelled into the phone as I glanced at Terricka and saw nothing but pure horror in her eyes.

She tried to come over and hug me to listen in, but I held my hand up to her as I stepped down off the porch instead. I waited for the girl on the other end to stop crying as I watched the police EMT's leave and Terricka broke down on the porch.

"As I said the first time I called Mrs. Hill, or should I call you Tisha. I am Lydia, Sha's girlfriend. My mother married Sha's dad and that's how we met." The girl said as I was taken aback by her honesty and the fucked up circumstance that lead them together.

I didn't judge them or their relationship based on that information, because I had no room to judge and I knew that you couldn't control who you loved. I was worried though about what had happened to Sha and how she ended up with him and his phone. "Okay Lydia, nice to meet you. NOW TELL ME WHAT HAPPENED TO MY BROTHER." I yelled on the other end as she sniffled and I watched Terricka fall to her knees.

"Mrs. Hill, I really don't know what happened. After Sha came back from Memphis we talked on the phone for a few days before he asked me to come to L.A. to visit. I came and we stayed at your house for a while as Sha got into school and we talked about starting a life together. I was going to transfer to UCLA with him and we were going to get an apartment off campus. Everything was going good too because just yesterday he found out he was accepted and we went and told your husband. We wanted to call and tell you but your husband said that you would be home in a couple of days and we would have a big dinner and tell you then. So, we left happy Tisha. I have never seen Sha as happy as he was that day. After that he and I decided to say in the city to celebrate and got a room at the Hyatt."

"All night all he talked about was how proud you would be of him and damn near smiled himself into a frenzy. Late last night everything changed for the worse, though and I wish like hell I could have seen it coming. After an intense workout, I ran out to get Sha's ingredients for his famous protein shake while he took a shower. I came back into the room to find the shower water running and Sha face down on the floor of the shower with a gash in his forehead and his cell in hand. I didn't know what to do so I'm sure I panicked for a few minutes before I grabbed his cell and called 911. They got there really fast and whisked him away to Cedar-Sinai Medical Center. I hugged him and told him that we would all be there but I don't think he heard me because he was unconscious when they left."

"I ran to the hospital and found out he was in emergency surgery and that is all they have told me so far. I tried to call your husband a few minutes ago but I guess he has already left for work and I don't have his cell number. That's when I pushed the button to see the last number Sha dialed and it was you. That's where we are at now. I don't know anything and I'm going crazy trying to figure things out. I'm so scared Tisha. I love Sha and I need him to be alright." Lydia cried in my ear as I balled right along with her.

I cried as I thought about the little, brave, strong boy who I loved with all of my heart, and who had already suffered so much. All I wanted to do was be by my brother's side at that moment, not in Memphis trying to save a lost cause. "I'm about to catch a flight immediately Lydia and I'll be there in a few hours. Please stay by my brother's side until I get there." I said to her as I put her on speakerphone and logged in to my airline to change my flight plans online.

I quickly found I flight that would leave a noon and moved my ticket before Lydia stopped crying long enough to respond. "I WON'T LEAVE HIM. I'LL NEVER LEAVE HIM. I'LL BE RIGHT HERE WHEN YOU GET HERE." Lydia cried as I told her to be strong and then hung up the phone.

As soon as I hung up and wiped the tears off my face Terricka was up on her feet as she ran over and tried to hug me. I quickly stepped to the side before she could touch me though and crushed her heart in the process.

"Sky take the kids and keep them with you until I get back. I'm going to file all the paperwork I need to get custody from home and have my lawyer here in Memphis handle what I can't handle from L.A. I will also need a statement from you, I'm sure but we will cross that bridge when we get there. Right now, I have to get home. I don't know what has happened but my brother is the hospital and they don't think he will make it." I said as my tears burst forward again and Terricka went hysterical behind me.

"OH SHA. WHAT HAPPENED TISHA? PLEASE TALK TO ME AND TELL ME WHAT HAPPENED? I'M SORRY TISHA BUT DON'T SHUT ME OUT RIGHT NOW BECAUSE WE ALL WE GOT. PLEASE TISHHHAAAA. WHAT HAPPENED TO SHA? LET ME GO WITH YOU. OHHHH" My sister cried as she wrapped her arms around the back of me and placed her forehead on my back.

For a second I let her head linger there as I rubbed her hand and closed my eyes while I remembered the many times we had been in the same position. I tried to remember the love and compassion I felt for her just three days prior too, but after I thought about all of the pain her actions had caused others I couldn't. Her sins, just like Denise's, were for everyone around her to bare and that just wasn't right.

I knew that she wasn't directly responsible for whatever Sha was going through but somehow I couldn't help but feel like if we didn't have to come to Memphis to save her none of it would have happened. That's why I couldn't console her like a part of me wanted to. Instead I suddenly pushed her arms off of me and stepped away quickly, headed to my truck. I didn't respond until I was next to the truck, but when I did open my mouth my words struck and destroyed like the venom from a snake.

"No, you can't go Terricka. It's not like you give a fuck anyway. All you care about is yourself and your drugs, not even your kids. You're just like Denise, poison and Sha doesn't need that around him right now. So go be free like you always wanted to be since Sky will have the kids. Just smoke your fucking life away sister, while I pick up the pieces as usual. Do us all a fucking favor!" I yelled out of my anger as I hopped in the car and pulled out of my parking spot.

As I drove out of the parking lot I looked in my rearview mirror to see my sister on the ground as she cried. I wanted so badly to go back and tell her I was sorry but I wasn't sure if I could. I regretted all of the horrible things I said to her even though some of them were true. I wished I could take back those last moments or say the magic words to fix it, but right then I just didn't have the energy to do it. All I could do was keep driving on and think about the sibling I had hundreds of miles away as he fought for his life.

I drove to the airport in a daze as tears periodically streaked my cheeks. Once in the parking lot I drove to the rental car entrance as I pulled out my phone to call Jerrod. "Heyyy my sexy baby. What you got going today down there in Memph-ghanistan?" Jerrod said as he laughed when he suddenly noticed I hadn't laughed with him and all I could do was cry as I heard his tone change and thought about Sha in pain again.

"What's wrong baby? Tisha, tell me what's wrong." Jerrod yelled into the phone as I tried to stop my tears and catch my breath. It took me a second to get it together as I walked into the rental car office with tears on my cheeks and a flushed face before I sat the rental contract and keys on the counter. I had to close my eyes and concentrate on my breathing as I nodded yes to the attendant who asked me if I was alright and listened to Jerrod yell my name. "TISHA! TISHHHAAA. TALK TO ME! DO I NEED TO BE ON MY WAY? TALK TO ME BABY." Jerrod yelled at the point of hysteria as I swallowed down the lump in my throat and signed the papers the girl handed me before I walked out.

I felt my lungs expand and retract and the blood began to flow through my body again when I stepped outside and the fresh, but hot, humid, mid-August in Memphis air hit me. I sucked it in deeply and made my way into the terminal as I finally got my bearings together enough to tell my husband what was going on.

"Jerrod, it's Sha. Some girl name Lydia called me and said he's in the hospital and they don't think he will make it. Baby I don't know what's going on but I'm on my way home. What happened while I been here Jerrod? What happened to my brother?" I cried as I made my way through the crowds to my boarding gate and plopped down in the first available chair.

My heart beat in my throat as I sat there and caught my breath while my husband explained. "Tisha, Lydia his girlfriend and she's a really cool girl, I met her about a week ago when Sha brought her to our house to stay. Shit has been going good since you been gone, I mean Sha got into school and everything. I told them not to call and tell you over the phone because I wanted to have a big dinner when you got back. I had it all planned out and everything. I don't know what the fuck has happened now though. Damn maine, this shit crazy." My husband yelled as I heard him sniffle and fight back his tears.

"I'm leaving right now and headed to the hospital. Where he at? Tisha? Tish, where he at?" Jerrod yelled as I heard him scurry down some stairs and I tried to search the scrambled memories in my mind for the name of the hospital. I quickly waded through the sorrowful scene in my memory until I found the conversation between me and Lydia. "Cedar-Sinai Medical Center. He's at Cedar Sinai, Jerrod. What the hell is going on? I'm about to be on a flight in the next ten minutes. I'll call you when I land at 4:30. I love you baby." I said to my husband before he said it back and we hung up the phone.

Once I was off the phone with Jerrod I sat there and cried for a while as I wrapped my mind around what had happened. Minutes later I boarded my plane just on time with the one bag that was in the truck and headed towards my next tragedy. As soon as I took my seat on the plane exhaustion set in and I couldn't help but to drift off to sleep. I tossed and turned the entire four-hour, non-stop flight as my life flashed before my eyes. All I saw was one nightmare after the next, which was the theme of my life. I saw all my mother had put me through and some of the things I had brought upon myself and I wanted nothing more than to break the cycle. I was tired of hurt and pain in my life, but something inside of me told me that there was more hurt to come. The vivid images of Sha's funeral that popped into my dreams about three hours into the flight was that hurt and it was a hurt my heart simply couldn't take. I woke up from that nightmare in a cold sweat as I looked around at the curious faces besides me.

"Are you alright?" The older white gentleman beside me on my right asked as his wife, an older black woman who sat on the other side of me offered advice. "Whatever it is that haunts you in your sleep you have to deal with it and move on young lady. Give it to God, make a mends if you can, and then let it go. Pain and hurt can eat you up inside just like hate and resentment. We have to both forgive and forget sometimes baby, in order to set ourselves free. Otherwise we end up just like those who hurt us. You understand?" The old lady asked as she smiled at me sweetly and took my hand in hers.

I smiled softly at her and nodded my head as I pondered her every word. I knew that she was right and I had to let it all go, but I also knew I had some things to deal with first. I knew I had to make things right with my sister after I found out what was going on with my brother, or my life would essentially be over. I was still nothing without them because they were such a big part of me, and I felt it was my duty to be that glue that held us all together. That was a burden I had inherited a long time ago. One I should have taken more seriously.

Just then I saw the look in Terricka's eyes when I told her she didn't care about Sha and she should just smoke her life away. I couldn't believe how evil I was when I told her that harsh shit and to do the world a favor by dying. That was the most hateful thing I had ever said to my sister and the realization of that hit me fast and hard. I had to jump up out of my seat and rush to the bathroom at that moment because I could feel my emotions about to explode. Once inside the tiny bathroom I let everything go as I cried for the disaster my life had turned out to be. I knew that all of the books, authors, awards, money, degrees, cars, and accolades meant nothing when I was about to fall the fuck apart.

"What the fuck is wrong with you Tisha?" I asked myself once my tears subsided and I could think logically again. I stared at my reflection in the tiny mirror over the sink before I splashed some water on my face and tried to wash away my sorrow. "Nothing is wrong with you other than being hurt baby. That's my fault though, not yours. But it's time for you to change things Tisha. You can't blame me or anyone else for everything that goes wrong in your life. It's time for you, your brother, and your sister to let go of my sins and the chaos they caused and start fresh on your own. Forgive and forget Tisha. Now, be strong. Dry up those tears and go take care of your brother then go get your sister. Everything is going to be okay. I can see that now, but you have to do this for yourself. Create your own happiness baby. I love you Shartisha." My mother's words rang in my ears and I saw her reflection in the mirror.

I smiled at the happy, sober, beautiful, wise Denise in the mirror as I wiped away the last of my tears. When I left the bathroom I felt stronger than I had in days and hoped that it would last once I got where I was going. I spent the rest of my flight wedged between two of the wisest, sweet, most in love people I had ever met as I soaked up their wisdom. I couldn't help but hope one day when Jerrod and I were old we would have the same type of bond that they shared. Their love for one another made me feel so hopeful and their kind words made me forget about my terrible fate. I didn't even want to say goodbye to them after we got off the plane and retrieved our bags, but I did and quickly called Jerrod to find he was already outside.

When I got outside in front of LAX I ran in to my husband's arms like the leading female character in one of those corny ass romance movies, happy to feel his love. Jerrod quickly lifted me up off my feet as I dropped my bag and he kissed me gently on the cheek before he buried his face I my neck. I could feel his warm tears run down my neck to my chest and his body shook gently and I tried to pull back to see his face. My heart raced erratically as I tried and tried to pull back but Jerrod buried his head deeper and cried a little harder. "WHAT IS IT JERROD? WHAT? TELL ME. PLEASE TELL ME. HE NOT DEAD, IS HE? PLEASE DON'T SAY THAT. JERROD PLLEEAASSEEEE. TELL MEEEE!" I cried hysterically as Jerrod cried more and rubbed my back.

I think I passed out for a few seconds after that because the next thing I knew I woke up suddenly and abruptly like I had been hit with a taser as my whole body tingled then fell numb. I blinked my eyes and looked around the car to notice that Jerrod had already put me and my bag inside as we pulled away from the curb. I opened my mouth to talk, but my throat was so dry from all the tears I had shed all I could do was make sounds. I turned and looked at the side of my husband's face as he drove with an intense expression on his face and didn't even glance my way as he handed me the bottle of water he had in the cup holder. I drunk the water fast, anxious to get my throat wet so that I could talk again and find out what had made him cry.

"Baby tell me what's wrong Jerrod. Please tell me." I said a lot calmer on the outside than I had been before, but still irate on the inside.

My heart told me to expect the worse and to prepare for something I never wanted to come true as I leaned over and tried to look at Jerrod's eyes but her continued to look straight. I tried to ignore the feeling I my heart that said death had found my family once again, but the feeling was too strong. Everything in me screamed the worst had found me, I just couldn't accept that though as I sat there and stared at Jerrod while he tried to find the right words to say to me.

I couldn't believe or accept that my brother would be dealt such a raw hand in life with nothing but one tragedy after the next. He had already lived through things some people only read about and cheated death three times so odds didn't appear to be in his favor. I couldn't believe that though so I shook my head vigorously as I erased those thoughts and reached over to grab Jerrod's hand. As soon as I touched him the damn that guarded his emotions broke and his tears and words poured out fast and hard like a raging river.

"Baby I went to the hospital after I talked to you and found Lydia in the hall crying. I didn't get much information out of her though so I sat there and waited for the doctor to come out again." Jerrod said as we suddenly pulled into the hospital parking lot and he turned off the car. I held my breath and watched his every move as he turned around in his seat to face me. Big tears fell from my strong husband's eyes when he looked back at me and I knew right then it was bad.

"It's not what you think baby, he's not dead but doctors say it doesn't look good. It seems after that incident with Shakeim, Sha received a traumatic blow that left bleeding on his brain, a hemorrhage to be exact. It slowly bled for the time he was with us at our house and while we were in Memphis, which is why he had no symptoms and didn't know anything was wrong. Doctors say the night he collapsed he must have pushed himself to the limit in the gym, which caused the bleeding to speed up and he lost consciousness before he slipped into a coma." Jerrod said through his tears as I began to cry right along with him.

I didn't know what to do or say as I replayed those words in my mind and thought about my brother laying there in another coma. Jerrod wrapped his arms round me and held me for a second s we both cried and tried to find strength in one another. "Oh my God Jerrod, no. The last thing he needed was another head injury. He didn't even tell me something happened to his head. I just knew that he fought with his dad. Damn, I feel like this my fault." I said as I began to shake.

"No baby this isn't your fault it's just something that happened. If anyone is to blame its Shaheim. I found out from Lydia he took a whole gang of niggas to the projects to get Sha the day they fought and he hit him in the head with a bat from the back. That's where the bleeding came from especially since his skull was already compromised from being thrown off the balcony. It wasn't your fault and it wasn't Lydia's fault despite what y'all think. This all Shahiem and that pussy will answer for all of this as soon as I know Sha is good. Now baby, doctors are giving him about a 20% chance to live, but we not listening to that." Jerrod said as I balled even harder and pulled away from his embrace.

"NOOOOOO. I can't lose him." I screamed as I fumbled for the door handle and Jerrod hit the locks. "NO baby, you're right we are not going to accept that. The Most High says have the faith of a mustard seed and that's what we will do. We will have faith that Sha will get better and with prayer along with our love I know that Sha can overcome this like he did everything in the past. He was supposed to have died at birth right, but here he is 19. When Denise dunked him in that scolding water as a baby they said he would die, but what did he do? He fought that shit. Just like he fought to recover from that traumatic brain injury when Denise threw him over the balcony and he came out like a G. Sha a soldier baby and he can get through this. We just gotta be soldiers too." Jerrod said as he grabbed my chin and then kissed me gently on the forehead.

"I'm sorry I cried like this and increased your anxiety I just hate to see the people I love hurt. But don't take my tears as admittance of the worse because it's far from that. I know Sha will come through just like I know Terricka will be alright and all of our lives will only get better. I believe that baby, just like I believe in our love. Now can you trust me like that and be strong?" Jerrod asked me as he wiped away my tears with his thumbs before he gently kissed my lips.

I wanted to break down again and tell him I was tired of being strong and I just wanted to give up, but I knew in my heart that wasn't true. Despite all the heartache I still had hope and the desire to end our pain once in for all. I had A'Miracle and Terricka's kids to look after so I knew to give up was not even an option. I had already lost my son so I was not prepared to take another loss. "I can do it baby, I have to. I'm just so scared." I said to Jerrod as he pulled me in and hugged me again.

"It's okay to be scared baby, I'm scared too but we have to believe. You are the strongest woman I know and I love you with my heart so know I will be right here every step of the way. We will all get through this like a family and before you know it Sha will be back home to crack jokes and beat me in video games. I promise." Jerrod said as he kissed the side of my head and I believed every word that he said. "Let's go Mrs. Hill, I got you." Jerrod said as he got out of the car and walked around to help me out.

Jerrod and I walked into the hospital hand in hand as my heart and mind raced a mile a minute. We didn't say a word as we walked through the hospital and got on the elevator to head to the trauma unit. When we got off on the fifth floor, Jerrod quickly escorted me into a waiting room where Lydia was and she ran straight into my arms. I felt kind of weird at first as I held the thick, light skinned girl with big grey eyes who clung to me like I was her life line. We both sobbed lightly as we held each other and she poured her heart out.

"Tisha, I'm so sorry and I'm so scared. Please don't be mad at me. If I had known about everything that happened I would never let him push himself like that in the gym. Please forgive me Tisha. I love Sha. Please forgive me." She cried as I rubbed her back and told her it would be okay. "No Lydia, it's not your fault and everything will be okay. Sha will pull through, we just gotta keep faith. Don't worry." I said to her as we sat down and the doctor suddenly walked in.

I quickly stood up as soon as the tall, dark haired, Indian surgeon walked up to me and I prepared myself for the worse while I hoped for the best. "Mrs. Hill." he said as he extended his hand to me and I tried desperately to read his expression. I tried, but he left no clues as he stood in front of me with a straight face before he looked at his clip board.

"Mrs. Hill, I'll just get straight to the point. As you know your brother has experienced some very traumatic brain injuries over his lifetime, and this one was no different. When they brought him in Sha was totally unresponsive and had no heartbeat. After we revived him I took him straight in to surgery where we worked over five hours to stop the bleeding. It didn't look good at first." The doctor said and I felt weak in the knees.

I stumbled a little as the doctor grabbed my arm and helped me in to the chair while Jerrod grabbed my hand. "Mrs. Hill please calm down because the surgery was a success. I won't lie like he is out of the woods but I will say everything is looking good so far. He is in recovery right now and you all can see him in the next hour or so. The next few weeks will be crucial as we wait to see if he wakes up the coma we had to induce to keep down his pain. Remain hopeful my dear and offer him nothing but love and support. Although he is in a coma, I'm confident he can hear you so staying by his side will be key. I will have a nurse come out to get you as soon as he is ready for visitors. Stay strong Mrs. Hill, Shamel will need it." The doctor said as I cried on Jerrod's shoulder.

I cried more out of relief as I buried my face in my husband's shoulder and thought about the almost optimist prognosis the doctor gave Sha. I believed him when he said he could recover and I was ready to do all I could to ensure. "Come on baby, you need to eat so that you can be ready when it's time to see Sha." Jerrod said as he stood up and pulled me to my feet.

"You too Lydia." He said as she got up and grabbed my hand.

We all walked to the cafeteria hand in hand as my mind went over what the doctor said. I tried to eat the burger Jerrod bought but I only took small bites before I decided to get up to make a phone call. I left Jerrod and Lydia at the table as I walked to the ladies' room and dialed Tania's number on my cell. She answered on the first ring and all of my emotions and the events of the past few weeks blurted out like word vomit. I told her everything from what happened with Terricka and what was going on with Sha. When I was don't my foster mother prayed with me and set my mind at ease.

"God got this baby, you just got believe. Everything in this life happens for a reason so just know this is a test to make you stronger. I will handle things down here with Terricka, I'll check on the kids and take them if I have to. You just focus Sha and keeping yourself well. I need you to stay strong if you think you can help anyone else. Okay baby?" Tania asked me as I dried up my tears and answered her.

"Yes ma'am. I will." I said as I prepared to hang up the phone and she stopped me. "You remember how just said everything happens for a reason? Well, I got a call today from someone who really wants to speak with you. He left a number and asked me to have you call as soon as possible. I just texted the number to your phone so promise me you will call Tisha." Tania said. "I promise I will ma. I love you." I said to her as she said she loved me back and we hung up the phone.

I took a minute to get my emotions under wrap and wash my face before I went back out to sit at the table with Jerrod and Lydia as they watched my face. "Baby you look so much better now. Everything okay?" Jerrod asked as he leaned over to kiss me on my lips. "Yes, everything is going to be just fine." I told my husband as I kissed him back and then checked the text that had just came through my phone from Tania.

William Randolph, 901-555-7115

Was the only thing the text said but somehow those simple words caught my attention and made me wonder who the person was. I sat there and stared at the text so intently it must have worried Jerrod because he suddenly stood up and bent over to see what had me so mesmerized. "Bae, who is William Randolph?" Jerrod asked as I shook my head.

"I don't know baby, Tania sent me this number and said he wanted me to call him. I'm curious as fuck, but I can't focus on this right now. We will call this number and find out as soon as we know Sha is okay though. Let's not worry about this now. Instead I just want to go give my brother some love." I said as I tried to ignore the worry, fear, and curiosity that danced in my heart.

When we got back to the fifth floor waiting room a nurse came out as soon as we sat down and let me know it was safe to go in. I felt like the floor was made of ice as I walked on wobbly legs to room 506 with Jerrod on one arm and Lydia on the other. When the door opened and I saw my brother as he laid there in the small bed with a bandaged wrapped round his head, a tube down his throat, and cords in every orifice I could see, I almost lost my confidence and freaked out but Jerrod was there to offer me strength as usual.

"It's okay baby. I'm right here. I got yo back." Jerrod whispered as I swallowed my fears and walked over to the left side of the bed with Jerrod behind me as Lydia went on the right side. Both of us grabbed his hand at the same time and two of his machines began to beep. "What's that?" I yelled frantically. "NURSE!" Jerrod yelled as she suddenly came out of nowhere. "Oh that's nothing to be alarmed about, it's actually a good thing." The nurse said after we told her what had happened and she checked the machines.

"That was his heart monitor and the other one monitors his brain waves. That just let us know that the surgery was a success and that your brother can hear, and feel although he is in a coma. That's a great thing Mrs. Hill. That makes his possibility for a full recovery increase by ten folds. Keep talking to him and showing him you care and I'm sure he will be out of here in no time." The nurse said before she smiled at us and left the rom

A tear fell from my eye as I turned back to my brother and kissed his hand then the monitor went off again. I knew that he felt me and he knew I was there and that was enough to give me strength. "I'm right here brother and I'm not going anywhere until I see you open your eyes. I am my brother's keeper. And I love you Shamel." I whispered in his ear before I kissed his hand again and his monitor continued to go off with each touch. "See baby. He hears you and he will get better." Jerrod said as he kissed my neck and I turned around to hug him.

Jerrod and I remained wrapped up in our embrace for a minute as we let Lydia talk to Sha and watched his monitor go off time and time again. It was like joy to my ears as I stood there and looked down at one of the strongest men I had ever met. Seeing him fight for his life once again gave me the fight I needed so I did the only thing I knew to do when my heart needed comfort. I sang from my heart.

"Nothing is forever what we're hoping for,

No more pain so don't you cry anymore.

Hold your head up high and dry yo tears,

Let me help you through and erase yo fears.

We'll overcome it all if we stick together,

We just gotta believe nothing lasts forever (nothing lasts forever)."

I sang with nothing but love as my brother's monitor went off again and I felt him grip my hand. "Jerrod, get the nurse he moved. He moved." I yelled as Lydia and I cried and Jerrod scrambled to get the nurse. I stood back with Sha's hand still in mine as she checked everything and I told her what happened.

"This is amazing Mrs. Hill. He is actually doing better than we ever thought. Whatever you're doing, keep doing it because it is the key to his recovery." The nurse said as she smiled at me genuinely with tears in her eyes and then quickly hurried away to get the doctor.

That is exactly what I did too as I kept my love all over my brother. I didn't leave with Jerrod when he went to pick up A'Miracle at three and I told him to just bring me some clothes when he came back the next day. I was not going to miss it when my brother opened his eyes so I camped out. The only time I left the room was around 10 pm when I went down to the cafeteria to grab Lydia and I a bit to eat.

While I waited on the food too get ready my curiosity caught up with me again and I took out my phone and dialed the number for William Randolph. I didn't know why at that moment, but my heart raced as I waited on someone to answer the phone and I almost hung up. I was glad that I didn't when a strong, warm, and loving voice said hello and I somehow figured out why I felt so nervous. From that first second I knew who the mysterious voice was on the phone, but I couldn't believe it. I couldn't even talk as he said hello again before he called my name and tears ran down my face.

"Shartisha baby say something. Do you know who this is?" The man said as I cried like a baby and shook my head even though he couldn't see me. "Daddy." I said through my tears as I heard the man cry on the other end. "Yes baby, it's your daddy and I'm so happy to hear your voice. Tisha, I'm so sorry for leaving you and not fighting harder to find you even though Denise did everything in her power to keep me from you. You gotta know though I never stopped trying, I never stopped wondering, looking, or hoping for you. I love you so much Shartisha and I hope one day you will give me a chance to make this all up to you." My father said as I thought about all the times I cried and hoped he would rescue me but he never came.

That abused, resentful little girl inside of me wanted to scream and curse as she spited the father who failed her.

However, the little girl and grown woman who just wanted love and closure spoke up instead. "Daddy, I have so many questions, but right now I'm going through something else and I can only deal with one thing at a time. I really want to give you a chance, but right now I can't make that commitment. Can we just say we will meet and talk when I get back to Memphis? That's all I can give right now." I said as I heard my dad gasp. "That's more than I could ask for Tisha. I will be waiting. Daddy loves you baby." He said to me as my heart melted and I waited until I heard him hang up the phone before I said I loved him too.

Once the conversation was over I got the food and sat down at a table for a second to let my tears past. I replayed our conversation in my mind twenty times before I instinctually dialed Terricka's number. I didn't know why but I wanted to share that with my sister and I hoped that it would show her how people could change. I hoped that we celebrate the call together and that our happiness could get our sisterly bond back. I hoped, but as soon as Terricka answered the phone all of my hope was gone.

"WHAT THE FUCK DO YOU WANT TISHA, HAVENT YOU TAKEN ENOUGH FROM ME BITCH. IF YOU NOT ABOUT TO TELL ME HOW SHA IS, THEN WE DON'T HAVE SHIT ELSE TO TALK ABOUT SO GET THE FUCK OFF MY PHONE." My sister yelled as I cried. "Terricka Sha is doing better but still in a coma. Sister we need to talk and come together right now because it's a lot at stake. Not only could we lose our brother but we could also lose yo kids. Sister, don't you care?" I asked Terricka as tears streamed down my face and she snarled like a dragon.

"HELL NO, I REALLY DON'T CARE. ITS JUST LIKE YOU SAID BITCH, ALL I CARE ABOUT IS MY DRUGS AND MYSELF. FUCK YOU, SHA AND THEM KIDS BITCH. BYE BITCH I'M GONE FOREVER JUST LIKE YOU WANTED!" Terricka yelled into the phone before she hung up.

Her words hit me like a million daggers and ripped through my already broken heart. I sat there and cried some more as her words bounced off the walls of my mind. I wanted to break down but something inside wouldn't let me. Surprisingly it was Denise's voice that came to me once again and helped me gain the clarity I needed.

"Pull yourself together Tisha and stay focused on what you have to do. Those are the drugs and the voices talking, not Terricka. She really doesn't mean it; she just needs time. You know sometimes to love someone is to let them go. You had to let me go. Maybe you just need to let Terricka go and hit rock bottom on her own so she can really appreciate your love and help. Focus on Sha right now baby. He needs you." My mother said as her voice rang in my mind and I found the strength to suck up my tears once again and do what had to be done.

I left that cafeteria with my faith and strength renewed knowing that I had found my father and there was hope for my brother. For two weeks after that I didn't leave Sha's side, not until October 15th when the thing I hoped for most happened. As I sat at Sha's bed side and read him a chapter from my latest book called A Broken Girl's Journey, I suddenly got the overwhelming feeling I was being watched. I ignored it for a second but when I felt something move on the bed I had to stop reading and look up. I looked up right into the beautiful, sad, brown eyes of my little brother as he stared down at me. I felt paralyzed as I stared at him while tears ran down my face and he smiled at me with his eyes before he reached for my hand. I quickly dropped the book and took his hand in mine as tears continued to run down my cheeks and my words got stuck in my throat. I felt flustered and overcome with happiness as I leaned in closer before I kissed his cheek and he made noises like he wanted to talk.

"No Sha, don't try to talk you have tube down your throat to help you breath. I already know what you want to say anyway, and I need you to know that I love you too. I love you more than anything little brother and I will never leave your side, no matter what. Now just rest because we have an uphill battle ahead of us." I whispered to my brother out of breath before I kissed him again and then sat back in my chair as I hummed and rubbed his hand.

Within minutes he was back asleep and I crept out of the room on wobbly legs to tell the nurse what had happened. I stood outside the room and cried tears of joy before I called Jerrod as the nurse and doctor went in to examine Sha. I could barely get my words out as I sobbed and I told Jerrod what happened before he and A'Miracle cheered on the other end of the phone. "I'm so happy mommy. Tell my uncle Sha I can't wait til he comes home. I can't wait til you come home either mommy." My daughter said as I suddenly realized it had been almost two months since I had spent a night at my house with MY family.

I felt like I had abandoned my baby for a second as her words replayed in my mind, but that thought didn't stay there long. "Don't you go to thinking crazy baby because I can hear it in your silence. A'Miracle knows you love her and we know what is going on. You have to be there for your brother. I got the baby and the house and we will be here when you all come home. You are just a saint Tisha with a heart of gold and there is nothing wrong with that. My baby gonna save the world and I'm gonna be right there to save her. Maine I love you Tisha." Jerrod said as I laughed through my tears and told him I loved him back.

After that call home I called Lydia and told her the good news. She informed me she would be back the next day after exams so that I could go home and I told her how much I appreciated it. "Give my baby a kiss for me and tell him I love him." She said before I agreed and hung up.

Once I was off the phone the doctors came out to tell me that Sha was doing great and would be able to get his breathing tube out and move out of ICU the next day. I felt as light as a feather, like the weight of the world had been lifted off my shoulders when the doctor said those words and left me there to bask in my happiness. I stood there and peered at my brother through the glass as he laid and slept peacefully and I thanked the Most High and angels above. "Thank you God for sparing my brother and all of the angels who watch over us. Thank you so much." I said as I wiped away my tears and prepared to go back inside.

Before I could step in though something stopped me and caused me to look at my phone. Without thinking I dialed Terricka's number so that I could tell her the good news. The phone at Terricka's house rang 12 times before a woman answered and the loud party that raged in the background almost drowned out her voice. "Hello." A woman yelled over the madness as I felt my anger overshadow my happiness.

I couldn't believe that with everything that was going on my sister was still doing the same shit. I couldn't help but to think my mama's voice in my mind was right. I couldn't help but to think that maybe to love was to let go. "Hello. Is Terricka there?" I asked as the girl on the phone laughed and told the people in the background to shut up.

I waited for her to get it quiet enough for us to talk and then I asked was Terricka there again. "Uhhh, no. That bitch gone. She just disappeared." The girl said as she laughed and my heart stopped in my chest. I couldn't believe what she said as I looked at the phone and made sure I had dialed the right number.

"Are you serious? This is her sister Tisha. What do you mean she just gone? So no one has seen her? For how long and where are the kids?" I asked as I felt tears well up in my eyes and fear fill my heart.

I feared the worst once again and I hoped that worse was not about to come true. I hoped, but that wasn't the case because what the girl said next sent me on another downward spiral through hell and I couldn't see how I would pull myself out.

"Oh you her sister huh? Well, heyyy sister. Your sister crazy, junky ass is gone Lord knows where and she been gone for about two weeks. Ain't nobody seen her since she got her ass beat by the dope man for stealing his shit. Rumor has it the bitch dead, but I don't know. As for them bad ass kids, they asses got taken by CPS. Ain't no telling where they at now. Anyway, bye bitch.

I don't have time to be a damn news reporter for you. Yo sister gone. Haaaa." The ratchet ass girl said before she hung up the phone and I broke down.

Part 3

WHERE DO I GO FROM HERE?

CHAPTER 7

Tisha: Out of Sight, Out of Mind…or so I thought!

After I found out Terricka was gone I cried like a baby as I slid to the floor in the hall of the hospital and laid my head against Sha's door. I cried for that hurt little girl my sister still was and hoped that I could still save her from herself. I couldn't help but to think as I laid there that it was all my fault and if I fought a little harder to get her to California, none of it would have happened. I thought about that and all of the possibilities of what could have happened to Terricka as I laid there and waddled in my own misery. I didn't want to believe what the junky girl who answered her phone had said, but it was hard not to when I considered my sister's history. I knew that my sister could be unpredictable, erratic and out of control so to believe she would just disappear wasn't so farfetched.

Something inside of me didn't want to believe that though. A voice inside my head screamed that she hadn't just left and that my sister may be in danger. There was also another voice who said she did leave voluntarily and if she was in danger it was because of her own actions. I listened to that internal battle between the voice of my logic and that of my emotions until I felt like my head would burst. I had to cover my ears with my hands and close my eyes to stop the thoughts and horrible scenes that played in my mind. I almost drove myself crazy as I laid on the floor and cried while my mind continued to go through dark scene after dark scene with each of them resulting in Terricka's death.

I know I must have looked like a madwoman sprawled all over the floor as tears streamed down my face, and my body shook uncontrollably. Suddenly I felt like that 18-year-old girl again, in the hospital and on the brink of insanity after the loss of her son. I felt myself start to fall down into that pit of turmoil and depression I had fell in several times before, and I desperately wanted to avoid it. That's why I tried to ignore my emotions and think about a logical solution to my dilemma. The only problem was, my sorrow was too deep and I saw no viable solutions. All I saw was pain on top of pain and the continuation of a hopeless cycle. That did nothing but caused me to balled even harder and stop traffic in the hall. Before I knew it Sha's nurse was at my side as she grabbed my shoulders and pulled me to my feet.

"Oh my God, Mrs. Hill are you alright? Come in and lay down." Nurse Shelly said as she led me by my shoulders into Sha's room and I plopped on to the let out chair. I quickly covered my mouth with my hand as soon as I sat down so that I could muffle my cries and not wake Sha. However, even with my hand over my mouth the soft moans I made as I cried could be heard throughout the room.

"Mrs. Hill are you okay? Sha is doing much better. See, I took out his breathing tube when you went out to make a call. He's almost ready for his move to a regular room. Is that why you're crying, because you're happy?" Nurse Shelly asked me as she gently rubbed my back. I closed my eyes and gathered my thoughts and emotions before I opened them backup and looked into her blue eyes. I wanted to badly to reveal my fears and thoughts at that moment but I knew that was not the place and she was definitely not the person for me to confide in. That's why I summoned the strength I needed to bury my emotions and ignored the worry in my heart. Despite how broken I felt inside at that moment I put on a brave face and smiled through my tears.

"Oh, I'm sorry Nurse Shelly I'm just so tired and overwhelmed. It seems it has been non-stop flights and tragedy with Sha being here and I think it is all just hitting me now. I guess I just need rest, but I'm not sleepy. I need to stay woke for Sha." I said as I began to softly sob again and the nurse rubbed my back again.

When she said that I quickly looked over at Sha and noticed that the breathing tube was in fact removed and I instantly felt guilty because I hadn't even noticed. "Oh my God. I feel like such a horrible sister. I didn't even notice that though because I was so wrapped up in my own pain. Oh, Sha." I said as tears formed in my eyes again and I attempted to get up but my weak legs gave out beneath me.

I felt drained emotionally and physically as I fell back into the chair and fought back my tears while my guilt and all of the horrible possibilities of what could have happened to my sister floated in my mind. "Oh Mrs. Hill, you're a wonderful sister and Shamel is lucky to have you. You're just emotional right now because you need rest. I'm going to go get you something to help you sleep and I will take care of Sha while you're resting. I promise." The nurse said as she squeezed my hand and smiled at me with compassion before she disappeared out of the room.

As soon as she was gone I let my emotions go as I covered my mouth again and cried out all of my pain. By the time I got it all out my hands were covered in tears, sweat, and snot and I felt like I had no emotions left. I felt numb as I got up on my shaky legs and waited until I felt stable enough to walk and not fall. I slowly walked over to Sha's bed and stared down at his pale, slightly swollen face as he took long deep breaths. "I love you little brother and I'm sorry for everything that has happened. I wish I could have protected you from everyone who has hurt you. I feel like I failed you. I feel like I failed Terricka, her kids, my son, and even myself. I just want to make things right. I have to make things right so we can finally have the life we always wanted, the lives we deserve. Just keep fighting brother and I will keep fighting too." I love you Shamel Nasir Lewis." I whispered into my brother's ear before I kissed him gently on the cheek.

I let my lips linger there for a minute as I felt the warmth of his skin and the depth of his love that he naturally exuded. I could feel strength and love all over me as I stood back up and looked at his face. When I did I almost jumped the fuck out of my skin because his big, brown eyes were wide open and he suddenly let his famous smile spread from ear-to-ear. I couldn't help but to cry as I leaned in and hug him and he wrapped his big strong arms around me and hugged me back. We stayed like that for minutes until he finally whispered in my ear.

"I love you too Tisha with all my heart. Thank you. Be strong." Sha whispered in a crackling voice I could barely hear but it was still like music to my ears. "Okay brother I promise. Now you close your eyes and get some rest. I'm gonna rest too soon so that we both can be strong enough to get you well, get you out of here, and get to living life. Soon all the sadness will be behind us Sha and happiness will be a familiar theme. I believe it. Now rest my brother. Lydia will be here soon." I said to Sha as I wiped away the single tear that fell from his eye.

I stroke his hand and kissed his cheek again as I watched him close his eyes and drift back to sleep. I watched him sleep for a few minutes with this peacefully, serene look on his face and suddenly I felt strong enough to face whatever came my way. I figured if Sha could go through all he had and still fight and be optimistic, then so could I. That's why when I finally let his hand go I crept into the bathroom inside his room with my phone in hand to make the calls I felt were necessary to get things on track.

First I called my lawyer Shelia Landry in Memphis and asked for the status on the temporary custody papers I asked her to file. I also got her to find out that the kids were in fact in CPS custody but that was all of the information she could give me.

After that I told her to push the petition for custody and that I would be back in Memphis the following week to finish everything. Once I hung up with Shelia I dialed the number on the card officer Black gave me and begged her to tell me where the kids were. It took a little time to convince her but before I hung up the phone I found out that Rodney Jr, Ryan, and Tania were still in a CPS facility while Talaya had been placed with a temporary foster family in Collierville, Tennessee. Just to hear those words put a fear in my heart that sent chills right down to my bones. That made me remember my time in foster care with the Reverend and I knew I had to get her out.

"Baby, I have to go back to Memphis." I said to my husband as soon as he answered the phone and I heard him take in a breath before he got totally silent. I sat down on the toilet seat and patiently waited on Jerrod to replay as I heard the nurse enter the room before she quickly knocked on the bathroom door. "Mrs. Hill. I have you a sedative here. It will be on the table next to your chair when you come out. Please get some rest." Nurse Shelly yelled as I held my hand over the phone so Jerrod could not hear.

I waited a second before I even tried to reply and put the phone to my ear to see if Jerrod had heard. It was still silent on his end except for the sound of a clock as it ticked so I put my hand back over the phone and responded to Shelly. "Thank you Shelly. I appreciate it. I definitely will." I said before I quickly put the phone back up to my face. As soon as I had the phone to my ear Jerrod finally spoke and poured his emotions out on me.

"You what Tisha? You're going back so soon? Why? What could be so important that you would go back so soon? And you think you're going alone? What the fuck Tisha? Answer me maine, forreal. "Jerrod said with a hint of anger I had never heard, not towards me anyway.

My heart raced a mile a minute as I contemplated on whether or not I should tell him everything or just what I wanted him to hear. The tone of his voice and the way be breathed all heavy and labored in my ear told me that I should tell the truth because a lie could cause me everything. "Jerrod, first off let me tell you the story from the beginning. So Sha is doing great. They took the tube out and he is breathing on his own. He even talked to me today. They are supposed to move him to a regular room later. I've been ecstatic about that for about an hour now. I babbled a little as I tried to give Jerrod the good news first to soften the blow. That didn't really work though because my baby was an ex-hood nigga with a business mind so he was not easily swayed by diversion.

"That's wassup. You know I'm happy as hell Sha is getting better. That's my nigga, he like my brother too so you know I'll be there to see him as soon as I get A'Miracle. That's beside the point though. I asked you why you had to go back to Memphis so soon Tisha. I want to know that and nothing else. You got it bad talking my ass in circles when I ask you a question that you don't want to answer, but it never works baby so just tell me wassup. You already know I got yo back no matter what so why is this so hard?" Jerrod asked me as I asked myself the same question.

Jerrod and I had already been through so much I knew that I could tell him anything and he wouldn't judge me or try to persuade me into anything I didn't want to do. I knew all of that but I was still afraid to tell him that I was about to go on a one-woman mission back into a war zone to find my bipolar, drugged out sister and she didn't even want to be found.

I just knew if I told him that he would try to keep me from going or maybe find a way for him to go too and I couldn't let that happen. It was my sister and my problem, not his sin to bare. I needed him to stay with A'Miracle to ensure she still had one level-headed parent around to care for her should shit go wrong. I couldn't have us both out in the streets to potentially get caught up and leave her alone to fend for herself. That is why I sugar coated the truth as much as I could and did my best to put my husband's worried mind at ease.

"Okay baby, I'm gonna tell you what you want to know." I said as I took a deep breath and let the back of my head rest against the wall behind the toilet as I spilled the sugar coated beans. "After I found out how good Sha was doing I called Terricka all anxious and shit, happy to make-up with her over the news that our brother would live. Well, I called and some bitch answered and said Terricka was gone. She said Terricka has been gone two weeks and last anyone saw her she had got her ass whooped by the dope man for stealing his shit. The girl also told me that the kids were taken by CPS and that's why I have to go back. I have to go get them Jerrod. I think it may be a lost cause for Terricka but I have to go get the kids." I said to my husband as I felt my emotions begin to crank up again.

I had to quickly get up, go over to the sink, and splash water on my face to keep back the tears that threatened to break free again. I didn't want to cry anymore, especially not on the phone with Jerrod. I knew I had to be strong so that he would agree to let me do what I was going to do anyway. At least that way he would feel less guilty about the fact he was about to let me walk into hell alone. That's why when I stood up and dried my face I dried up my tears too and put the phone back to my ear as Jerrod began to talk.

"Damn baby, I had no idea. What the fuck going on? It seems like all this shit happening at one time. Like bad luck or some shit." Jerrod said as I heard him sigh and then punch something. "It's the curse Jerrod. I told you we were cursed, but I am about to break this muthafucka and end it once and for all." I said with conviction as I heard Jerrod gasp a little before he began to talk again.

"You ae not cursed baby, none of you are just blessed that's why you're tested so much. This a fucked up situation and now I understand why you must go back, but I can't let you leave right now. You have to come home first and let's discuss this Tisha. Hell, you don't even have a plan." Jerrod said as he tried to get me to slow down but he didn't know I already had a full plan in motion.

Unbeknownst to him though, I had already figured out how I would go about everything and I already knew who would go along with me for help. "Baby, I actually do have a plan. I contacted my lawyer in Memphis before I left and had her set up a petition for custody of the kids. I talked to her today and she told me it would be ready when I get there next week. I also called Officer Black. You know the female officer who was at the scene when Terricka called the police on me. You remember I told you about that on our ride from the airport right?" I asked Jerrod as he sucked his teeth while he tried to remember. "Oh yea, I remember. She's the one who told you she would help get the kids?" Jerrod asked and I replied.

"Yes, her. So I called her and she told me where the kids are. The three oldest are still in CPS custody at some orphanage type ass facility and Talaya is at some foster home in Collierville. In Collierville Jerrod in a foster home. I'm so scared for her and that's what makes this such a fucking urgent trip. Anyway, I know where they are and I got the plan to get the kids by late next week in motion now I just need to attempt to find Terricka or at least just retrieve some things from her house I know she and the kids would like to have. It's some fucked up shit going on over there and I gotta see wassup. I know you looking at the phone crazy and shit right now cause I'm talking about going all the way to Memphis to face some bullshit alone, but baby I don't think I have to be alone on this one and you can stay right here in Cali to take care of A'Miracle and Sha." I said to Jerrod as I waited for his response.

I didn't have to wait long though because he was curious as fuck to hear what I had to say. "Who Tisha? You know I need to know this before I can let you go. If I let you go alone or with a muthafucka who ain't capable of protecting you and something happens, I will never forgive myself and there will be hell to pay for everyone associated with it. That's my word. So who is gonna take on such a responsibility baby? Who else besides me, Terricka, Buddy, and Sha do you trust with your life?" Jerrod asked me as he increased the intensity in his voice.

I could hear him as he grew impatient and I sat there and thought about whether or not I should tell him about my father. I wasn't sure how he would react because I knew how he felt about absent fathers, but regardless of the way he felt I knew I had to say it. "My dad." I blurted out as I gasped and then covered my mouth with my hand. I said it so fast and so light I was surprised that Jerrod had heard me but I instantly knew that he did when he began to fire question after question at me.

"What do you mean your father? When? What? How did you find him Tisha? Where has he been all these fucking years? Why now? What the fuck is going on? So you trust him baby? Huh? Talk to me baby and just tell me what's happening. If you trust him, you know I will too but I need you to give me way more specifics on this forreal. I can't just up and entrust the most precious thing in my world beside my daughter to someone I don't even know. I mean baby you don't even know him. I wonna be with you for something like this Tisha. How about I just leave A'Miracle with your assistant Patti and let them stay at our house so we can monitor everything going on via our cameras and I go with you to Memphis? That way we can handle everything together. Let's do it that way. Come on Tisha." Jerrod said.

I sighed as I sat back up on the toilet and stood up to pace the floor. I knew that Jerrod wouldn't want me to go and I also knew he would try to do something to change my mind, but I wasn't willing to waiver on the subject. "Baby, let's just talk about this later. Once you get A'Miracle from school come to get me. That will be around 5 and I know Sha will have moved to a regular room and Lydia will be here. Then we can go and eat as a family and maybe even catch a movie. Once we get home from that we can discuss this. Alright? Is that okay with you my king? I asked Jerrod as I heard him smack his lips and then loudly blow out his breath.

I could hear the frustration and fear all in his voice as he continued to breath and grunt before he finally responded to my questions. "It's whatever you want my queen. You know I have your back 1000% but I'm not just gonna let you make me forget or dismiss this. Can I at least talk to your father and see if I can get a feel for him? Please Tisha? I have to make sure you will be alright and that will make me feel better. Other than that everything sounds straight. I can't wait to spend some time with you, laugh with you, and love on you. I know our daughter can't wait either. So what do you say? We got a deal?" Jerrod asked me as I smiled to myself.

I loved that man so much because I knew that's exactly how he felt about me. Sometimes I would just sit and smile when I thought about how we met and how he protected and loved me from the very start. No matter what his love always made me feel like that scared, insecure little girl who he met, taught her valuable life lessons, protected and helped to find the strong, confident woman inside of me. That's why I couldn't deny him, no matter what it was, and why he couldn't deny me. Our bond was unbreakable.

"Okay baby, I promise. When we get home, no matter how late it is I will call him and see if he will do Skype with us so you can really get a feel for him. Okay?" I asked my husband as I heard his mood instantly change. "Yeah, now that's wassup. Okay baby. I can't wait to see you later. I love you with all of my heart Shartisha... Witcho ole fine ass. I can't wait to smack that big..." Jerrod began as I quickly stopped him and we both laughed. "Ole nasty man just wait for it. I got you. I love you too my king. See ya later." I said to my husband before I made a kissing noise into the phone and he did the same and then we hung up.

When I hung up with Jerrod I felt a little better because I was one step closer to Memphis. After I used the facilities and freshened up a bit, I walked out of the bathroom to find Sha still asleep and my pill along with a cup of water on the table just like the nurse said it would be. I quickly sat down and popped the pill into my mouth and then swallowed it down with the water before I sat back, let out the chair, and then closed my eyes.

Within minutes I was in a deep sleep, trapped between a beautiful vision of the future and a horrible nightmare of the past. I tossed and turned while trapped in the nightmare of the past as Denise beat, burned, and locked me in rooms while me and my siblings had to run for our lives. I felt my body relax and my restless soul begin to rest when I saw a glimpse of my beautiful future with my entire family.

In that vision could hear Terricka's laughter and see silhouettes of her and her happy family, husband included as they ran through a field of flowers, while Sha and Lydia laughed and trailed behind them. Then there was my family, which included three kids in the vision and a happy mom and dad. I saw all of that as I slept but what I didn't see was what had led us all there.

I couldn't for the life of me see the trials I would have to go through to reach that happy ending. I couldn't see the chaos and pain either. So much was still unknown, however; I was grateful that here was a happy ending at all and I knew all of us was there. I knew that I made it through so I didn't even mind the pain I knew was sure to come. That happy vision was enough to let me put my mind at ease and do nothing but sleep peacefully until the nurse woke me up sometime later.

I opened my eyes to see Nurse Shelly's smiling face as she told me Sha had already been moved and she had waited to wake me. I quickly got up and got myself together as she finished paperwork and then met her at the desk. "Soo you ready to go see where your brother is now and see some more incredible progress?" The nurse asked me as she smiled while she walked around the desk and I returned the smile and my heart raced.

I could do nothing but nod my head at that moment because I could feel my words were stuck in my throat. The nurse understood my elation so she simply walked around me and grabbed my arm to carry me to the elevator. Once inside she filled me in on what had happened since I had been knocked out for four hours and I was taken aback by his speedy and incredible progress. Shelly informed me that while I was asleep she came in to catch Sha as he reached for the remote and she almost fainted.

She told me how they expected his ability to move his limbs would be a long rehabilitation process like it was before, but Sha seemed to have skipped all of that. She said he was the only person she had seen come of the ventilator and be able to move in the same day. That's why she said he was moved while I was sleep and was doing fantastic when she left to come get me. I couldn't believe what she said when she finished so I had to ask her was she telling me the truth.

"Yes, Mrs. Hill, I am telling you the truth. Your brother will definitely be back to normal really soon." Nurse Shelly said as we got off the elevator on the second floor and walked to room 219. At the door I stopped to hug the nurse before I thanked her for all she had done. After that I entered Sha's room and was shocked by what I saw. I couldn't believe what I saw as I walked closer to Sha propped up in bed with the remote in one hand, Lydia's hand in the other, and a huge smile on his face. He looked just like the big, little brother I had kissed before he walked into the airport weeks earlier, all handsome and strong.

"Hey big, sis!" Sha said with a slight slur and drag in his voice, but still that silent, subtle confidence.

He looked stronger than he did earlier and a lot happier as Lydia stood up and kissed him before she rushed around to hug me. "Hey Tisha. Look at him. They say it's a miracle and he's some type of robot. I told the nurse no, he's just awesome." Lydia said as she laughed and turned to look at Sha and I agreed with her. "You are definitely right about that. He is my awesome little brother beanie baby." I said as I walked over to Sha and kissed him while he tried to jerk away because I called him his childhood nickname Terricka and I came up with.

After that all three of us laughed and talked, and we didn't stop until A'Miracle and Jerrod showed up at 6. By that time Sha was a little tired and had laid down to let the pain medicine he had just received work so we allowed A'Miracle to get her kisses and Jerrod spoke to Sha before my family and I left. I told my brother how much I loved him and gave him a big kiss before I left and he told me not to worry. I couldn't help it though as I walked out of the room and down the hall while he stayed behind. I couldn't help but to feel like I was leaving him just like I had left Terricka and that's when shit got bad for her. After that I pretty much felt that every tragedy in her life was my fault. That was why I carried around and umbrella of guilt, which made me feel I was required to make things right. That was the same guilt I still carried with me as I walked hand in hand with my daughter and husband out to our car.

We rode to A'Miracle's favorite restaurant, Carl Jr's, wrapped up in happy chatter as my daughter told me all about what I had missed. I felt guilty and a little jealous as I listened to her giggle about her recital I had missed and how fun dance class was with daddy and Patti. I couldn't help but to think that I was doing so much to help my extended family, that I was slowly losing my immediate one. My husband and daughter had to rely on each other or my assistant as I went out to save the world. That's why I couldn't help but to think how I would deserve it if Patti took my husband and family. Why wouldn't she when I was always too busy to do what I had to. I knew in my heart that Jerrod would never do that, but it still crossed my mind and hurt me bad as fuck. Just the thought of him with the perky 25-year-old, red bone with perky breasts drove me insane and made me mad as fuck. I wasn't mad at him or her though, but I was mad at myself for creating the situation to begin with.

I was trapped between my love for my family and my loyalty to my sister and brother and I didn't know what to do. I was in pure emotional agony as I sat there with a fake ass smile on my face and pretended to listen to what my daughter had said. I pretended but in reality my mind was everywhere but there at that moment, and my heart was so heavy that I felt like I was about to drown. Somehow I didn't let it show though and shielded the innocent, beautiful little brown doll who stared up at me.

I was able to convince A'Miracle I had heard her as I laughed along to the end of her joke about a butterfly. When she finished laughing I turned around in my seat to kiss her forehead and then kissed Jerrod's cheek as I turned back around to sit down. Once I sat back he turned to stare at me and the look in his eyes told me that he saw my worry. I opened my mouth to say something when he closed his eyes then opened them again as he shook his head and mouthed the word, "Later". I smiled softly and agreed with him before I reached over and grabbed his hand and all of us joked and laughed until we pulled into the restaurant's parking lot.

I spent the rest of the night wrapped up in love and laughter with my husband and my daughter. By the time we made it home it was well after 10 pm and A'Miracle was knocked out. I walked around my home and remembered all the good times as I took off my shoes and let my toes sink deeply into the plush camel hair carpet of my den. I looked at all the pictures of our happy family that lined the walls and wished for that happiness forever. After a few more minutes of enjoying the fact that I was home I went upstairs to kiss my daughter as Jerrod and I tucked her in bed. After that we retired to our bedroom where I quickly took out my MacBook and sat down. "Come on baby, you ready? I asked Jerrod as he kicked off his shoes and came over to sit beside me.

He kissed me softly and quickly before he pulled back to look me in the eyes and shook his head yes. "I just gotta make sure you good baby so you can go accomplish your mission and come back home to us. We miss you Tisha and we need you here sometimes too." Jerrod said as I saw a glimmer of a tear in his eye and quickly kissed it away. "Oh baby, I'm sorry and I love you too. I love both of you. I'm gonna make this right." I said as I dialed the number for William Randolph in my cellphone and then waited for him to answer.

Jerrod kissed me from my forehead down to my neck as I held the phone up to my ear and it continued to ring. After 10 rings my father finally answered in a sleepy yet excited voice and I felt my heart race. I don't know why but I got tongue tied and sat there and just held the phone as he yelled hello. I sat there so long Jerrod reached over and grabbed the phone to do what I obviously couldn't do.

"Uh, hello sir my name is Jerrod Hill and I am the husband of your newly discovered daughter Shartisha Lewis-Hill." Jerrod said in the sophisticated voice he always did when he imitated someone who lived in Beverly Hills.

His sudden silliness caught me off guard and broke the trance I was in. I quickly scooted closer to Jerrod then to hear my dad introduce himself and Jerrod get straight to the point. "Okay sir, now with all of the trivialities out of the way let me get right down to it. Now, I don't know you just like Tisha doesn't so I'm a little fucked up about that but I won't go there right now. I will say she believes its true so I'm gonna roll with my baby. Now our dilemma. Tisha has to come back to Memphis soon because of some bullshit surrounding her sister and I can't come. Now, since I can't go Tisha needs somebody who can watch her back in the jungle and she said that person was you. Me, personally I don't know you so I can't say if you can get down with the niggas she may face, which brings us to this conversation. Since I can't be in Memphis I'd like to meet you via Skype right now if you can. I already got a vague idea of your aurora now from the way you conversing with me but I still wonna lay eyes on you too. So if you will give me your info, we can hook that up right now." Jerrod said as I heard my dad agree and watched Jerrod type the info into the computer.

Within minutes Jerrod had hung up the phone and dialed up my dad on Skype. I jumped up out of the bed and stood at the foot, behind the computer screen as soon as I heard it began to ring. I felt nausea and excited like I had just gotten off the extreme tea cup ride as I stood there and shook while Jerrod looked confused. "Baby what's wrong? Why are you nervous Tisha? Come here baby." Jerrod said as I shook my head no.

Suddenly the ringing stopped and I heard the deep, strong voice of my father as it echoed through the computer speakers. "Hello again Jerrod. It's nice to meet you in person my guy, or something like in person." My father said as he did a nervous laugh and Jerrod smiled while he nodded his head. I could see right away that my father had depth because he had quickly gone from a calm and professional, to hood and super relatable to Jerrod. In seconds they were wrapped up in a deep conversation like they were old friends as I stood and watched in awe.

"Yeah so, back to what I was saying on the phone. Jerrod, I never stopped looking or fighting for my daughter. When I got out after she turned 13 I came to the house to get her and Denise wouldn't let me. She called the police on me and had them pick me up for attempted kidnapping. I went back for six months after being out one hour, although I eventually beat that charge. I beat it but I went through hell, yet I didn't stop there though. I petitioned and called CPS for help and every time she would move and it would take me months to find her or CPS would visit and quickly close the case. I even tried to go to the school and find her but Denise had that covered to. She did all she could to erase that girl from my life bruh, but she couldn't erase her from my heart. That's why I got this tattoo." My daddy said as I watched Jerrod's eyes light up and my curiosity overpowered my fear.

I quickly ran back around to my side of the bed and sat down before I placed my face in front of the screen. When I did I got a glimpse of my beautiful 13-year-old face in an intricate, portrait tattoo that was taken from a picture my school had put in the paper. Tears instantly began to fall down my cheeks when I saw that and Jerrod wrapped his arm around me before he kissed my head.

"I got this tattoo right after I got out. I stopped at a store right across the street from the bail bonds man down town and picked up a paper at the counter. As I searched the paper for the want ads I came across the beautiful face of an angel, my angel. I knew it was her as soon as I stared in her eyes even though I hadn't seen her in years at that point, I didn't even have to read the name. She had the same eyes as me, the same smile. She was my princess. I went straight to the tattoo shop from there G and got it because I knew one day we would be reunited and I always wanted to keep her close to my heart." My daddy said as he pulled his shirt down and then sat down back in front of the camera.

As soon as our eyes met both of us were stuck. I couldn't move, breath or think as I sat there and felt as if I had looked in a mirror. My father had the same peanut butter complexion as me with big brown eyes and subtle dimples. He had a short, waved haircut and tattoos on his neck and arms. He was handsome but I could also see that he could be ugly if necessary just from the cuts and scars thrown in between and beneath most of his tattoos. Despite his rough demeanor as he sat there in his basketball shorts and white t-shirt, I could see love and compassion ins his eyes as tears streaked down his cheeks.

"Tisha, I love you baby. Daddy sorry. I'm sorry I couldn't protect you princess. I's sorry but I promise I will be here now. I love you Tisha!" My daddy cried as I cried along with him and told him how much I loved him.

After that we talked for another hour and my dad promised to pick me up from the airport the following Monday. That meant I had five whole days to love on my family and that's exactly what I did. I enjoyed every day with my husband and daughter as Jerrod took off and we went skating, on hay rides, and pumpkin carving with A'Miracle when we weren't at the hospital with Sha. By the time October 1 rolled around I was satisfied that my family was good and I would be safe when I got to Memphis. I got word from my lawyer Shelia Landry that Monday morning as Jerrod drove me to the airport and was happy to hear that my petition had gone through. I found out I was granted custody of all four children and could have them in my home in less than two weeks once I finished the required interview and paperwork. That made me so happy that I squealed and hung up the phone without saying goodbye as Jerrod turned to see what was wrong.

"We got custody baby. We got them. I just got a week or so to wait of I have this interview and then we're coming home.

Yes. I told you everything would work out. Now dad will take care of me while I'm in Memphis and you can rest easy my king. You wonna know why? Cause I'm coming home. I'm coming home!" I sang as I laughed and leaned over to hug and kiss Jerrod while he drove and laughed too.

At the airport I kissed my husband goodbye with a light and happy heart determined to conquer everything I set out to do. I thought of nothing but how good it would feel to have the kids in my arms and know that they were safe as the plane took me closer to Memphis. I hoped that I would be able to save Terricka as well, but I wasn't so optimist. I wished that Jerrod could find Buddy because I knew he could find her and get through to her even when I couldn't. I wished and hoped the entire plane ride without any fear only determination to overcome whatever obstacle.

When my plane landed at four that afternoon I was hyped and ready to do what had to be done. I was happy to see my dad was there at the gate, just like he said he would be. For a second I was taken aback by the 6'5", peanut butter colored beast that stood there and waited with a mean mug on his face. He looked just like a muthafucka fresh out the pen on a murder charge with all his muscles and tattoos. Anybody else would have walked away, but I didn't I just stood there and waited for him to catch my glance. When he did his smile lit up and warmed my heart from across the room. I ran into his arms like the lame people on the movies as soon as I saw that familiar smile and he picked me up to hug me like I was a precious jewel.

"Aww Tisha, I love you and I'm so happy to finally hold you. Daddy sorry baby and I promise to make it up to you. He whispered in my ear as he held me and then put me down to grab my bags. I wiped away my tears and then grabbed his hand as he led me out of the airport. The entire ride the Spaghetti Warehouse downtown, I remained silent and just listened to my dad talk about how he looked for me, how he would help me, and how sorry he was. "Tisha I hope this can be a new beginning for us. I'm happy you called me and I would have been upset if you didn't. You need somebody to ride with you through this and since your better half isn't here, daddy will step in. I got you okay?" My daddy said as I cried and he reached over to wipe away my tear. "Okay dad. I love you and thank you." I said as I smiled at him and let him wipe away my tears.

After that we had a great dinner and just before we left my dad made a call to his goons to meet us in Breezy Point. I sat there at the table across from him and just stared at his face as I watched him switch from loving, professional like dad to straight up goon ass nigga in a matter of seconds. After my dad arranged for them to meet us we left the restaurant and headed straight to the bay.

I explained to my dad that I wanted to go to my sister's house to get all of the kid's things, some of my sister's important stuff, and to try and find out where she was. I said all of that but to my true reason for going back was to find my sister. I hadn't even told Jerrod that, but I think my dad knew from the jump because he told me he already had his ear to the street. "I got word out that she is not to be fucked with and I'm sure that anyone who sees her will let me know." My dad said and I felt a little better.

My dad and I chatted all the way to Frayser and when we pulled down the street from Breezy Point my dad got a call from one of his goons. "Here I am coming upright behind y'all. Follow me." My dad said as hung up the phone and drove in. The sun had just set in the early October Memphis sky when we pulled in and the air was warm with a cool undertone as it breezed through the open window and caressed my cheek. I looked up at the sky as my dad pulled right in front of the apartment and I said a silent prayer for anyone who may have hurt my sister because they would be dead before sun up. My dad looked over at me as I turned back around before he pulled two hand guns from under the seat.

"You ready princess?" My dad asked me as he handed me one and I checked to make sure it was locked and loaded. "Yeah, I'm ready dad. Let's get this over with. Make sure everybody knows that we only shoot if necessary. Me and you and one more can go in just have the others stay outside. I just wonna gather some information on my sister mainly, only hurt a bitch if I have to. Okay?" I asked my father as he nodded his head while he texted my instructions to his goons.

After we received their confirmation my dad and I got out and the goon he talked to earlier whom they called Unc, jumped out with us. We all tucked away our heat as we walked up to the door and the junkies outside on the porch scattered. I stood back and put my ear to the window as my daddy banged on the door like a real G. I could hear people scatter in the living room as rap music played and the t.v. blasted loudly at the same time. I glanced at my dad and nodded that they were in there when he banged again.

"I know you muthafuckas hear me knocking. OPEN THE GODDAMN DOOR!" My daddy yelled as Unc got impatient and kicked in the door. He kicked that bitch so hard it flew off the hinges and we rushed in before they even knew what had happened. I rushed right into the living room to the big black chair I knew Vito called his throne. Sure as shit stinks there his junky, frail ass was with some bitch between his legs as she sucked his tiny dick. Just to see him there as he enjoyed himself in my sister's house while she was missing made me so furious. It made me so mad that I pulled out my strap and ran over there to slap his ass with it before he could even look up. I hit his ass so hard teeth flew out of his mouth and blood ran down the front of his dingy wife beater. His eyes snapped up to me just as the junky who had her face in his groin looked up at me with dope hazed eyes.

"Hey, who is this bitch Vito?" The girl yelled through slurred speech as I reached out and grabbed a handful of her matted braids. As I grabbed her Vito grabbed his mouth and then jumped up out the chair with the shit. He jumped up with the intentions of kicking my ass like I heard he did my sister on occasion, but what he didn't know was that my daddy didn't play that shit. "Tisha bitch I'll kill you." He yelled when he was in the full upright position and my daddy hit him with a Friday uppercut and slumped his bitch ass right back in the chair.

That one punch from my dad's massive, ring covered hand opened up Vito's chin on contact and I instantly saw bone and white meat pop out as he cried like a bitch. I turned my attention from Vito back to his hoe for a second as he continued to cry, and I drug that bitch to the door as I slapped her across the face occasionally. "Hoe stay the fuck out my sister house." I said as she yelled and I finally recognized her voice from the phone.

That made me go even harder on the bitch so I drug her out on the porch and then threw her face down on the ground. The impact of her body on the concrete made a loud thud and I let her hair go when her face hit the ground but didn't bounce back up. "Oh shit, somebody just beat Mika. AHHHHH she slammed that hoe. Aye, they in there fucking them folks up." Some boys on the next porch yelled as my daddy's goons formed a human wall around the door to block their view inside.

After I kicked the bitch up her ass once, I ran back inside and found my father with his now gloved hands around Vito's throat as he choked the life out of him. His grip was so tight around his neck I could see every vein in Vito's face as he gasped for air and his eyes popped out of his head. "Daddy, daddy please let him go. I need to find out where my sister is. Daddy please let him go." I yelled to my father as he shook his head no and Unc drug another bloody nigga into the front room. "Aye Big Folk. Let him go maine or we ain't gonna find the girl." Unc yelled at my daddy as he suddenly looked up with tears in his eyes.

"He already told me he beat her then shot her up with dope and left her in a stolen car with guns and pills. This bitch made ass nigga called 12 too and turned her in. Like a lil vindictive ass girl he set her up. Didn't you pussy? Mad cause you wasn't man enough to love her right and get her away from the bullshit. Let me kill this nigga Tisha. I'll go back to jail for you and anybody that you love." My daddy said as he continued to choke Vito and I watched his face turn blue.

Part of me wanted to tell him to do it and kill Vito's evil ass. However, I couldn't take the thought of losing my dad again so I begged him to let Vito go. "Please daddy. Let him go. Don't leave me again." I said with tears in my eyes as my daddy looked up into my eyes and released Vito's throat.

As soon as he did I ran over and grabbed my dad's arm as Vito lie, lifeless on the ground. I kicked him in the stomach and he squirmed so I knew he was still alive. After that my dad drug me to the door before we all jumped into our cars. As soon as the door closed to the truck me and my dad were in gun shots rang out from the upstairs window in Terricka's apartment. That was the last thing I heard before a hail of bullets erupted and my dad dumped out of the window as he backed up out of the parking spot. We pulled out of the parking lot going 80 miles per hour with my daddy's goons blasting right behind us.

My heart raced like a hamster on crack who had just got a new wheel as we sped towards the expressway and the police sped past us in the opposite direction. Right before we got on the on-ramp my dad stopped so that he could check to make sure we weren't hit. After that he called his boys as he cut on his police scanner and heard they had a description of the cars. We disappeared after that as we sped on to I-40 straight to Arlington.

I laid low in Arlington at my dad's house for that following week as I kept my eyes on the news and found out three niggas had gotten killed at the shootout and Vito was one of those niggas. I was relieved when I found out the police had no leads and believed the attack was drug related. That was enough to turn my focus from that and back to the mission I came for and that was the kids and my sister. That Monday, one week after I had been there I found out my sister was in jail on a $50,000 bond. I called around all day until I found a bails bond man who would take the 10% cash I had on me to get her out of jail. When I finally found one I was relieved to find out that he could get her released as early as the following morning. That was perfect since I was going to pick up the kids that afternoon and our flight didn't leave until the next day. That would give us all time to catch up before the kids and I went away.

In my mind the plan was perfect so as soon as my dad got home from his landscaping job, in which he owned the company, he and I headed to Just In Time Bonding and I paid the $5,000 necessary to get my sister out. I also had to sign a pink slip on the most expensive piece of book printing equipment I had in my office as collateral, which I would lose if she didn't go to court. I didn't care though I was just ready to get everything over with and get home for good. I didn't think twice as I signed the paper and the man told me she would be out the next day. I gave him my number after he told me he would go see her in the next hour and asked him if he would tell her to call me. He agreed and I left there happy, but still a little apprehensive of everything going as planned. I felt better though once we pulled up at the CPS office and I walked in to see four smiling little faces. I kissed and hugged my nieces and nephews as they told me how happy they were to see me.

"See I told y'all Te Te was coming and everything would be alright." Rodney Jr. said to his siblings before he turned around and gave me a big smile and hugged me tight.

"I love you Te Te and I knew you would come back for us. Can we go home now?" Rodney whispered in my ear as tears fell from my eyes. I kissed his little tear streaked cheeks before I stood back up and whisked Talaya up in my arms before I kissed Ryan and Tania on their heads. "Yes, tomorrow morning we go home!" I said as they all cheered and my dad helped me get them all out and into the car.

Once in the car I told my dad to take us to the Robinson's before the kids began to ask a million questions. I explained to them who my dad was and why we had to go to the Robinson's first. None of them seemed interested in waiting for any reason, especially not a dinner and I couldn't tell them we weren't leaving right away because I wanted them to say goodbye to Terricka. I just tried to encourage them to forgive her and say goodbye IF we saw her before we left. "I know how you babies feel; believe me I do. But you will regret it I you don't say bye because she's still your mother my loves. I will protect you though so don't worry. So if we see her while we're at grandma and grandpa's house for this big dinner, be sure to tell her you love her." I said as I looked at them in the rearview mirror and they all shook their heads to say okay.

Just then my phone rang and I looked at the ID to see a number I didn't know. I answered it and to my surprise I heard Terricka's low and raspy, but sweet and sober voice. "Hey little sister, my savior. Thank you for doing this." Terricka said as I felt tears well up in my eyes and I glanced in the mirror at the kids. I debated whether or not I should let them know it was her on the phone and after a few minutes I decided not to. I didn't want to upset them unless it was necessary and it would only be necessary if she showed up at the house the next day. So to shield their little hearts I played like she was a friend of mine on the phone.

"Oh you're welcome doll, but how are you doing? It's been a long time since I've seen you. I'm still here in Memphis and will be at home with the Robinsons' until late tomorrow afternoon. I hope to see you. Love ya girl." I said as I wiped away the tears that fell from my eyes and pretended I was okay. Terricka got quiet for a second after I spoke and almost made me think she had hung up until I heard her sniffle on the other end. "Oh my kids must be in the car. You don't want them to know it's me huh, and that I'm in jail? Well, I guess that's best sister. Let them know I love them though and I'm gonna get better for them. I love you too sister." Terricka said as I heard her cry between her words.

I almost couldn't control my emotions as I listened to the hurt and desire to change in my sister but lack of motivation to do so. I wanted to reach out and help her like I had done so many times before, but I felt it was a lost cause. I had done that too many times and every time I extended my hand to help she smacked that muthafucka away. It was only so much I could take, especially when I felt that I was doing more harm than good. That's why I felt it was time for that tough love my mama used to talk about because nothing else had worked so far. "You tell them yourself tomorrow when you come to the house. Be there forreal though because this is the last chance to see me...us." I whispered into the phone.

"Okay, I'll be there. Thank you again for getting me out." My sister replied really quickly before she hung up and left me dazed with the phone still in hand. I held in the tears that burned behind my eyes and smothered the hurt and fear in my heart as the kids began to sing to a song on the radio and my daddy joined in. I turned to face the window as I silently cried and my tears dripped down the glass like rain. In my heart I knew what would happen before it did, but I didn't want to believe it was true. Instead I dried up my tears and found a thread of hope and strength to get through another night.

I had a good night too at home with the Robinson's and the kids as we enjoyed a nice dinner, I put the kids in the bath, and then we watched movies until we passed out. That night I fell asleep but I didn't dream anything, instead I had a long peacefully slumber. I woke up the next morning anxious to see what the day would hold. I was down in the kitchen before my foster mother Tania was with breakfast already on. After we all ate at the table together and I had the kids dressed we went outside to play on the swing set. I sat on the swing and watched my sister's kids laugh and play like I had never seen them do before. Every now and then I would pick up my phone to make sure that it was on. At two o'clock when it suddenly rang, I fumbled to find it and answer it before the person hung up.

"Hello. Hello Terricka." I yelled into the phone after I answered only to be met with silence and then the person hung up.

I looked at the number with a 731 area code and wondered who that was that had called. The kids diverted my attention from that though when they ran over with leaves in their hands and began to attack me with them. I threw my phone down in my seat and jumped up to chase them and forget about my worries for a minute. We played like that for an hour as we rolled in the leaves and laughed. At close to four p.m., an hour and a half before our flight, I stood up with tears in my eyes because what I already knew had come true. There was no Terricka in sight and there probably never was going to be, because she never intended to come.

"She played me just like Denise used to do people, and now I'm done. Sometimes to love is to let go." I said to Tania as she met me on my way to the house. "What happened baby?" She yelled after me as I opened the kitchen door. "She did exactly what I knew she would ma and that's okay. Get the kids together so y'all can take us to the airport because it's time to go." I said as Tania shook her head with a sad look on her face.

I marched into the house and up to my old room as I redialed that mysterious number that had called me earlier. I let it ring over and over again until the answering machine finally came on. When it finally did come on I froze in my tracks as I listened to the nasty recording Terricka had left just for me. I had to replay it a dozen times in order to understand everything she said through her slurred speech.

"Hello you've reached Terricka and if this Tisha ole Bougie ass bitch bye. Okay you got me out so what I'm supposed to be your slave. You got the kids and that's what you wanted so bitch go. Go y'all asses on back to California and leave me the fuck alone. YOU CAN'T SAVE ME TISHA CAUSE I DON'T WANT TO BE SAVED. STOP TRYING BITCH! Bye HOE and I hope you didn't put yo house up cause I'm not going back to court. Hahaaaaaa!" Terricka said before the recording ended and I cut off all feelings for her.

I cried for a second as I finished the packing then I wiped away my tears and went down stairs with bags in hand. I put on a brave face as we all loaded into the car and Tania grabbed me to hug me. "You did all you could do baby, now it's time for your sister to help herself." Tania said before she kissed me and we got into the car.

I rode silently to the airport lost in my thoughts as my sister's words rang in my ears. I still didn't give up hope that one day she would change but I knew that time to change hadn't come yet. I felt a sudden wave of hurt and sorrow take over me as we pulled in front of the airport and I realized that could be the last time I talked to my sister. I almost broke down at that thought, but I pulled myself together as soon as my phone rang.

"Hello." I said as I hopped out and my foster dad helped me with the bags. "Heyyy big sis, I'm backkkkk. Your boy out the hospital and everything. I'm at home now waiting on you. Soooo where ya at?" Sha said as I jumped up and down in happiness and told him I was on my way.

After that I kissed my foster parent's goodbye and boarded the plane with my four new babies right with me. Once I had them settled in the four seats in the row in front of me I snuggled deep down into my first class seat and put my forehead on the window as our plane went up into the air.

"Well, I guess some dragons can't be slayed and sometimes you do have to let go in order to truly love. Goodbye for now big sister. I hope you take care of yourself." I said as I looked out into the clouds and then closed the blind on the window.

Chapter 8

Sha: Gathering The Pieces

I felt like the luckiest nigga in the world as I hung up with my sister then turned over in bed to hug, kiss, and squeeze the big plump ass of the sexy red bone next to me. I gripped that ass and let my tongue dance around in her sweet ass mouth for a minute as I thought about how I almost died…again!

"Damn baby, to think I almost didn't make it. What would have you done without me?" I asked Lydia as she stared up at me with tears in her big gray eyes and begged me not to think like that. "Please Sha don't say shit like that. I don't know what I would do without you. Go crazy perhaps. One thing fasho, I would have fucked yo daddy's punk ass up because it's all his fault. I hate him and I don't want to ever go back there, but I know I have no choice. I gotta be there for my siblings cause you know my mama crazy. I guess we both have to carry the sins of our parents and feel obligated to protect our siblings." Lydia said to me as my mind drifted back to my own sisters.

Suddenly I thought about the tone in Tisha's voice when she answered the phone and the fact that she said her and the kids would be home soon and not Terricka. I couldn't help but to think the worse as I turned over on to my back and looked up at the ceiling as my mind wondered. With all the shit I had been through and all the shit I still had to fight, I felt nothing was more important than the fight I had to endure for family. All I wanted was for my sisters to be happy because I had seen them sad, hurt, and suffer for far too long.

I felt like Tisha and Terricka deserved a stress free life with nothing but love all around them because that is what they tried to give me all of my life. No matter how much they were beaten and raped they still tried to shield me from what was going on. They would hide me and take beatings on my behalf just to spare me the pain that they knew all too well.

My sisters went through all of that and I did too because they didn't know it, but I saw and heard everything that went down. I hated all my mother did to them and I would often hide in the shadows and wish I was strong enough to kill her and the men who hurt my sisters. As I laid there I remembered one night when I was ten and I tried to stab my mother. I could see the images vividly in my mind as I laid in my kind sized bed and Lydia turned over to put her head on my chest.

I could still hear the cowbell she had placed by my sister's door ring loudly as she and the big, nasty man from around the block named Jerome, walked into the room. I could still feel my heart race as I climbed out of the vent into the hall and crouched down by their closed door to listen and look through the peep hole. I wished I hadn't saw what I did as soon as I looked in though because the first fucking thing I saw was my sisters cowered together on the bed with pink baby doll gowns on. I can still remember their faces as they sat there and looked scared as hell while tears ran down their cheeks.

I remember how I wanted to yell out their names as my mother barked out orders and the man smiled at them before he took off his shirt. I could still feel the cold, hard, metal scissors in my hand that I held as I stood up and positioned myself right behind the door. I made it up in my mind at that moment that I was going to stab the shit out of my mama as soon as she came out. I tried to do that shit too.

As soon as she walked her naked, nasty, cracked out ass out of the room I lunged at her back and barely nicked her with the blades. That was the worst mistake of my life too because she hit me so hard in the nose that my 90 lb. ass flew into the wall and passed out. When I woke up I was on my back in the closet of my room and my head hurt like I had been hit by a car. I opened my eyes to see the evil red eyes of my mother as she bent down over me. "Try that shit again lil bastard and I will stomp yo head in worse you little retarded bitch. Now go to sleep hoe." My mama yelled in my face before she stomped me so hard in the head I did pass out again.

I remembered that shit like it was yesterday as I laid there next to the girl of my dreams almost 10 years later. That was a memory that was seared in my brain and it brought back a pain I feared I could never escape. "What's wrong baby? Why you crying?" Lydia asked me as she suddenly looked up and then kissed away my tears.

I didn't even realize a nigga had shed a tear because I was so wrapped up in my memories. I quickly sucked that shit up and looked down at Lydia as she stared up at me with those, sexy, compassionate eyes. I ain't even gonna lie, even though my heart was heavy right then I couldn't stop my dick from getting rock hard just having her near. Suddenly all I wanted to do was touch Lydia's sexy ass and feel myself inside of her. I needed to be inside of her and feel her love, her warmth. I needed to feel something, anything but the pain that always seemed to lurk around every corner.

"I don't know baby. I didn't even realize I was crying. I guess I'm kinda fucked up in the head because everything so fucking uncertain right now. I just don't know what's gonna happen in any faucet of my life. I don't know if those muthafuckas gonna go ahead and let me in school. I don't know if I will find a job and we can move into an apartment. I don't know if my sister Terricka is okay and I'm worried about Tisha too because she takes on so much. Then to top it all off, I don't know if I will be able to keep you. Maine, I realize my life fucked up and I got some demons to fucking deal with and you don't need that bullshit." I said to Lydia as she shook her head no and I continued.

"I know that just being me fucks up my chances, but I really fucking like you Lydia and a nigga want to be with you. Like for real. You make me want to do better. You make me want to be better. I have been through some really hard shit in my life, me and my sisters. I never told you this before but our mama was bipolar, schizophrenic, a manic depressant, abuser, drug addict, and sexual deviant. I won't go into great detail, but she did some very horrible shit to me and my sisters. Some shit you wouldn't even do to your enemies. She's the reason I don't truly know how to express my emotions because if I did as a kid they would be beaten out of me. I barely talked as a young nigga and usually stayed hidden. I figured out of sight, out of mind, so I went ghost to not get hurt. I was wrong though because no matter where I hid she would find me. She hurt us bad baby and fucked us up at the same time. Now we all are just trying to gather the pieces." I said as I held back my tears like a real nigga and my girlfriend cried on my chest.

I felt Lydia's body shake as she buried her head in my chest for a second and then I reached down to pull up the left side of my shirt. "You see this burn?" I asked Lydia as she shook her head yes while she ran her fingers over the patches of burned skin. "My mama did this. She tried to drown me in boiling hot water when I was a baby. I was too young to remember that, but after being beat for years and having her throw me over a 15 ft. banister when I was 10, the effects of her abuse has really taken a toll on me. I ain't gonna lie baby, it's hard for me to trust and get close to other people, especially females. My mammy is to thank for that.

She got me to the point where I second guess whether or not anyone could truly love me. That's why I never really had a girlfriend before now. I just couldn't bring myself to trust anyone not to break my heart when they found out how fucked up I really am. That's how I still feel. I feel like I'm not god enough for you and that I carry too much baggage to be loved. I'm scarred up inside and out baby and to tell the truth, I don't know if I will ever heal. Maybe its best if you get out now." I said to Lydia as those tears that burned behind my eyelids suddenly dripped down my face in four huge drops.

I quickly reached up and dried my tears with the back of my hand and tried to be hard. Lydia saw right through that shit though as she hoisted her body up until we were nose to nose and then she kissed the traces of tears from my eyes. You don't have to be afraid to be vulnerable or show your true emotions to me Sha. I love you just the way you are. I have had a fucked up life too and I have a lot of scars that you simply cannot see. That doesn't make me unworthy of love and neither are you. I love you unconditionally and I have since the moment I laid eyes on you. I know you have demons and I have some of my own, let's conquer them together. I just want to be with you Shamel. I want to be with you in every way possible because I love everything about you. Even the things you think are ugly. Like this." Lydia said as she suddenly began to kiss down my body from my neck to my chest.

I kinda felt like a bitch as she kissed me and I laid there and squirmed, but that shit felt so good I couldn't resist it. My dick got harder than two-week old bread when she licked the rough, disfigured skin on my side from under my armpit all the way down to my waist. I felt sensations run through me that I had never felt before as she kissed across my waist to my groin and then looked up at me with those big, passionate eyes while she pulled my jogging pants off.

That was all it took to get me to the point where I was about to burst so I quickly sat up, grabbed Lydia around her waist, and flipped her on to her back on the bed. I moved so fast and with such precision she didn't even have time to think before I had her pinned down and my lips were all over her as I kissed her face and neck. "You know what Lydia, I love you too. You're the only female I've ever told that to other than my sisters. All I ever want is you. I want you to be my wife someday girl. If I asked you, what would you say?" I asked Lydia as I blurted out my true emotions before I could take it back.

To forget about my nervousness from saying shit too soon, I kissed her lips and watched tears well up in her eyed before she responded. "You would make me the happiest woman in the world if you asked me to be your wife." Lydia said to me as I felt a tingle in my heart that I had never felt before.

It was like lighting had struck my heart and caused it to explode into a million little cracked out butterflies that flapped around erratically in my chest. I knew that feeling I felt had to be love and that scared the shit of me. To love someone and possibly be hurt was a fucked up thought, but I knew it was a chance I wanted to take so I grabbed the girl who made me better and kissed her long and hard before I began to rip off her clothes. I quickly undressed Lydia as she stared into my eyes and we got wrapped up in a deep passionate kiss. I felt tingles all over as she rubbed up my back and I kissed and licked down her neck until I got to her subtle, perky breasts. I took a deep breath before I took one into my mouth and flicked her nipple with the tip of my tongue. It got hard instantly as I blew on it and then latched on to her breast like a breastfed baby.

"Oh Sha yessssss." She moaned as I continued to suck and lick her neck and breast before I used my hand to trace down her body to her wet center. I could feel the heat and moisture from her vagina as soon as I got in that region and that was enough to awaken my pure animal attraction to her. Before she could even catch on I stood up and ripped my t-shirt and boxers off before I jumped back on top of her in position. I used my hand to rub my 10 inch dick up and down her vagina lips as I nibbled on and kissed her neck while I whispered in her ear.

"I love you Lydia and I want you to know this thang is forever with me. I want us to be together for a lifetime not just for one moment of passion. I know I'm a thug street nigga, but this street nigga has a heart and I'm smart enough to know that when you find a good thing you don't let it go. Let me love you forever baby. Okay?" I asked Lydia as a phantom tear fell from my eye and landed on her cheek to mingle with hers.

We kissed a long passionate kiss after that as I ran my hand through her hair while I still held my wood in the other hand. When we ended our lip lock I pulled back a little to look at her face again and to see if she was ready to answer the question. The smile on her face followed by the way she flicked her tongue at me and then bit her bottom lip let me know that she was just as ready as I was. "Sha I couldn't promise forever to anyone but you. You are my king. I need you. I want you." She panted as I gave her what she asked for.

I used my hand to run my dick up and down Lydia's clit one last time as I licked from her ear around to her mouth. As soon as our lips touched I entered her tight, wet womb and it felt like I had slipped into heaven. She moaned out in ecstasy as I dug down deep directly to her g-spot. I could feel her contract and expand the walls of her vagina with every thrust of my dick and that shit felt like her pussy was giving me head. That was some shit I had never felt before with all the no edges and no walls bitches I had fucked in the hood. Baby's shit was definitely different though, so different she made a nigga moan.

"Ssss Oh shit girl. Damn this pussy good. This my pussy though right?" I asked her as I put both of her legs up on my shoulders and beat that shit like a drum. When I did that she let out a low, light howl that made my dick even harder and her pussy seemed to get juicer by the pump. Before long we were both sweaty as fuck, moaning and her pussy was skeeting all over the place.

"Damn baby you got me so wet, this has never happened before." Lydia said as he body began to shake and I looped my hands under her armpits, around to her back so that I could hold her by both shoulders. When I did that I leaned in closer and dug my dick so far up in her I know I felt an ovary. "Ohhh shittt." She yelled as I began to grind in a circular motion making sure I stimulated that clit with each stroke. After about three more good strokes and a dozen scratches to my back, Lydia's body began to tremble and shake as she reached her second orgasm. "Ohhh I love you Shamel." She yelled as I kissed her long and hard then licked down the space between her breasts.

When her body finished trembling I kissed down her stomach until I was face first in her wet honey pot. I slurped that shit and sucked her clit until she flapped around like a fish out of water and begged me to stop. "Ohhh baby please. Give me that dick Sha." She yelled as I came back up and quickly flipped her over on to her stomach. Once on her stomach I coached her up on to her knees so that I could hit that pussy from the back. "Arch your back baby. Let me get up in that thang." I said before I leaned down to kiss her left ass cheek and then used my dick to smack the other.

I watched her toot that fat ass up in the air so that her face was all the way down and her waist laid on the bed to provide the perfect elevation. That fat ass monkey sat up in my face all big and wet, and made my fucking mouth water. I smacked her on the ass and watched it jiggle as I teased her hole with the dick. Every time I did it she backed up on my shit and used her pussy walls to grip it before I pulled out and smacked her ass. That shit felt so good I damn near nutted so I had to quickly dive in before that happened.

Without notice I rammed my dick balls deep into her pussy and nailed her into the bed. I grabbed the back of her long, thick, hair and wrapped it around my left hand as I beat that pussy up and smacked her big, red ass with my right hand. She fucked me back and moaned the entire time as I felt a familiar feeling build up from my toes. The more she threw that pussy back and I tapped her g-spot the harder we went and the stronger my nut felt. Within seconds her and I began to shake together and I knew I was in trouble. I started to pull out just when I felt my nut about to burst, but Lydia reached back with both hands and grabbed me around the waist as she continued to throw that ass back.

"No, don't pull out. Let's have a baby Sha, I love you and want to be your wife." Lydia said as I let it go and released 19 years' worth of semen build up inside of her. Both of our bodies shook violently as I felt my entire load go inside of her and I knew for sure I had gotten her pregnant at that moment. As soon as out bodies finished shaking I fell back on to the bed, wet and out of breath. Lydia fell down beside me and let her head lay on my chest after she kissed me and told me she loved me again.

"I love you too baby and I will never let you go. I hope you are pregnant right now. I will be the best father, way better than my own and I know you will be 100 times the woman my mother was. Yes, let's gone have Shamel Jr." I said as I looked down at Lydia and she looked up at me with happy, glossy eyes.

We laid there wrapped in each other's arms as we talked about what our future would hold. Before long we were both fast asleep, lost in our own separate but beautiful dreams. While asleep I had my first nightmare free dream of my life, one I didn't have to immediately forget as soon as I opened my eyes. There was no one chasing me or trying to kill me in this dream, just Lydia, me and our love.

I saw us happy and together as her little belly grew into a big, round ball. I saw myself with her, right by her side every step of the way and I knew that was exactly how it was going to be. I was going to be that involved dad and supportive boyfriend, there for every doctor's appointment, prenatal class, and anything else she needed me to do or be at. I wanted to be better than every man I had ever saw in my life and I knew that started by being a great man to the mother of my child.

I woke up sometime later in my bed, still wrapped up in Lydia's love with her arm across my throat and her leg sprawled across my waist. I opened my eyes and looked directly into her beautiful face as she slept peacefully with this big smile on her lips. I couldn't resist the kiss I laid on her and I smiled when she wrinkled up her nose and moved her head. She was so beautiful, even when she was sleep and annoyed, and I felt I could stay like that, all in love with her forever. I laid there and stared at her for a few more minutes before I suddenly got the overwhelming feeling that someone was watching me. I quickly lifted up a little and glanced around the room before my eyes caught the short, little chocolate figure who stood in the door.

I damn near jumped out of my skin when I saw Rodney. Jr.'s face as he stood in my door way and smirked. I quickly pulled the covers up over baby's sexy body as I kept my eyes on my nephew as he tried to memorize every inch of her. "Ohhhh. Hey uncle Sha. Everybody looking for you, but I'm happy I found you." He said as he giggled and then covered his mouth with his hand while I jumped up and slipped my jogging pants on.

"Oh really lil freaky, sneaky young nigga?" I said as I rushed over to fake punch him in the stomach before I balled him up and held him over my head. He giggled and squirmed as I shook him and then lowered him back down to the ground. "You can't be looking at my girl, young nigga. That's wifey right there, your soon to be auntie. Aite my guy?" I asked my nephew as I tickled him and he smiled up at me.

I tickled him again as he laughed his head off and I got a warm feeling in my heart. I loved all of my nieces and nephews with all of me but Rodney Jr. and I had a special kind of bond. Not only did he look just like me and not his father, but that young nigga had my quiet, calm demeanor as well. Like me, Lil Rod as I called him, was also a productive of his environment, a boy forced to grow up too fast with no guidance. My nephew had a smart mouth and witty mind accompanied by a quick temper he inherited from both of his parents. He had depth and demons already before the age of 10 destined to be a true hell raiser if that wild side wasn't tamed. He was my lil mini me in so many ways and I loved him. I loved all of my sisters' kids and I felt having them around was going to be good for all of us.

"Let me run into the bathroom to freshen up though. I would tell you to just go ahead and I'll be down there when I'm done, but I know you're just like me and would never leave even if I told yo bad ass too." I said as he smiled sneakily at me and he nodded his head yes while I laughed back at him. "See, that's what I already know so I'm just gonna say stay right here until I'm done. Sit yo lil nasty ass right here by the door until I get out and don't go over there fucking with the covers or shit. Aite?" I asked my nephew as I made a serious face and a scared look spread across his.

I quickly laughed when I saw that face, to show him I was playing before I mushed his head, grabbed my clean boxers, t-shirt, and sweats, off the dresser, and dashed into the bathroom.

"Okay uncle Sha. She beautiful ANDDD thick, but anyway everybody wants to see you." Rodney Jr. said as he laughed and yelled at me through the door.

I damn near fell as I got into the shower when he said that. I could do nothing but catch myself and laugh after that. "You a wild, smart, and smart mouthed ass young nigga. I fucks with you though." I said to Rodney, Jr. as I laughed while I speed washed and he laughed too. I laughed and joked with my nephew through the door the entire time I showered and got dressed. By the time I came out of the bathroom fresh and fully dressed both of us were giggling like lil females.

"Yea, you came out just in time. She was almost my girlfriend." Rodney Jr said as we both laughed and I wrapped him up in a chokehold really fast. I held him around the neck with one arm as I tickled him with my right hand and he begged for mercy. "Please okay, okay uncle Sha I was just playing. I'm gonna pee!" Rodney Jr. said as he laughed and I instantly let him go. "Oh hell nawl, no pissing youngin'." I said as we both laughed and I pushed him in the back away from my door.

"Okay, I ain't gonna pee, but I will get yo girl." Rodney, Jr. said as he laughed and I smacked him across the back of his head. "No, okay forreal uncle, I'm happy to see you. Everybody want to see you bad." Rodney Jr said as he turned from little, mature hood boy to the little innocent kid he was at heart. "Well lead me to them smooth young nigga." I said to Rodney before I turned back around to yell at the sleeping beauty I had inside. "BABY GET UP!! EVERYBODY AT HOME!!" I yelled to Lydia before I turned around and laughed as I jogged down the steps behind Rodney, Jr.

As soon as we got down stairs and I turned the corner to walk into the family room I was attacked by a half dozen little bodies as the hugged and clung to me. "UNCLE SHAAAAAAAA!" The all yelled as I picked the girls; A'Miracle, Tania, and Talaya, up one by one and kissed their foreheads while I told them how beautiful they were. They all giggled, glowed, and kissed my cheek before I sat them back down and they smiled their beautiful smiles. After than I turned to give Rodney, Jr. another dap then hugged Ryan in my arms.

"Damn young nigga, you big ass hell now. You remember me?" I asked him as he smiled that little shy, smile and shook his head yes. "They all remember you. That's all they talked about the entire ride here, seeing their uncle Sha. It's clear that they love their uncle Sha, and I love you too my beanie baby." My sister Tisha said as he got up from the couch besides Jerrod and came over to hug me.

I hugged her tightly in my arms and enjoyed the feeling of her loving embrace. I was happy to have my sister home safe and sound, or at least where I could help protect her. I felt like a nothing ass nigga as I laid up in that damn hospital bed and my sister risked her life trying to make shit better for all of us. I hated that and that's why when God gave me yet another chance at life, I vowed to never repeat past mistakes by taking care of my business and helping my sisters any way I could. "I love you too big sis. Thank you. Thank you for everything you do for so many people." I whispered in her ear as I kissed her on the cheek and she began to weep. "Awww, don't start all that crying and sht. Jerrod said as he laughed and came over to grab Tisha out of my embrace just as a beautiful, messy haired Lydia walked into the living room and everyone roared to life.

After I formally introduced Lydia to the kids we all sat down on the couches to talk while the kids got engrossed in a game of bowling on the WII. "So Lydia, how did your transfer to UCLA go? My co-worker said his sister is still waiting to get her letter." Jerrod said as we all sat on the couch and talked, which drifted my mind back to my own sister.

Suddenly Terricka was all I could think about so I stood up and asked Tisha if she could come talk to me in the next room as Jerrod and Lydia finished their conversation. As soon as we were in the kitchen I could sense the nervous energy in my sister as she went over to the refrigerator and pretended to look for something. I stared at her as she moved around juice, and then went through the fruit drawer and pulled out an orange. "Tisha, stop all this dodging and shit. Wassup big sis? Where Terricka at? What happened Tish?" I asked as my sister stared at me with suddenly sad eyes and I knew shit was fucked up.

My heart raced like a muthafucka as I followed Tisha with my eyes and she walked around the island to the barstools where I sat and she took a seat beside me. I could tell she was about to lay some heavy shit on me when she suddenly touched my hand and said my name. "Shamel, bruh." Tisha began as I sat there in a daze, focused on every word that she said.

I sat there numb as fuck, while I listened and she went through every sordid detail of what had happened since we left her in Memphis. She told me all about how Terricka's mood changes and how she went back into her drug haze and even how she paid to get her out and Terricka said kiss her ass. She told me everything I didn't want to hear as a piece of my heart broke with each word that she spoke. I closed my eyes and tried to stop the screams inside of me that said just go find my sister and make her listen. I had the same desire that Tisha had and that was to fix Terricka, however; deep in my heart I knew I could never do that.

"Sometimes to truly love is to let go lil brother, I'm learning that. It seems the more we try to save Terricka and pull her in the harder she pulls away. I just don't know what it is lil brother, but it's like she wants to dwell in her pain." Tisha said as I shook my head and tried to deny what I knew was the truth. "No I can't believe that big sis. I can't believe anybody wants pain. I don't want to believe that. We gotta do something else. We gotta find a way to pull her out." I said as I looked at Tisha and she shook her head.

"Ain't no pulling out a drowning person if they never extend their hand Sha. We can't make her want to live and be a mom. All we can do is love on the kids she brought into this world and hope that we can end the vicious cycle that began long before we were brought into the world. That's all we can do without constantly hurting ourselves and allowing her to hurt us. Do you know I put up my printing press up as collateral for the other $45,000 worth of property on her $50,000 bond? Wonna know what she said to me when we talked and she was out of jail? She laughed in my face and said she hopes I didn't put my house up because she wasn't going to court. My sister! Our sister!! She said fuck me and all I worked so hard for. Sha, I think the Terricka we once knew is gone." My sister said to me as tears welled up in my eyes and I put my head down and covered it with my arms.

In seconds I felt Tisha's arms around me as she hugged me and told me everything would be alright. I wanted to believe her but that was easier said than doing seeing that our situation was hopeless. "It's okay little brother. We have to be strong, keep living life, and make things better for the kids. When Terricka get ready to change we can still be there for her. Jerrod found Buddy yesterday and he had already found her new cell number and talked to her on the phone. I'm confident he will find her and get her back on track. In the meantime, let's stay focused, okay? Now, what is this good news I heard you have?" My sister asked as I tucked away my emotions, wiped my face, and then looked at her and smiled.

I smiled away my fear and sorrow as I accepted what could be the evitable and tried to focused on the rays of sunshine that had finally began to shine on my life. I told my sister about getting the chance to test and re-interview for UCLA. I told her about how much I loved Lydia and how I found a job, and wanted to get married and have kid. I was surprised that when I finished talking my sister was totally on bard with everything I said. She was happy I want to finally begin to live life and offered to support us in any way that she could.

"You know I got you Sha and I'm so proud of you little brother. I can't wait for you to be a husband and a father, let me tell you being a spouse and parent are the best roles in the world. I think Lydia and you will make great parents and be very happy together. I will help you with the baby and from no on you don't have to worry about work. I see you still draw even though you told me you quit. Well, yo ass just unquit because I need a new lead graphic designer down at Pen Hustlas Publications. And we pay $68,000 a year with full benefits to start off. That's enough to start a family with. So what do you say lil brother?" Tisha asked me as I sat there in a daze and tried to process what she said.

"Hell yeah big sis. Oh damn. I don't know what to say to no shit like this. I don't really know what you will expect from me in this role, but I promise I will work my hardest to get it. This is exactly what I need to get on track in case she is pregnant. Thank you big sis." I said as I hugged my sister and felt like everything was falling in place.

The rest of the day I kicked it with family as Jerrod and I cooked crab legs, lobster tails, and crawfish for the entire family and we all sat out on the back patio and enjoyed a wonderful dinner. I went to bed that night happy as fuck with Lydia by my side and love in my heart, and once again there were no nightmares to keep me awake and remind me of the torture I once had to endure. The next morning, I woke up feeling better than I had in years and rushed down stairs to cook breakfast only to find my sister had already done it. I inhaled all of the delicious smells deeply and smiled at her as she sat on a barstool with a satisfied look on her face and letter in hand.

"What Tisha? What is it that had you looking all happy and shit?" I asked her as I took a seat next to her and she put the envelop in my hand. I stared down at the UCLA emblem and almost died when I saw admissions office. I turned the thick, heavy envelop over in my hand as I looked at the seal and thought about whether I wanted to open it or not. That envelope was the key too my future and the life Lydia and I talked about. As I sat there with it in my hand I was too nervous to open it and find out.

"Here, open it please." I said to my sister as I handed her the envelop and then put my hands on my head before I leaned on the counter. I listened with my eyes closed as she opened the letter and read to herself until she got to a line she was sure I wanted to hear. "CONGRATULATION MR. LEWIS YOU

HAVE BEEN ADMITTED INTO UCLA ON A FULL SCHOLORSHIP FOR OUR GRAPHC AND CONCEPTUAL ARTS DEGREE PROGRAM!" Tisha said as she yelled and I opened my eyes to look at her and be sure I had heard her correctly.

"WHAT?" I said as I grabbed the letter out of her hand as I stood up and held it to the light. I read over the same words she just had and as soon as I finished I squealed like a project girl who was just given ten free bundles of Brazilian hair. "Awwwwww shit. They gave a nigga a chance. It's on now big sis!" I said as I jumped around and Tisha ran into my arms to jump too.

We hugged and yelled for the others to come as my heart cried for the little boy who should have died long ago. "We made it big sis. We became everything they said we would never be. Everything she said we never be or overcome we have done it. We beat all odds and yet we're still not done proving them wrong. Two out of three ain't bad odds big sis. I love you sis." I whispered to Tisha as we continued to yelled and jump while Lydia, Jerrod, and all the kids ran downstairs.

We all celebrated that day, a Monday, by having a big breakfast and going to an amusement park after the kids left school. The next day I went in to UCLA, finished my admissions, got my classes, and found out I had student housing in the form of a two-bed room apartment on campus. The only thing I was responsible for was my daily needs and the lights in my place, besides maintaining good conduct and grades. I figured I had that down pact since I would be with Lydia all the time and I didn't party so I could study.

After I got all that situated I went to the café on campus where I had applied for a job as a cashier. I walked in to tell them never mind since I had a job with Tisha, but I walked out with my uniform in hand. I figure I really couldn't get in trouble if most of my time was occupied so I took the part-time job for the weekend during the morning hours just to have something else to do. After that I fell into a happy little routine really fast with classes weekdays from six in the morning until noon and work at the publishing company from two in the afternoon until seven in the evening. I worked like that with the café on the weekends for about a month until Lydia and I moved into my apartment right before Thanksgiving break.

That was around the time things started going to good and I knew something bad was on the horizon. It all started when we got a call from Buddy in which he told us that Terricka had been in several fights and he heard she had broken her arm recently. He said she was with him for a few days and he had her on track until she ran away one day he was at work and he hadn't seen her since. That really fucked up my head that morning he called as I walked to the café for my shift. I tried not to let it show on my face as I went about my job, but my co-worker Janey could instantly tell something was up when I kept snapping on customers.

"What's wrong with you Sha?" She asked me after I had excused myself from the register and went to bust tables so I wouldn't have to talk to people. I almost went off on her lil short, pudgy, nosey ass too when she said that, but I knew her question came from a good place and I was just on edge. "I'm okay Janey, I just got some bad news about my family this morning." I said to her as she walked closer with a smile on her face.

I glanced at her out of the side of my eye as she continued to smile and look towards the door, then I shrugged it off as I continued to work. "Ohhh I knew it was something. Well, maybe I have something that will lift your mood." Janey said as she grabbed my attention. "It's a gentleman by the door looking for you and he said he's your father." Janey said as I instantly snapped to attention and glanced at the door where Shaheim stood and looked right in my direction.

I felt rage boil up inside of me as I looked at him with that smug ass expression on his face and he motioned for me to come over. In my heart I knew from the jump that meeting was not going to be good and that I should have just walked into the kitchen, but I didn't. Instead I told Janey to tell the boss, Mr. Donaldson, that I was about to step outside and asked her to cover the tables for me. After that I stormed to the door and out of them right past my father as I yelled for him to follow.

"COME OUT HERE DOG!" I yelled as I walked out and I heard him laugh as he trailed behind.

When we got out there and I turned to stand face-to-face with him as he clapped his hands and looked at me from head to toe. "Well, well, well, if it ain't my son, the college boy. Look at you Sha, working and in school and shit. I bet you think you something now huh? Think you big shit huh? Bet these people don't know the truth." He said in a loud tone as I realized he was drunk. A couple of people on their way into the café stopped to see what was going on as I stepped up into Shaheim's face and put my mean mug on.

"Look here ole drunk, pussy ass nigga. Don't come up here to my muthafucking place of employment and try to blow up the spot. Yea I'm in college working and doing very well. I'm doing everything yo bitch ass said I never would and it burns you up don't it? Well, that's yo problem bitch, not mine. However, it will be yo problem if you bring yo weak ass up here again. That's my word." I said through clenched teeth as I bumped past him on my way back in and he grabbed my arm.

I jerked my arm back as soon as he touched me and spent around ready to whoop his ass while he smiled and a small crowd lurked around us and whispered. "Oh the retard mad. You gonna show them who you really are huh? Show them the crazy, violent, retard, thief that you really are." My dad aid before I reached out and grabbed him in his collar to pull him closer to me. "Listen bitch..." I began as he cut me off with a demand of his own. "No you listen little bitch. Now if you like the way you're living now I advise you to listen up. I know you're living with your sister and work for her company, and that this lil job a cover up. I know you make real money now so its time you pay restitution. Now I can tell the police where you are and let them come snatch yo bitch ass up, take you to jail, and end this college shit before it really begins. I'd get my restitution then. Or you can play nice and give me uhhhh, $10,000 and I will call it even. The choice is yours though boy. I'm sure your sister would be hurt if all that happens. I now where y'all live to so make this easy on her. I'm sure she doesn't want any more drama right now with her sister missing and all. Think about it young nigga." He whispered as I suddenly though about Tisha and all of the people around me as they stared and I let him go.

I glared at my father with nothing but hate as he stood there and smiled while he fixed his collar and I turned to walk in. "Oh and leave Lydia alone. She don't really like you. I guess she's just sad that I don't want to touch that hot pocket anymore since her little sister so hot n ready." My daddy said and struck that one nerve he knew would drive me insane.

Before he or I knew it, I had turned around and lunged at him with my hands up ready to choke the life out of his ass. Lucky for me though my big homie and star quarterback Chop was nearby at a table with his girl and he jumped up quickly to pull me away. I cursed at my dad as he pulled me inside and I was greeted by my manager. Needless to say I was released from that job right then, but my manager didn't report the incident to the university so I was grateful for that. I couldn't go home my head was fucked up when I left so I hopped in the Impala Tisha bought me and headed home to her house When I got there she was already gone to take Tania, A'Miracle, and Talaya to their Saturday dance class and Jerrod let me in. He was really who I wanted to see anyway since I didn't want to worry Tisha with more problems.

"Wassup lil bruh?" Jerrod said as he opened the door and I waked in after I gave him dap. I guess he could tell by the way I stormed in or how hard I hit his hand that something was wrong because by the time I made it to the family room to sit greet my nephews who were on the floor playing with cars as the watched the game, Jerrod was behind me with questions. "Wassup Sha? You look a little on edge my guy." Jerrod said as he walked up to me and I motioned at the kids.

"Boys, would y'all please go outside and play in the backyard for a while until I talk to uncle Sha? Y'all can even ride your 4-wheelers. With helmets and leave the curtains open so I can see y'all outside." Jerrod said as the boys got up and agreed before they ran outside. I sat down and watched Jerrod as he went over to open the curtains they had forgotten before I began my story.

"Maine big bruh, it seems every time shit going right in my life something goes wrong. Let me tell you about this bullshit." I began as Jerrod came around and sat down beside me and I told him everything. I watched Jerrod's usually calm and composed demeanor turn back to that of a gangsta like I remembered as a kid while I sat there with an evil expression on his face and his mind worked. After a few minutes it was like I could see the lightbulb in his brain go off and he stood up.

"Okay this what we're gonna do. You're gonna call that ole bitch ass pedophile nigga and tell him to be here tomorrow to get his 10 stacks. I'm gonna make sure all of my cameras inside and out are working tomorrow, matter of fact I'm gonna add some more in here. One is gonna be visible so he can't say he didn't know we have surveillance. You gonna let him come in and spill his fucking guts. Then after he does that you gonna make him wonna fight so I can come whoop his ass. Since he wonna play with 12 and ruin niggas lives like that damn Dense tried to do me, we gonna let him see how it feel. Muthafuckas in prison don't take kindly to pedophiles though. He'll find that out fast. You game?" Jerrod asked me as I stood up and shook his hand.

"Bet then bruh, its perfect. Be over here at noon regardless of when you tell him. Sunday is my day so Tisha and the kids are usually out until about nine at night. That gives us plenty time to get this bitch nigga. I got you lil bruh. Don't worry." Jerrod said as we dapped again then went outside to play football with the boys.

The rest of the day I thought about the plan until I pushed it to the back of my mind before I entered my apartment.

I got inside to find Lydia gone and that said she had to go home to her mother's house with my dad because her sister called her upset. I called her a dozen times with no answer before she finally picked up and told me Shaheim had done something to her sister Alysia but she wouldn't tell her what. I told her to come home right then and bring her sister too, but she said they wouldn't let her sister go and that she couldn't leave her.

I understood that from experience so I told her to barricade themselves in the room and for her to text me every hour. Once we hung up I freaked out for a second as I cried and punched the air while I imagined it was my father' face. I calmed down when I got a text from Lydia that said she was fine and they were locked in the room. After that I grabbed a bottle of vodka and took a few swigs before I dialed my dad's cell number.

As soon as he answered I said what I had to say and told him to meet me at my sister's by two if he wanted is money. I hung up before that bitch could answer and hit the bottle three more times before I fell asleep with vengeance on my mind. I woke up the next day at nine a.m. and began to clean up my apartment to keep my mind occupied. By the time 11 rolled around I was done, dressed, and headed out the door to meet my father. I pulled up to find Tisha was gone and Jerrod had parked his car in the garage. I parked in the driveway and went inside to find him in the living room as he rolled a blunt.

"Wassup lil bruh you ready? Is the pussy nigga really coming?" He asked as he handed me one of the blunts he had already rolled and I shook my head yes. "The pussy said he is and as money hungry as he is I know he should. I guess all we can do now is wait." I said to Jerrod and he finish rolling his blunt and we both lit ours at the same time.

We got high as a muthafucka as we waited on my dad and when he knocked on the door at two on the dot, I jumped up ready to end his bitch ass and slay a dragon of my own. "You got this bruh, remember get him to confess then make him made so I can beat him." Jerrod said as I nodded and he went to hide. I felt anxiety and anger build up in me as I walked to the door and opened it for my dad. As soon as he walked in he jumped with the shit as he stormed past me right into the family room.

"Yeah, yo lil bitch ass wised up fast, I guess you smarter than I thought. Anyway, nigga where my money. You up here in this mansion and shit all bougie. Muthafuckas got a camera like somebody wonna steal yo house. Nigga y'all still ain't shit but some dusty ass project kids. The offspring of a psycho, junky hoe. Hahaa!" My dad said as I felt fire burn behind my eyes. I almost forgot the plan and beat his ass but I quickly got my shit together and started to question him instead.

"I got yo money right here ole bitch ass nigga." I said as I pulled the 10 racks Jerrod had given me as decoy money out of my pocket. "I got it but you gotta tell me some shit first. Tell me you didn't know what my mama was doing to us all of those years. Tell me you haven't been hurting Lydia and Alysia since they have been in yo home. Tell me it wasn't yo intention to kill me, yo son when you brought them niggas to the Cottage and I almost got shot. Tell me nigga and you can take this money and walk away." I said as I held the money out and watched the evil smile spread across his face.

I watched him as he contemplated whether or not he would answer me truthfully as he examined the camera behind me. "Tell you huh? Truth or dare huh young nigga? Well, fuck it. I'm a tell yo lil bitch ass the truth because I don't care about you enough to lie. Hell yea I knew. I knew the bitch was crazy, she was beating y'all and selling them lil hoes pussy. I knew it all the entire time and pretended not to because it wasn't my business. I even snuck over there one night she has them hoes unconscious and got me a piece of those sweet pussies. I tell you that young hoe Tisha was the best." He said as I clenched my fists and fought that blind rage that pulsated through me.

I could imagine what Jerrod was doing as he sat in the next room and had to hear his wife's rapist brag with no remorse. In fact, he was happy as he spilled his guts. "Nigga I knew it all. I just felt sorry for you after the bitch tried to kill you the second time, by throwing you over the banister so I came to get you. I thought that check would be good and I could actually bond with you, like I had missed something but I quickly found out I was wrong. I found out you were every kind of retarded muthafucka she said you were. Now to get to what you really want to know, HELL, YEA, I been fucking yo bitch since y'all were 15 and I married her mama. I have my way with every pussy in my house. What the fuck are you gonna do about it?" He yelled as I had enough and rushed towards his ass.

I came at him like a runaway train, but that time he expected it and stepped to the side as he pulled a 9MM from under his shirt and aimed it right at my head. "Yeah, lil bitch nigga you thought you was gonna snuff me again, huh? Got me over here to confess on camera then try to whoop my ass huh? Lil retarded bitch I don't give a fuck about a confession because after I kill you and ransack this house I'm gonna take the tapes anyway bitch. You better hope me and my goons don't come back. I see its three little beautiful bitches I can have fun with up in here. You know like em' young and tender. You think I won't?" He asked me as tears fell from my eyes and I prepared to die.

"Yeah, cry lil bitch. Those the last tears you will shed. Tell yo maggot ass mammy I said hey when you get to hell." My dad said as he pulled the trigger and Jerrod busted in the room at the same time. The click from the gun as it got jammed was like music to my ears as I punched my father so hard he flew into the wall like a rag doll. Before I could get over there to work his ass out Jerrod was on him as he kicked and stomped him like a madman. I watched as teeth and blood flew everywhere a Jerrod continued to beat him with no mercy. I had to pull him away when he stomped his head into the china cabinet by the door and I noticed a big plug of meat fly out. "Bruh, bruh stop. Don't kill the bitch. Tisha will never forgive me if you go to jail. The 12 on the way I already pushed the alarm." I said as I felt Jerrod's tense body relax in my hands.

Minutes later sirens could be heard as Jerrod and I sat at the table and smoked a blunt of medical. We continued to sit there and smoke as the cops rushed in and we told them what had gone down. After that my dad was taken in and we were questioned before we were given a summons for court to testify. I felt like part of my hell was over though as I watched the police car with my father in it drive away. Once they were gone I helped Jerrod clean up the house then I thanked him before I went home. At home I texted Lydia, laid down, and unexpectedly fell asleep. I woke up at six the next morning to the sound of my phone ringing. When I answered it Lydia's voice poured over the line as her cries filled my ears and I sat up to talk.

"Lydia, what's wrong baby? Talk to me." I said as she cried and hiccupped before she was able to clearly tell me what happened. "Shaheim was arrested last night on several child molestation charges, mine and my sister's included. My mama went crazy on us. She put both of us out and now my sister is suicidal. What is she gonna do Sha? She has nowhere else to go. You know our brothers only care about themselves." Lydia said as she cried and I stared at the phone.

I couldn't believe she was questioning my loyalty after all we had been through. I had to prove to her that I was there for her no matter what. "She good baby, she can stay with us. I make enough money to take care of us all, don't worry about nothing. Your sister is my sister so there is no question of where she will go. Y'all just get her now. Do I need to come get y'all?" I asked Lydia as I reached over to grab my shoes and she told me I didn't have to because they had her sister's car.

"Oh baby thank you I love you Sha and I'm sure our baby will love you too. Okay, bye baby." Lydia said fast as she tried to rush me off the phone but I caught on. "Wait a minute, pump yo brakes. What the hell did you just say?" I asked her as my heart raced and I stood up to pace the floor. "I said your baby will too. I'M PREGANANT SHA!" Lydia said and my world turned from bleak to beautiful.

I cheered in her ear as she cried and I told her how much I loved her. I must have said that shit fifty times before she hung up the phone and I jumped around my living room and hunched the air like I was the man. All that excitement made me have to pee so I ran to the bathroom to relieve myself. Just as I walked back into the room with a big ass smile on my face my phone rang again and I thought it was Lydia. I answered the phone happy as hell, but as soon as I heard the voice my tone changed.

"Sha. Sha this your sister. I love you Sha. I just wanted you to know that. Tell Tisha and my kids I love them too. I called you for the address because I really have to send something." Terricka said in a slurred, drugged out voice that broke my heart.

I almost hung up in her face but the love for my sister no matter how fucked up she was wouldn't let me do it. I quickly gave her the address before I began to question her and she shut down. "Terricka I love you too, but where are you? Are you okay? Why you leave Buddy? Sister yo kids need you. Come to California Terricka. Will you." I begged my sister as I heard her do a dry, druggy laugh in the background.

I could almost see her all drugged and dirty as she swayed and held the phone to her ear. "Oh my saint little brother. He wants to save me just like Tisha. Baby ain't no saving me Sha so please let me go. All of y'all just let me go. Believe me my kids are better off without me just like we were better off without Denise. Hell, everyone's lives are better without me so just let me go. I'll be at peace soon anyway; free from pain, hurt, memories, and guilt. I'll be home soon Sha so don't worry. Anyway, bye and keep yo eyes on the mail for my gift." Terricka said before she hung up and I sat there and yelled her name.

When I hung up with her my heart dropped and I instantly called Tisha and told her what happened. I could hear extreme worry in her voice as she told me what I wanted to hear.

"I'm sending this information to Buddy right now so that he can go get her. He knows exactly where she is. He will hold her down until we get there. It's Monday now, so we can fly out Friday. Don't worry little brother. We will try again to save her.

We won't give up." Tisha said before we expressed our love to one another and hung up.

Once off the phone I cried like a baby until all my tears dried up. I couldn't help but to think my sister had given up and that was the last time I would hear her voice. I went into the bathroom and splashed water on my face before I looked at the man in the mirror. "Every time I'm occupied gathering the pieces of my shattered life, something else crumbles. I won't give up though. This curse will end." I said to myself as I prepared to fight the toughest battle of my life.

Chapter 9

Terricka: Slipping, Falling… I can't Get Up!

Tears fell from my eyes like water once I hung the phone up with my brother. I quickly jotted the address he gave me down on the big, yellow envelope I had in my hand before I staggered away from the porch I was on and towards the blue mailbox that sat on the corner. I scanned the blocked through swollen, bruised, and blood shot eyes as I looked up and down Watkins before I hit the corner where everyone could see me. I was not trying to run into Meech again when I had just barely escaped him hours earlier after he had me locked up and fucked up all night long.

That nigga put me through some real hostel shit for a funky ass eight ball of powder and twenty measly ass 30's. Hell, I knew I was wrong when I stole the shit but I never expected him to go as hard on me as he did. I could still feel how my heart raced when he walked in the room and I stuffed his shit down my pants. I could still feel that fear as I scurried up to the mailbox and dropped the envelope in and it was two hours after I had escaped. After I dropped the envelope off, I quickly dashed my ass down the street and into the store in front of Apple Tree Apartments as my memories and the voices took over me.

As I ran into the store and went to sit on the cooler in the back I often sat on, the voices in my head told me I was already dead so I should just commit suicide. They encourage me to kill everyone that hurt me and then myself as I softly whispered no and held my ears while I rocked back and forth on the cooler. I didn't even really speak to the store owner Cooley as he walked past and called my name because I was so wrapped up in my paranoia and the memories. Suddenly I felt like Meech's big, angry ass was right there in front of me again. I saw him as clear as day even though no one was there, yet I still trapped in the memory as I saw him when he lunged forward and snatched me up by my neck. I could still feel his hands all over me as he pounded me in the face while he kept one of his hands around my neck to shake and strangle me. "No Meech, I'm sorry. Here yo shit back." I yelled as he continued to punch and shake me while I stuck my hand into my stinky, dirty pussy and pulled out his sticky, crusted bags.

I pulled them out as he continued to choke me and lifted me up off my feet to shake me. His grip was so intense that my hands naturally flew up to my neck and the sticky bags flew right into his face. I guess he took that as disrespect like I did that shit on purpose because the bags flew right on to his lips and in his mouth. As soon as they did and the stench hit his nose he slammed my ass into the ground like a sack of potatoes. I could still fell him kick and stomp me as he yelled what a whore I was. He beat me until I passed out and when I woke up sometime later I was in a bath tub of ice cold water as he poured liquid soap and straight bleach on me while every cut and wound on my body burned.

"YOU NASTY, ROGGISH BITCH. YOU THREW THAT SHIT RIGHT IN MY MOUTH, OLE DISREPECTFUL, DIRTY HOE. AFTER ALL I HAVE DONE FOR YO BUM ASS YOU GO AND THROW ROTTEN PUSSY JUICES IN MY MOUTH? BITCH YOU GONNA PAY FOR THAT. I'M GONNA MAKE SURE YOUR NASTY ASS NEVER TRIES A NIGGA LIKE ME AGAIN. HOE YOU AIN'T GONNA WONNA SMOKE, SNORT, SHOOT, OR GET HIGH OR HOE AT ALL WHEN I'M DONE WITH YO MAGGOT ASS. IT'S GONNA BE SO MUCH SHIT STUCK IN EVERY HOLE YOU HAVE HOE, YOU AIN'T GONNA WONNA EVER SEE SHIT DICK SHAPED AGAIN. NOW WASH YO ASS BITCH." Meech yelled at me as tears ran down my swollen eyes and I used the rag he threw in the tub to wash my face.

I cried as I sat in the already dirty water and Meech chuckled while he watched me wash. I cried but not for what he thought. No, my mind was somewhere else. I know he thought I sat there and had tears in my eyes because he was gonna beat my ass some more and let his homies come over and gang rape me. Had I been an ordinary woman that would have been the cause of my tears. However, Meech didn't know that the pussy shit he was about to do to me was my mama's type of torture most of my life. That wasn't enough to make me cry because I knew his pussy ass wouldn't kill me even though I didn't give a fuck about death. No, that wasn't it.

As I sat there and scrubbed my body with the bath brush Meech gave me and liquid soap, I cried for all the dope I didn't get to use, but was about to be punished for. I cried for the additional bodies that would be on my conscious when I eventually merked Meech and whoever else he had to touch me. Most importantly I cried for the four little kids I brought into the world and would leave behind because I knew that the chain of events which were unfolding would lead me to one and one only solution. I knew that my end would be just as violent as my beginning I just hoped it would be on my terms and I could finish all I planned before then.

"Hurry up bitch cause I got real plans for you. Let that damn water out then standup and take a shower, wash all that damn dirt off. My niggas already ain't keen on fucking junky hoes. The least you could do is be a clean one. I mean you ain't ugly anyway and from what I heard you used to be a baddie, down ass bitch. Straight up GD and nice with them hands and a strap. I heard you fell off once your mama died and yo sister and brother jumped state. I guess that shit fucked you up huh? Well, that still ain't no excuse to steal from me and just be a bummy ass bitch now. Hoe they took yo kids too didn't it?" Meech asked as I shook my head yes as I looked down at the water.

"Yeah, you one of them worthless hoes so what I'm about to do to you ain't gonna matter anyway. Ain't nobody gonna miss yo nothing ass. I might as well do what I was gone do at first and rid the world of your scurvy ass. Might as well huh bitch?" Meech said as he laughed and then reach over to punch me in the mouth when I didn't respond. I held my lip that he busted on impact as the fresh blood dripped into the water and I fell straight into a flashback. Suddenly I was back in time and couldn't even really hear Meech as he yelled that I had ten minutes to finish before he left the room. I just remained in that position, frozen stiff in a daze trapped in a memory with my hands up to my mouth as blood dripped from between my fingers.

I closed my eyes as the memory seemed to embody me and I opened my eyes as 17-year-old Terricka back in the tub at my mother's house while the blood from my sore, battered, once virgin vagina tinted the bath water I sat in. I could still feel the pain between my legs from the ripped flesh as I cried my heart out. As I cried I vowed to one day kill my mother and make her feel the pain I did. I prayed out loud with conviction too and begged the Lord to give me a chance to help him exact vengeance on my mother.

"Please Lord punish Denise and let me help you. Make her pay for all she has done. I know my sister says it's not good to hate, but I hate her and I know you spite the devil that has manifested in your vessel so please Lord just take her away and make her accountable for her own sins." I prayed through my sobs as the door to the bathroom suddenly opened.

When that door opened I felt betrayed by God as Satan himself walked into the bathroom in the form of my mother. She had on a pair of red leather booty shorts and matching top on with red devil horns on her head. Although I knew that was one of her costumes for the trick she had in her room, I felt it was totally ironic at that moment. It was so ironic I laughed before I knew it, but in a cold, flat tone I barley recognized that caught me off guard. I guess it caught my mama off guard too because she suddenly turned to look at me with big eyes.

"Oh its funny huh bitch? It's funny? We'll see how funny it is in a minute. I heard you in here praying to that God you and your sister cherish so much, but let's see if he helps you now hoe. You wonna rid the world of me huh? You want your

God to punish me and make me pay for my sins huh? Bitch my biggest sin was you. YOU TERRICKA. Having you began my hell. Hell, you whole conception was a sin. I know you have heard so much from you grandma on how I was a hoe and all y'all have different daddies. I know you think you daddy some junky nigga I fucked while we were high out of our minds and Tisha daddy some gangsta nigga I drove away. Y'all wrong though." My mother said as she turned around and looked at me with hate and malice.

"YO DADDY WAS MY FUCKING GRANDFATHER AND MY MAMA KNEW IT. She pretended not to know her daddy liked little girls and would volunteers to keep all the girls in the family and never the boys because he wanted to have his way with us. She pretended she didn't know but she did. Even when I got older and would be beaten by him and held down by my uncles the point where I had bruises all over when I came home, she ignored it. So hell yeah, I ran away. I started to do any drug I could to get high and numb my pain. I hit the streets on my own at 15 after he beat and raped me so bad I bled for days. That was the day you were conceived. After that I was gone. I did so much shit while I carried you I just knew you would be born retarder or some shit, but you weren't. When I had you, you were perfect all beautiful and shit and I vowed to protect you no matter what and I did for a while. Then I met Tisha's dad and he showed me love. He loved me but something inside wouldn't let me accept that love." She said.

"By the time Tisha was born something had begun to change inside of me and the robots began to open my eyes to so much. I fought their help for a while and for a while we were happy, but then one day I just snapped. I snapped and he left and that's when everything became too much. All alone with two babies, no money, no education, no family, and these damn robots trying to help me, I fell into depression. They robots seemed to be the only thing I had so I listened to them. I listened and they showed me you were the root of it all. You started this curse so it must end with you." My mama said before she began to slice me with the cord from the curling iron she picked up off the bathroom counter.

She beat me like a runaway slave as blood flew all over the walls and her. I remembered how I screamed and cried while she beat me and I pulled my upper boy up and over the side of the tub. When I did that she wrapped her arm around my waist and jammed the curling iron she still had in her hand up my ass. I cried and bucked as she sodomized me with the curling iron in between punches to my back and head while she yelled how much she hated me and the curse had to end. Once she was out of breath and tired she let my battered, bloody body fall back into the tinted water as I cried and stared at her with hate.

"See that look you giving me right now proves what I thought. Bitch you just like me. You're just as evil and the true cause of the curse. If I go by that bible I hear y'all quote that means you're an abomination that has to be purged. I hate I have to be the one to do it but regardless of my ties to you, I have to end this." My mother said as I sobbed and watched her walk two feet over to the counter and plug in the curlers she had just sodomized me with.

I had no idea what she was about to do as I sat there and sobbed while every inch of my body burned or throbbed with pain. I begged her to stop as she turned to walk back to me but that dead look in her eyes told me that my mother was gone. It was the drugs and mental illness that beat and hurt me not her but I really saw no difference.

"Please mama. TISHAAA." I yelled as she walked closer while she swung the curlers from side to side. "Don't please mama, me now bitch when you just prayed the lord would kill me. Now you want mercy. Fuck you!" My mother yelled as she pretended to throw it, but quickly pulled it back.

I felt my heart stop when she did that because I could just feel myself being electrocuted if she would have let those curlers go. I cried as my heart raced and I closed my eyes to brace myself and my mother laughed. "Look at your tough ass now, scared as shit. Well, good bye evil little bitch. Goodbye to you and your curse." My mama yelled as her voice was suddenly cut off and I opened my eyes to see Tisha on the ground on top of my mother.

My little sister had bust in and tackled her right before she threw the curlers into the tub. She had saved my life. I quickly jumped out as my mother punched and kicked until she got up then she beat us both with the curling iron that was hot and still plugged into the wall. "Nooo, mama I remembered I yelled in my flashback as Meech suddenly grabbed me by the arm and pulled me out of the shower, which brought me back in time.

He snapped me out of my flashback and I was back there in his trap house as he pulled me naked by my arm and hair into his living room. When he pulled me inside I got a little scared when I saw all of the big, ugly niggas who waited with their dicks in hand. After that I blocked everything out, much like I did that memory of when my mother said I was the root of the curse. I blocked out all of the dicks and foreign objects they stuck into every orifice on my body as the robots told me that was my fate but I could end it all if I did what my mother had tried to do. The only thing I didn't block out and could still feel as I sat there on the cooler in the corner store, hours after the attack was Meech's hand on my arm as he held me down. "Terricka. Terricka!" Cooley yelled as he shook me by my arm and brought me out of my memory within a nightmare.

I opened my eyes and looked into his face as my heart still raced in my chest. "Damn Terricka, what's wrong with you today? You're even more fucked up than you usually are? What the hell happened to yo face?" Cooley asked me as I turned to the left and stared at my swollen, bruised face in the beer box.

He was right I did look fucked up, just like a drugged out zombie with my swollen and battered face, dull, dry skin, and disheveled appearance. I grimaced when I looked at myself because no matter how bad shit had gotten I had never looked like that. "What the fuck did happen to me?" I asked myself out loud as I jumped off the cooler and walked closer to stare at myself in the glass on the beer box.

I stuck my hands in my hair and turned my head from side to side as I looked at myself, just like a crazy person would. "That's what the fuck I just asked you Terricka. What the fuck happened to you? Anyway, whatever happened you gotta get the fuck up outta here because you running off my customers. Besides I don't want Meech in her tearing shit up and I already heard you on his bad side. Sooo Bye Felicia." Cooley said as I continued to stare at myself I the cooler and the voices in my head got louder. "FUCK YOU COOLEY! I'M OUT THIS BITCH OLE UGLAS!" I yelled as I stormed to the front of the store as the robots in my head told me to buck.

On my way out of the store I knocked down rows of cookies and candies, grabbed a big bag of chips, and opened them before I poured the entire bag on the counter. "Terricka you raggedy bitch!" Cooley yelled as he ran around the corner and chased me out of the store. I laughed as I ran out and crossed the street with old times on my mind. I saw me and my sister as girls as we ran around the same corner after we stole soap and food from that exact store. "See Tisha, I told you we would get away." I said to my sister as she ran beside me and we both laughed.

I ran all the way up to the first street non-stop as I continued to laugh with my sister when suddenly her laughter stopped. I looked to the side to see what was wrong and like a ghost, Tisha was gone. "TISHAAA." I yelled as I spent around in a circle and looked for her behind bushes and in people's yards. "TISSHHHAAA. Why you keep leaving me? You're gonna miss me when I'm gone." I yelled to the wind as people in the cars that whizzed by me stared while I talked to myself.

Suddenly the voices in my head filled my ears again and I couldn't take what they had to say. They told me I was about to lose it and they were the only friends I had left. The voices said to kill Meech and his goons then out myself so I wouldn't feel anymore and that's exactly what I wanted to do. I mobbed down the street with murder on my mind, the voices in my head, and an itch that started from my toes and worked its way up. That was an itch I hated but loved at the same time because I needed my cocaine to function. That's why I knew I had to abort my mission momentarily and get to Millington with Tangie to load up and get my mind right. That would calm the voices and give me the strength I needed to do what needed to be done.

"Yeah, let's call Tangie." I said to myself as I pulled out my phone and one of the semi-logical voices in my mind told me not to get high and for a second I listened. I fought the urge to snort until I couldn't anymore and possibly fill my veins with the drug I craved. It was the only thing that made me feel sane sometimes and I wanted it. I wanted it but I listened to the voices as I walked up the hill and entered Breezy Point. I staggered to my apartment still in a daze as horrible visions from the past and my own guilt threatened to drive me deeper into insanity.

When I got close to my apartment just the sight of it made me weak because for a second I was sane enough to remember what I had done. For a second I saw myself when I came back from my binge once Tisha had bonded me out and I got my kids back from Sky. I saw myself as I did good for a couple of days and then everything went downhill. After that I saw the day they came to take my kids and I flapped around the floor like a fish out of water and cried. I saw their little faces as I walked up to the door and tried to turn the knob only to notice there was a padlock on the door.

"WHAT THE FUCK? WHY THE FUCK IS THERE A PADLOCK ON MY DOOR? WHO THE FUCK IN HERE? VITO, BITCH OPEN THIS MUTHAFUCKING DOOR!" I yelled as I banged on and kicked the door. I stood there for minutes and beat like a madwoman until finally the man from next door came out to tell me what was going on. "WHO THE FUCK OUT HERE BAMMING?" the drunk man named Doug next door said as he came out on the porch in late November with a wife beater on and boxers.

I watched him and laughed as he swayed from side to side while I did the same and it seemed we both did our best to focus. "Oh Terricka it's you. Witcho crazy ass. What the fuck you want girl? Why you out here beating and shit?" He asked me as he lifted the fried chicken leg that dangled from his hand and bit it like a starving dog.

I rolled my eyes at him as I folded my arms and looked his dumb as from head to toe. I Didn't know what the fuck he meant by why I was there? Hell I was there because it was my house and I was ready to go home, bathed and then hit the streets to get high before I ended it all. "What you mean ole drunk muthafucka, this my house. Where the fuck Vito at and why he lock my damn door?" I asked Doug through clenched teeth as I took a Newport out of my pocket and lit it.

I inhaled the stale nicotine deeply and blew the smoke out in Dough's direction as he staggered across to my porch so that he was right in front of me. He stood there in my face for a few minutes with a smug expression on his face. "Oh…you don't know do you? Witcho ole crackhead ass, talking about I'm drunk. I'd rather be a drunk than a fuck up. First you get yo kids taken now you ain't go nowhere to stay." Doug said as I looked at him like he had lost his damn mind.

I had to step back a little then step back up almost nose to nose with him to try to understand what he said. "What the fuck you just say ole man?" II asked Doug as I clenched my left fist and hit my cigarette with the other. One of the voices in my head told me to hit his old ass since he wanted to test my gangsta. However, I was too preoccupied with what he had just said to even listen to the voices.

"You heard me bitch. You know they took yo kids, but I guess you didn't know yo ass put out huh?" He said in a sing song like a little kid who had just snitched on the other. I shook my head no to let him know I had no idea I was put out as he shook his head in disbelief. "You mean to tell me nobody ain't told you what went down at yo place?" He asked me as I stared at him and shook my head no again before he took my hand.

I let him pull me over to the edge of the porch before I sat down on the top step right next to him and concentrated on the silence beyond the voices. When we sat down he put his wrinkled, dirty hand over mine and looked at me lovingly and with a glimmer of pity for the first time. We usually went back and forth about who was the worst person and cursed each other out like sailors whenever we saw one another, but not then.

Even on my bad days when I couldn't get high or the voices were just too powerful I would attack him if he even looked at me wrong. This day was different though and that was what scared me the most. I didn't want him to be nice to me because in all actuality I was a piece of shit. I didn't want him to be nice to me at that moment because I felt like it was a cushion for a shit storm of hurt that was on its way. I was right too and he proved it when he opened his mouth.

"I hate to be the one who tells you this Terricka, but Vito is dead. While you was gone somebody came over her and shot this house up. Vito got shot and two other niggas. Some girl even drug the Meeka bitch up out yo house and stomped her in the ground. I heard some people say the girl was yo sister but you know I don't listen to these messy hoes over here. Anyway, after that and they couldn't find you the office put a stay out notice on the door and padlocked it. It's been like that for a minute. Terricka you know this mean you can't get Section-8 again so what you gonna do? How you gonna get yo kids back?" Doug asked me as everything he said swirled around in my head.

I didn't want to believe what he said as I sat there dazed, but I knew it was gonna come anyway because I had already gotten locked up. That automatically kicked me off of all forms of public assistance, which meant even if I wasn't a crazy ass bitch, I still wouldn't have been able to take care of my kids. Either way it went homeless or still in subsidized housing, I knew that my reign of terror had come to an end and it was over for life as I knew it, and at that point I was okay with that. I quickly stood up and walked off the porch as Doug called my name behind me. "TERRICKA. TERRICKA! WHAT YOU

DOING? WHERE THE HELL ARE YOU GONNA GO?" Doug yelled behind me as I began to slow down while I laughed.

I turned around to face Doug as tears ran down my cheeks. I didn't even know why I had tears in my eyes as I stood there and leaked like a stripper. Maybe it was because I knew that there really was no purpose for me living or maybe it was simply because I was crazy as fuck. Whatever the reason was, I stood there and cried my last tears as Doug looked on with pity. "I'M GOING TO HELL DOUG. STRAIGHT TO HELL. DON'T WORRY, I WON'T BE ALONE THERE LIKE I WAS HERE. I'LL FINALLY BE REUNITED WITH MY MAMA." I said before I laughed a deeper laugh and Dough looked at me crazy before I turned around and walked off.

I could hear him call my name and tell me he would help as I continued to walk towards the exit of the apartments. I walked out without even a glance back as my mind and body went blank, but the pain in my heart raged on. I did a silent cry with no tears or words for Vito as I turned the corner on to Delano and walked back towards the store. Halfway down the block I took another cigarette out of my pocket and lit it right before my phone began to ring.

I slowly took the phone out of my pocket as I dreaded who would be on the other end. Once I looked at the ID and saw Buddy's number, I changed my mind and fought through the cloud of crazy in my brain. I shook off the hate and the horrible visions of all the things I had done to him. I hated the fact that I always hurt him the worse than he ever hurt me, and at that moment I wanted to change that.

I wanted to apologize to him for leaving when he was at work, and for the fact I took his grandfather's ring out of his draw. I wanted to apologize and to ask him to forgive me so that we could be a family again. I figured I had hit rock bottom so there was nowhere to go but up if I had him by my side like the old days. I knew that with him there to love me I could get control of my meds and even leave the drugs alone. That's why I fought the voices with all I had as I sat down on the curb in front of someone's house, cleared my mind, and answered the phone. I put on my best, I'm better now, Terricka voice as I waited for the caller to respond.

"Hello." I said in a singsong voice as someone grunted on the other end. I waited a few seconds as the person just held the phone and breathed then I spoke again. "Hello, Buddy? Don't be playing on my phone bae. Say something baby daddy." I said as I giggled and the person on the other end had obviously had enough.

Suddenly I heard a female's voice on the other end as she growled then sucked her teeth. "Bae? Bae? Bitch ain't no bae for you over here. Listen up ole crazy junky bitch because I am only going to say this once. Bitch this is Melissa, Rodney's fiancé, and I am soooo tired of you. I'm tired of your junky ass fucking up. I'm tired of your bipolar ass being needy. And frankly bitch I'm just tired of you, kids included. My man has told me everything about yo maggot ass and I cannot see how he fucked with a nothing ass bitch like you in the first place." The girl said as I laughed and she tried to dig deeper to push my buttons.

"Laugh now bitch but you will cry later. Hoe you are an unfit, junky ass mammy who beats her kids and stay gone for weeks at a time. Hoe, you are the scum of the earth. Now I see why he left you. Bitch, I don't care what y'all had T-E-RR-I-C-KA, that's in the past bitch because I'm the future. Now I advise you not to call my man ever again and don't be expecting him to sweep in again like captain save em and whisk you away… Bitch please. All of that shit is over. We gonna get custody of yo dusty ass kids, the two that are his anyway, IF they are his, and then we will be done with you forever. Soooo just go smoke yo life away bitch. Just gone commit suicide cause you doing the same thing fucking with my man because I will body you bitch. You understand?" The girl Melissa yelled into the phone as I sat on the curb and fumed on the inside as wondered who she thought she was talking to.

On the outside I was totally calm as I sat there and listened to the bitch laugh as she waited on my response and thought she had gotten under my skin. I wanted so badly to go off and tell that bitch how I was unfazed by all of the shit she said but I was gonna cut her heart out just for acting tough. However, I chose to stay quiet and just show her instead. I let the voices advise me on the best way to get her as I sat there silent and she began to grow impatient as she waited on my response.

"Uhhh bitch I know yo junky ass heard me. Do you understand or do I have to say it in retard? Ter-ric-ka. STAY AWAY FROM MY MAN OR I WILL KILL YOU!" Melissa said slowly as she slurred each syllable like she had a speech problem.

I sucked in my breath and held in the screams and curses inside of me as a wicked smile spread across my lips and visions of her blood on my hands filled my mind. "Okay bitch I gotcha. Guess what, I'll see you soon." I said calmly as I heard her gasp on the other end then I hung up the phone in her face.

As soon as I hung up I screamed and growled like a mad woman as I threw my phone in the grass and began to pull up flowers out of the ground at the house I sat in front of. I went crazy on the plants as I dug up soil with my hands and threw pots into the streets. I screamed and destroyed shit until someone came out of the house and asked me what the fuck I was doing. When I heard that I picked up my phone without turning around to look at them and then dashed towards the corner in a full sprint. By the time I got back to the store I was out of breath and dirty from head to toe.

I didn't give a fuck about that though all I wanted to do was get buzzed and forget about all my pain. I wanted to forget I had no kids, no place to stay, no sister and brother, no mother, no father, no Vito, and probably no Buddy either. For the first time I was really all alone like I always said and that shit was a hard pill to swallow. All I wanted to do was not feel. That's why I waited until a big group of boys went into the store and snuck in behind them where Cooley couldn't see me. Once inside I filled the legs of my jogging pants and coat with Bud Lights and Four Loco's.

That wasn't the high I was looking for but I knew it would do the trick until I got to Tangie and got on. The only thing I had to do was get out of the store. I got my perfect opportunity to scape when an old drunk last began to argue with Cooley at the counter of $.46 and started to throw shit across the room. As soon as I saw him and his brother Jeff come from around the counter to put her out I bolted straight to the door. I ran fast as I could with 15 cans of beer down my pants and more in my coat. I almost made it out unseen too until one can fell out and rolled across the floor. As soon as that happened Cooley looked up and mouthed the words funky bitch as I laughed out loud at him.

"The funky bitch is the bitch that had you." I yelled back as I jolted out and around the building. I could hear him yell and his footsteps hit the ground behind me as I ran out of his lot and right into the Apple Tree Apartments that sat right behind the store. As soon as I was safe behind the gate I stopped as Cooley stopped too. I knew he wouldn't chase me in the store because his bitch ass was scared to get jumped and robbed so I stood there and taunted him.

"Ahh Hahh Coley fuck you and these cheap ass beers." I said as I took one out of my pants, popped the top, and drunk it down in a matter of seconds. "Fuck you Terricka junky bitch you will get yours. You already dead anyway." Cooley said as he shook his head and waved me off. "You right muthafucka I am and soon a lot of other muthafuckas will be too." I yelled as I threw the can I had in my hand at him and took out another to open.

I drunk that second beer down fast too as I felt it go straight to my head. After that I called Tangie and told her to come get me. That bitch flexed for a minute all high and shit as she talked about her boyfriend needed gas. That's when I hit the bitch with the words she wanted to hear.

"Bitch I got cash. Meech caught up to me yesterday so I was over there getting money. Then he fucked up and showed me where he stashed his shit so I took all I could find, but his bitch ass walked in and caught me. He beat the fuck out of me after that and called the niggas to train my ass. I woke up at about 7 this morning bloody and fucked up. Before I snuck out that bitch though I found his re-up money and took all that shit. Hoe I got over $600 in my hand right now and I want to dope it all." I said out loud as I swayed from side to side while I counted the money and stashed the other $1500 I didn't tell her about. I could hear Tangie tell her boyfriend what I said on the other end before she got back on the phone.

"Say no more. Where you at?" She asked as I told her then sat back down to drink some more. After about 15 minutes of sitting there and drinking while I smoked one cigarette after the other, Tangie and her boyfriend Link, a dread head heroin addict, robber, pulled up and I hopped in. From the second I got in the car I started to get high as Tangie passed me the crack pipe she was about to hit. "Here we ain't got no powder, we finna go get it though. Hit this. It's the same damn thang." She said as I shrugged and put the pipe into my mouth before I lit it.

I hit that shit hard too as the thick white smoke invaded my lungs and sent me on a trip I had never been on before. All of the voices around me even the ones in my head seemed to slow down as soon as I inhaled the dope and everything was a blur. It stayed like for three days too, while I remained lost in my hurt, insanity, and a cloud of drugs. I did everything I could to mask my pain as I spent most of my $600 loot.

When Thursday afternoon rolled around I woke up in Millington at a nasty ass hotel butt naked on the floor as Tangie, Link, and three more dudes laid out sleep everywhere else in the room. As soon as I opened my eyes I quickly jumped up, dressed, and quietly searched the room. Within minutes I found an assault rifle, bullets, heroine, and the keys to the junky car someone had pawned Link and he picked me up in. Once I gathered my shit I snuck out the room and hopped in the car. I pulled off the lot as soon as I crunk up the car and headed back to Frayser. Since my drug haze was gone the voices and bipolar tendencies were back and they were out for one thing and that one things was blood.

"I'm about to fuck all their lives around starting with that bitch Meech. I hear y'all. I know what to do. Soon this will all be over. You hear that mama. Soon I will be right there with you to prove bitch I'm nothing like you. I'm woman enough to kill myself and end my kids pain." I yelled to myself as I looked in the rearview mirror and turned down Frayser Blvd.

I was back in the hood in minutes as I strolled the track and tried to find out where Meech and his crew had crashed. Soon I saw one of my smoking buddies named Trish in front of Cooley's store and I drove down on her. "Yo Trish. Where Meech nem at?" I asked her as she ducked down to see who I was then ran over to the car.

Within seconds she told me where they were, I gave her a $1 bill, and then I headed straight to the house on Brook Meade where they were. I pulled three houses down and parked the car before I got out and tucked the fully loaded weapon down the front of my coat. My mind and the voices in my head moved a mile a minute as I walked up to the door and thought about what I would say to get in. I started to knock and play like I was gonna beg, but something told me to check the knob first. When I did that bitch turned and like a beast I was on go. I slipped in and closed the door behind me as I quickly scanned every room of the 1-bed room house. I found Meech big ass in the back room with his strap on the bed and quickly retrieved that bitch before I went back up front.

As soon as I was back in the living room I began to fire shots into the sleeping bodies of the three niggas in the living room. I shot off a dozen rounds into those bitches as feathers and blood flew through the air. By that time, I could hear Meech yell from the bedroom followed by his footsteps as he ran to the door with his hidden strap in hand. He didn't even get a chance to get a shot off though because before he could even think I lit his ass up. I shot him until the gun was empty then I threw that bitch on the floor and picked up the other gun he had. I walked out of there that morning, in broad daylight with blood all over me and gun in hand. I didn't even care as I walked slowly to my car and people all around screamed and called the police. I knew that I was going to die anyway so I didn't give a fuck about who knew it was me.

I hopped in the car and rode towards Rodney 's house in silence as the conversation with me and his fiancé replayed in my head. I wanted nothing more than to see that bitch die as I drove towards their cute, three-bedroom house in Raleigh right by the hotel I was gonna hide out in. When I pulled up on their block I left the car at the end of the street as I got out and hit the pipe filled with heroine I had just prepared. When I inhaled that shit I got times higher than the crack and lost all reasoning and sanity. I was like a deranged lion as I stalked up the driveway and got a glimpse of Melissa as she cleaned her living room. I wasted no time as I kicked the little, fragile ass front door and barged right into her perfect world.

"Yeah bitch remember me?" I asked as I stood there in front of Melissa and she looked shocked and scared shitless with her tall model looking ass. She was pretty as fuck, I had to admit as I pointed both of my guns at her. She was cute but that didn't mean shit while I had the scrap to her head. "Who are you? What did I do? What do you want?" She said as I began to laugh and walked right up to her face. "I'm the crazy, junky, baby mama you told to go kill herself so now its yo turn bitch. Kill yoself." I said as I laughed and she began to cry harder. I ignored her cries and pleas though as the voices in my head said do her. "Nah don't kill yoself, let me do it. Bye Bitch!" I said as I shot Melissa six times with each gun and left her full of holes.

As soon as I did that and the smoke cleared I was gone and so was my mind. I don't even remember how I got to the hotel but the next thing I knew it was after midnight on Friday and I was lie face down in the hotel bed. I felt nauseous and weighed down as all of my thoughts fears emotions and memories hit me at once and I wanted to break down and cry. Instead I got up and dressed before I went to the store around the corner to grab breakfast and another big, yellow envelop. Inside the store I waited in line as the local news played on a small tv on the desk. I listened as the female news reporter talked about murder after murder I had committed and I remembered when I had been in that situation before. I remembers how I had watched the news for days after I killed my mother just to confirm she was really dead. That's when her face popped up in my mind, vivid and so clear I thought I could reach out and touch her as I grabbed the girl in front of me.

I apologized to the girl as I gathered my shit well enough to purchase my sausage breakfast plate and envelope then I left the store. Back in my room I ate and then filled then began to dismantle the childen's book with voice recognition in to conceal the money I was sending. I filled the book to the brim before I recorded a message and told my kids how sorry I was and how much I loved them. After that I laced it in the envelope, sealed and addressed it, then took it to the hotel office to be mailed. Once back in the room I called Buddy as I hit the glass pipe I had grown to love.

"Hey Terricka. Where are you? I need to talk to you as soon as I got back in town." Buddy said as soon as he answered the phone. I sat there and listened for a minute as he pretended to know nothing about his bitch calling me or her murder. The voices told me he knew but was setting me up. I just didn't give a fuck. I quickly told him where I was at and then he said he would be there about 9 when he got in town. After I told him I loved him I hung up the phone and went into the bathroom to prepared.

I bathed while I thought of my plan then decided to go get kerosene when I was dressed. Once I got that I went back to my room where I smoke for hours on end until I passed out. The heavy knocks on the door at around 8;45 woke me up and jumped up still kinda high and ready to end it all. I quickly rushed over to the door and let Buddy in as he instantly hugged me up in his arms and I looked over his shoulder into the parking lot. I expected cops to barge in right then but they didn't and I felt relieved I could still go through with my plan. As soon as he came in I invited him to sit down as I poured him a glass of heroine laced vodka as I went to the bathroom. I stood and stared at myself in the mirror and Denise's face appeared as she told me not to do it.

"Fuck you." I whispered to her before I turned to walk out of the door and heard buddy get off the phone with someone. I wondered if her called the police as I came back into the room and sat down next to him with a curious look on my face. "Terricka baby wassup? I been looking for you. What happened why you leave me?" He asked as he looked sincerely into my eyes.

I felt conflicted as I looked into the eyes of the only man I loved and the sane part of me wanted to make up while the crazy side encouraged me to end us both. I tried to shake all the voices as I closed my eyes and breathed deeply but nothing would work. "Buddy I just have to ask you a question and I need you to be honest. Are you engaged?" I asked as he closed his eyes and sat back with a sad look on his face.

I knew the answer to my question right then and I felt sick in my stomach but relieved that I had already set my plan in motion. I didn't even wait for Buddy to answer before I fired another question at him and watched him begin to sway in his seat. "So Buddy, is it true that you said you're tired of saving me? Am I a lost bitch you want to leave you alone?" I said to him as tears fell from my eyes and he fought to keep his open.

As I looked at his slumped posture I could tell right then the drugs were working and Buddy was about to be out. That's why I rushed him to answer me and prepared to send us both to hell. "Maine Terricka why you questioning me like this, that's that shit that made me leave. Yea, that's my fiancée and sometimes I get tired of saving yo broken ass but I still love you. Terr…" Buddy said in a slurred but forceful tone before he suddenly passed out.

When he did I wasted no time as I got up and began to pour kerosene all around the room and on both of us. After that I sat down at the table and smoked all of the heroine I had left and drunk the rest of Buddy's drink. Within two minutes I began to hallucinate and saw Denise as she sat next to me on the couch. That shit scared the fuck out of me after I reached over to touch her and felt her warm skin. I ran over to the bed and jumped in it to pull the covers over my head as she called my named. I yelled out for it to stop as she kept talking and I found the matches in my pocket.

Suddenly I couldn't hear her voice anymore only the voices in my head as they told me to do it. I jumped up in that instant and ran over to the couch and struck and match before my feet even stopped. Without any thought I threw it over the couch right on to Buddy and he burst into flames. I stood there for a second and watched him burn as his body twitched and he moaned. Then suddenly Denise's voice was back as she called my name. I turned around to see her but no matter what direction I turned to she wasn't there.

My hands trembled as I grabbed another match and struck it as she called my name again. I didn't notice until it was too late but that time the voice came from outside the room. I never waited to find that out though as I threw the match on my head and I was engulfed in flames. Through the searing pain and my own screams, I could hear my name as Sha and Tisha yelled it from the other side of the hotel door. I tried to open my mouth to yell, but flames went down my throat and everything went black. That was the end I had searched for. The end of the Lewis curse!

Part 4

Releasing The Sin

Chapter 10

Epilogue
Cycle Broken: No More Sins

The sun shined brightly as it poured through the window in the vitiation room at Shelby County Jail East- Women's Correctional Facility. It was so warm and inviting I almost forgot the somber occasion we were there for. I looked over at my eight kids as smiled as they talked quietly to one another or squirmed in their seats. I had to stop for a minute and smile at the happy bunch of well-rounded kids they had become. My two nieces Tania and Talaya sat quietly to the side far away from where the inmate sat. At eight and nine years old they had grown into beautiful, soft spoken girls who loved everything except that bi-monthly visit to the prison. I sued to have to fight them to come but after a while they stopped resisting the evitable. Instead they would just sit there and say nothing like they weren't even in the room.

My nephews Rodney Jr, and Ryan were different though they looked forward to the visits to vent. As ten and eleven-year-old young men they had lots of questions every time and weren't afraid to ask them. A'Miracle was always full of questions too, but in her soft delicate way. As a twelve-year-old mature young woman she always tried to be polite but express how she felt. She would ask questions then give her opinions and forgive in the same breath. Then she would fade into the background to either comfort Tania and Talaya or take care of my three youngest kids; Jerrod, III who was four and the twins Janaye and Jaylene who were just about to turn two. She as Sha would help me after their time to talk and often take the kids out to the car to divert their frustrations.

I on the other hand, was always very talkative whenever I was there and this time was no different. The only difference was I didn't allow anyone to leave not even Lydia with Sha, Jr. who hated to sit still or Jerrod who just hated to go be there period. No, I made them al stay to help celebrate even if they didn't want to.

I held my breath as the doors to the holding area opened and I watched the guard wheel my sister towards the table. I noticed as other people in the visitation room cringed and whispered among themselves as she was wheeled down the aisle and they got a good look at the grotesque burns that covered her entire body. In five years most of the wounds had healed, however; the emotional scars were still so fresh they were visible in her eyes. They were still fresh for me too. I could barely look at her without breaking down after I thought about all she had done to others and herself. It was a week after she set herself and Buddy on fire in that hotel room before I found out she killed five other people before that. I was devastated when I found that out, just about as devastated as I was when Sha and I kicked the hotel door in and the flames inside came flying out. I could see her as she rolled on the floor engulfed in flames and like a fool I ran in to get her.

I ran in against my better judgement all because I loved my sister more than anything and I wore the scars to prove it. I had a similar burn to Terricka's down the center of my back to my waist and one on my right arm. That didn't matter to me though because I had managed to get her out. I didn't think she would live though when I saw how her skin peeled off and dripped on to the ground and left skin patches everywhere she rolled. All I could do was pray and cry as Sha ran off to get the ambulance. Moments later they were on the scene and she was loaded on to a stretcher. She spent five months in the hospital's burn unit, barely alive behind that, but miraculously she survived what doctors never thought she would.

Even though she lost her left eye, an ear, and could barely talk from the flames that went down her throat, my sister lived and was now about to celebrate her 31st birthday behind bars, where she would remain for the rest of her natural life. Just going to see her there knowing that she would never get out was just as hard as seeing her recover and knowing that she was recovering from an act she committed on herself. All of that was just as hard for me as it was for my family, but I sucked it up a put on a brave face because she was my sister. She was my sister and she had done something none of us could have ever done. She ended the curse and released us all from our personal hell, pain, and guilt. It was a harsh reality that sometimes sounded cruel, but when Terricka did what she did, she really did end the curse.

From the day my family and I returned to California after Buddy's funeral life got nothing but better. The kids began to excel in school and Jerrod and I became closer than ever. A'Miracle was ecstatic because she had other kids around and I even expanded my company into a multimillion dollar empire. The happiness didn't end there either because Sha and Lydia got married a month later and she had Shamel, Jr. a perfectly healthy 10 pound baby boy shortly after. Sha advanced quickly at my company and became a board member after several of his graphics sold for millions and he helped us gain some of the top authors in the country. Jerrod also expanded his business to three other states and on his days off got me knocked up with three more bundles of joy.

Everything in our lives flourished after that and I can't help but think that was mostly in part to Terricka. Not only did I receive those envelopes full of money she sent and used that money to invest in a newer book printer and advances for better authors, it doubled so fast I reinvested some in Jerrod's company and added substantial amounts to all of the kids' college funds. It was like she knew what we would need before we did and she sacrificed her life so that we could be good financially. She helped me and Sha out a lot mentally and emotionally too when we read the contents of the first envelope she sent us. That's when we found out all about our mother's past and the true identity of Terricka's father. I can still remember how Sha and I cried and held each other as we apologized to the mother we never understood.

After reading that and a heartfelt letter from Terricka that expressed her love and her own personal regret, somehow Sha and I were able to let everything go and look forward to new beginnings. We figured it was like Terricka said in her letter, we had lived through too much bad to give up right before the good. So we kept fighting and living. That's why I felt like I owed my sister the world and I would still be there no matter. That's why every year I brought her a birthday cupcake whether she ate it or not. This year was no different as I watched a tiny smile cover her lips as the officer parked her in front of me. I could still see a glimmer of the Terricka she once was sparkle in her eyes as she looked at me then everyone else in the room. I looked at the guard to make sure it was still okay for each of us to give her a birthday hug like usual and he nodded as I stood up and motioned for all of the kids to get up one by one.

I watched as Sha, Jerrod, and A'Miracle hugged and kissed her after they said happy birthday and whatever else they had to see, and her four stood in the back with my babies. After that me and my little babies walked over and kissed and greeted her quickly before I handed them off to Jerrod and stood back to watch the kids. I had been waiting for years for the breakthrough the psychiatrist said they would have in which they would finally feel the love and loss for their mother. I hadn't seen it yet so I was unsure if it would come as they all walked up to her slowly. Rodney Jr led the pact as usual with his tall lanky self as he tried to look strong and serious. I could see the emotion in his face though as he bent down to hug her and I knew we had finally reached that breakthrough.

"Happy birthday mama. I love you so much and I forgive you. Can you forgive me?" Rodney Jr. said as he wept and buried his head in Terricka's chest.

I watched as tears ran down my sister's face and she did her best to hug her son with her deformed hands as she kissed the top of his head. "I …Love you…too son." Terricka managed to say in a voice just about a whisper as all of her other kids ran over to hug her with tears in her eyes.

I stood back and cried softly as I watched Ryan go up and tell her happy birthday profess his love and how much he missed her followed by Tania. Tanis cried the entire time and kept hugging her but she managed to say the same thing. When it became time for the smallest one to talk, Talaya the little genius, I watched her closely as she walked up with the voice activated story book Terricka sent that was filled with money. She clutched the book to her chest as she walked up and hugged Terricka around the neck. I watched my sister rub her back as tears ran down her face. I couldn't stop my tears either as she told her mother she loved her and missed her more than everything and that she would always remember her through the book. Then she opened it so that we could all hear Terricka's voice.

"Hello my babies, this is mommy and I am just sending this to tell you all I love you very much... I know sometimes it's hard for you to believe that because mommy is so mean but please know baby that was not because of you or anything you did. It was because mommy is sick. Mommy is sick so I am going away but I want you to always know I will look over you. I love you all with all of my heart and although there will be some hard fact coming your way really soon I want you know you have to be strong. No matter what know that you were loved and that I always loved you. So when you start missing me look in the wind and open this book. Remember this song my babies and let it be your strength." Terricka's voice blasted through the speaker of the book and tears continued to fall from her eyes and Talaya wiped them off.

"Nothing is forever what we're hoping for,
No more pain so don't you cry anymore.
Hold your head up high and dry yo tears,

Let me help you through and erase yo fears.
We'll overcome it all if we stick together,
We just gotta believe nothing lasts forever (nothing
lasts forever)."

My sister sang as we all joined in and then everyone hugged her again. Soon after that we sung her happy birthday and she blew out the candle on her cupcake. We all laughed and joked as she ate her cake for the first time and we saw a slight smile on her deformed face. When the guard and siren announced visitation was over I sent the family ahead as I said my one last goodbye. I bent down in front of my sister and looked in her eyes as I saw her love look through me.

"I love you Tisha and I thank you for never giving up on me. For a long time, I thought, maybe I'm just like my mama, and I became that. I know now I was never her. I know now I don't have to carry her sins just like you shouldn't carry mine. Be happy sister, curse free. I love you. Take care of my babies and be strong. Sisters Forever." Terricka said in a low raspy tear filled voices as I reached over as kissed her face.

"Sisters Forever." I said back as I cried and she held me.

Within seconds the guard was there and he quickly wheeled her away from the table. I watched her disappear out of the door before I turned around and walked out. I left the jail that day headed to the airport and back to my life with a light, happy mind, but heavy heart and I couldn't figure out why. The next morning, I woke up to the soft subtle tweet of a bird as it sat on my windowsill. I sat up in bed as Jerrod laid beside me still in a deep sleep and the bird stared right at me. I watched it as it pressed its little face up against the glass and it felt like it looked right through me. I got up slowly and walked over to the window as it continued to sit there. I slowly raised the window with the expectation it would fly away but to my surprise it didn't.

Instead it just sat there as I stuck my hand out the window and gently rubbed its back with two fingers.

I watched as it seemed to snuggle up on my hand and tweet a beautiful sing that caused tears to stream down my face. Then suddenly it was gone as it flew high into the sky and the moment we shared took my breath away. I had to dip my head out of the window to catch my breath and watch it disappear. I dried my eyes and closed the window just as my phone began to ring. When I answered it my heart stopped when I was told my sister had just died 5 minutes ago. I cried softly on the phone for a minute before I informed them I would be back in town in a couple of days to make her arrangements when I hung up the phone I went back to the window and looked out for the bird, my sister's spirit as I cried. Suddenly I felt Jerrod's arms around me as he wrapped me in his love.

"What's wrong baby?" He asked me as he kissed my neck and I watched as the little bird flew back into the windowsill. "My sister just died baby, she finally at peace. Now she can stop living with other people's sins and guilt, and finally be happy as she runs through a field of flowers with her Mandingo. Finally, the curse is broken and the cycle of despair ends here. Finally, the Sins of Thy Mother can die." I said to my husband as the little bird flew away forever.

The End

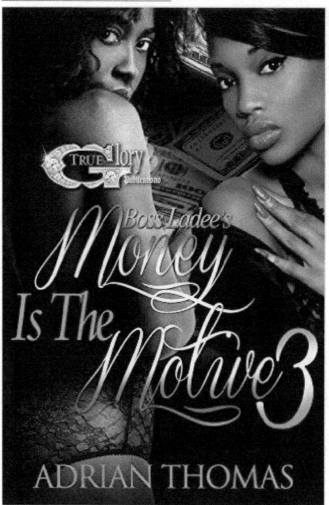

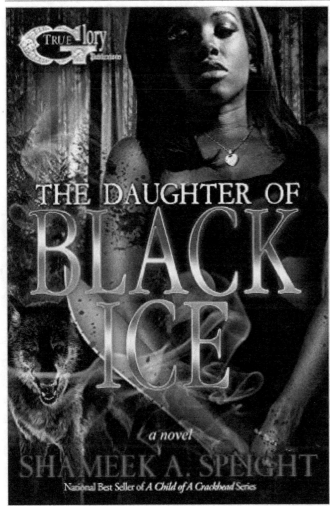

THE DAUGHTER OF

BLACK
ICE

a novel

SHAMEEK A. SPEIGHT

National Best Seller of *A Child of A Crackhead* Series

My Bitch Yo Bitch Everybody bitch 3 (My Bitch,Yo Bitch Everybody Bitch)

CPSIA information can be obtained
at www.ICGtesting.com
Printed in the USA
LVHW012326250720
661537LV00021B/2255